Waiting

Almost There

JOHN MOEHL

RESOURCE *Publications* · Eugene, Oregon

WAITING
Almost There

Resource Publications
An Imprint of Wipf and Stock Publishers
199 W. 8th Ave., Suite 3
Eugene, OR 97401

www.wipfandstock.com

PAPERBACK ISBN: 978-1-5326-8186-8
HARDCOVER ISBN: 978-1-5326-8187-5
EBOOK ISBN: 978-1-5326-8188-2

Manufactured in the U.S.A.   02/10/20

Waiting

ALSO BY JOHN MOEHL

Phobos & Deimos: two moons, two worlds
Closer to God
Ann—a story of intolerance
The Agate Hunter

Contents

Author's Note

THIS IS A WORK of fiction. The story, its actors, and their actions are fiction. While some of the sites are fictitious, in other cases, incidents may take place in real, well-known geographic locations. However, the story recounted at these locales is fiction. Similarly, at times historical persons or events are incorporated into the story to complement its telling. This does not imply any relationship between the story and these true historical personages or these real historical deeds. The tales told are complete fiction.

While the characters and their actions are fiction, it may be worth noting that the human issues confronting these characters are real and pedestrian. The story, in its broadest terms, is a common one—applying to many, if not most of us. Few have the foresight and ability to control the pathways of their lives. So often, we end up where we never thought we would go. The whims of this world push us all, at times, in unknown, frequently seemingly random directions.

This story does not endeavor to explore Divine Provenance—real or imagined. It simply recounts how one person, seemingly unwittingly and often with the best intentions, ricochets off the guardrails that trace her life's path, as she tries to make sense of the senseless, and hopes it is all worth it.

Finally, in crafting this story, I would like to acknowledge the stimuli provided by the written words of Dr. Albert Schweitzer; his memorable quotations as well as passages from *On the Edge of the Primeval Forest & More from the Primeval Forest*. This reinforcement of my work was further bolstered by John Steinbeck's *Travels with Charley*, Chinua Achebe's *Things Fall Apart*, and the words of Sir Richard Francis Burton along with the sentiments of Doris Day and Jimmy Cliff as well as the aspirations of Emma Lazarus.

Preface

THIS IS PAULA'S STORY—as told by Paula.

Paula is a product of Middle America. She is like many of us; a happy kid, an average student, and a loved daughter. From a small everyday town, a girl who doesn't look too far beyond the schoolground or the neighborhood. Nevertheless, just over the next hill—not to mention across the seas— is another unknown world that lies in the shadows, remote, and unseen. But this is truly a case of "out of sight, out of mind." These alien elements do not bother Paula—they do not penetrate her life.

Then they do.

This is all, Paula is sure, purely by chance because (although she should) she has no master plan—no guiding star. Adrift in a complex, but compelling world, Paula moves down a path that often seems ill-conceived—a path that initially does not appear to be hers, but that then somehow miraculously metamorphoses into her life.

Apprehensive at first, she ultimately owns it: it is hers. And, she decides to try and make it count.

In the end, she understands all too well, however, it will not be she who is the judge and jury reviewing her precarious (even fragile) life—it will be "them." "They," the others, they will be the reviewers—the evaluators. She fears she will never know their verdict.

AÉROGARE

Fluorescent lights wash all in a blue-white sheen
as the bustle of hundreds of bodies seems to produce its own pulse of
energy.

There is the aroma of stale coffee and rancid cooking oil
as the legions, moving down the glassed corridors, create a dissonant
clamor.

There is no morning, no evening—no sun, no moon.
There is only constant and almost purposeless movement.

Plastic chairs lined in front of sightless windows,
a world within a world with rules of its own.

There is an electronic ping that pierces the ears.
A faceless voice calls, "Flight 667 now boarding for Conakry."

A cluster, a subset of the greater horde, moves to a gaping hole,
sucked into another space—another time.

Prologue

I HATE WAITING.

Mother always said she couldn't wait until I was born. I was never sure if she was talking about being in a hurry to get through and over her pregnancy, or being in a rush to see her child? Whatever the reason, she apparently imparted in this child a great dislike for waiting for anything.

Now, in what some ridiculously call the "autumn of my life," I hate it even more. Hardships of time and age have dictated many things, and I presently find myself in a managed environment where I am forced to continuously wait for others. Although we all have our own rooms, and even our work areas, where we can be more in control of our own lives, many routine activities take place in common areas where our overseers and their helpers are in control. They are a group, in my hopefully not too biased perspective, with no concept of being quick or efficient. In my opinion they are quite simply unfit to be the stewards of so many—custodians of my verve and vicissitudes.

Yet, here they are and here am I.

Again, and I hate always going back to Mother, but as she used to say (incessantly), "What's worth doing is worth doing well." My keepers have no clue! They hardly know when something is done, let alone have any inkling of when it might be done well.

What's worse, they can't concentrate enough on their charges (read this as take their eyes off their cellphones) long enough to be able to tell you what they think they've done or tried to do. Many of my co-detainees say, "It's just the new generation." I say, "To hell with it all." Then I catch myself and say, "This too will pass."

I just have to be patient.

I just have to wait.

I hate to wait.

Before the Beginning

MY MOTHER REALLY LIKED Albert Schweitzer. I don't know whether she was impressed by his work, intrigued by someone like him going to live in Africa, or just infatuated by a guy wearing a pith helmet in a steamy tropical forest? I guess, as this happened before I was born, at the very least this interest was sparked by Dr. Schweitzer's appearance on the cover of *Time* magazine in July 1949. Mother liked *Time*.

For whatever reasons, Mother was cutting clippings about the good doctor for her scrapbook. When I was old enough to read, she would pass these to me—somewhere I should still have a bedraggled manila envelope full of yellow snippets.

When Albert—as Mother began calling him, appeared on the cover of *Life* magazine in February 1965—at the time of his passing at the age of ninety, Mother was both grief-stricken and ecstatic. He had made the cover of *Life*, but he was dead (I'm not sure she saw the irony). She bought me my very own copy—it's somewhere with the manila envelope, I suppose.

This was one of many ways I did not follow in my mother's footsteps. I still think Albert Schweitzer is an interesting person—but in a much more abstract way than my mother. I even wrote a report about him, at Mother's insistence, in fifth grade.

In the ensuing decades, I have seen how his life has escaped from the pages of something like a Joseph Conrad novel into a much more objective assessment of his work and philosophy. I did even—very briefly—visit Lambaréné where, in 1912, Dr. Schweitzer practiced medicine at a hospital operated by the Paris Missionary Society on the Ogooué River.

In 1952 Albert Schweitzer was awarded the Nobel Peace Prize. In accepting the honor, he discussed the problems of maintaining world peace—a discussion that is still considered as applicable today. He maintained he had a personal philosophy incapsulated in a "reverence for life"—believing civilized life was falling apart due to a lack of ethical behavior. People needed to respect each other, establishing moral civilizations. In spite of his strong Christian upbringing, a number of his thoughts evolved into a theology perhaps more closely akin to Eastern religions.

Like many upon whom the spotlight has shown, when the light dims there are often numerous imperfections noticed. Nevertheless, I still believed Albert Schweitzer was an interesting man, saying interesting things.

Childhood

Man is a clever animal who behaves like an imbecile.

—ALBERT SCHWEITZER

AS EVERYONE, I HAVE my own story. I obviously did not start out life as being the ward of some unknowing and uncaring institution. I have always thought of myself as caring—hopefully, somewhat knowing too. In fact, as the story goes, I was so caring that, in view of Mother's rush to get over the childbearing part, I decided to make my appearance a month early to reduce her anxiety.

I grew up in what was, in hindsight, a pretty typical family in the 1950s. My father went to the office every day—I was in third grade before I knew he was an insurance salesman. My mother stayed home, took care of my younger sister and myself, fed the dog, and kept the house spick-and-span as well as our stomachs full of what passed at that time as nutritious food. On Saturdays we all worked in the yard—following the seasons—cutting grass, raking leaves, or tending modest flower gardens that accentuated our small three-bedroom home. On Sundays, sometimes (at least Easter and Christmas), we went to church. On non-church Sundays we'd finish the work outside that we had not quite completed, go for a drive in the countryside, or visit my parents' friends. It was all pretty much the usual thing. My life did not seem to vary very much from that of my classmates. We all got measles, complained about the work our folks made us do at home, and liked recess.

School, Sam Jackson Primary, was about a twenty-minute walk from home. I walked morning and afternoon, rain or shine, with neighbors and other kids from our neighborhood. The walk was better than the classroom. My sister, three years my junior, joined our group when she was six, wearing my hand-me-downs. It was months before she was known as Susan rather than as Paula's sister—not one of her happier periods.

We lived in, what I was to learn in school, was called The Great Basin. A subset, as I later also learned, of what many called Middle America. This was all meaningless to us as we slowly floated to the surface of Sam Jackson. As a child who was growing up where I had been born, I was simply home.

It was years later, as I looked back at how this home had affected me—one of its seedlings—that I began to look more at the internal and external components of the place from which I came.

I came to think that those who chose the label Middle America were looking more economically than socially—certainly not geographically. Our town was definitely not the middle. We were physically located in the far west—one of those influences I would later dissect, but I shouldn't get ahead of myself. We were also, nationally-speaking, not the socioeconomic middle—but none of that mattered to a girl entering fifth grade.

Girls from this rural community were already spying their future in fifth grade. There seemed to be clusters looking through a similar lens. Some saw themselves as working—in those days, principally being teachers or nurses. Others saw themselves as their mothers' successors—becoming wives and homemakers. Some even considered themselves movie stars or beauty queens. Regardless of the fifth-grade vision of one's trajectory, this was nearly always the germination of a seed fertilized by the parents—sometimes trying to push their offspring in a direction where they felt there was a good fit, sometimes trying to live vicariously through their descendant.

When I began to peek from under the covers and gaze into an unknown future, none of my cohort's aims seemed appealing. My waffling was the more noticeable, at least to me, because my parents did not provide prescribed guardrails or family-honored targets. My parents would say, "Do the best you can, follow your heart, and you will do well."

In fifth grade, I had no idea what this meant.

My extracurricular hours were spent reading comic books, taking walks in the nearby woods with our golden retriever, Ralph, and the occasional cherished fishing trip with my father. My planning horizon was never further away than the end of the school year.

I have no idea if my classmates were more forward-looking than I, but my own shortsightedness hit a pothole when, in eighth-grade study hall, we were introduced to career planning. Granted this was not very much, but for me it was a tremor that I probably should have interpreted as a shockwave. We had to choose what we wanted to be. Stunning.

The activity was not as open-ended as I might, at least in retrospect, have hoped. Mr. Corrigan, our homeroom teacher, brought out a stained and weary cardboard box from under his desk that contained dozens of what once were white brochures entitled "So You Want to Be," followed by doctor, lawyer, teacher, or whatever possible profession.

We were then to select the brochure that corresponded with our life's plan and write a brief composition on how we would line up our lives on these new-found targets. There were no brochures for movie star, beauty queen, wife, mother, or even just flat rich, so a lot of kids just had to make do. My classmates greeted this exercise with the same enthusiasm as a math quiz. There was no angst about not finding the topic of which one had dreamed for the past three years. It was much more like trick-or-treaters putting their hand in the neighbors' candy basket and taking a random sweet. My comrades just haphazardly picked a booklet, retiring to their desks to rotely follow Mr. Corrigan's instructions—more energized by the upcoming lunch break than the pathway to their future.

It would be a gross exaggeration to say I alone felt this to be a momentous occasion. Nonetheless, I did take it seriously. I needed to choose. I found it difficult—almost unpleasant.

Both my grandmothers had been teachers. Many girls in class were thinking about becoming teachers. It seemed sensible. Thus, I chose "So You Want to be a Teacher." I went back to my desk to read the few pages and seriously ponder the next steps.

At home I informed my mother I was going to be a teacher. She said, "Fine. Just work hard and have patience, my dear. All comes to those who wait."

That evening I wrote my essay for Mr. Corrigan about how important teachers were. I used my growing vocabulary and the flowery words we heard at times in church to heap accolades on a profession that I guessed I had chosen as my objective—not realizing I was, at the same time, heaping flattery on he who would grade my work.

To no one's surprise, in a week all was forgotten. Many went back to their earlier dream tracks to someday become something they wanted to be and do something they wanted to do. I, too, promptly forgot my essay for Mr. Corrigan, going back to the woods with Ralph or into other worlds with my comic books.

Then, in ninth and tenth grade, things changed. Girls started noticing boys. Although we had spent almost a decade of our schooling together, it was kind of like having dogs and cats as pets—they were different, but they were both your pets. The dogs ate dog food and the cats ate cat food. The dogs went for walks, the cats had litter boxes. Boys and girls were like that. And, then they weren't.

Sarah had been my best friend since first grade. She lived four houses down, her father a dentist. We walked to school together. We did homework together. We went to Sears and Roebuck together. We went to the Polar Bear to get hamburgers and Coke together. We cried together when her grandmother died. We laughed together when her aunt's dachshund had puppies.

Then, we went to Union High together and she met Bobby.

It was over. Sarah and Bobby were always together. She barely said hi to me in the hall. She wore his ring, hugged his arm, and made cooing noises in his ears.

Sarah was not alone. It made me think of the stories in Sunday school about Noah where he brought the animals into the ark two-by-two. My schoolmates were all melting away two by two.

I may sound like I was an outsider looking in. I was not. Like my consorts—male and female—I was finding a new interest in the opposite sex. I began wondering if the cats and dogs were really that different and separable. Equally novel, boys seemed to be looking at me. Sometimes they would want to talk about some totally un-understandable subject. Sometimes they would snap my bra. Sometimes they would offer me a stick of Beech-Nut gum. They were hard to figure out.

My first relationships, dalliances I should really say, were more out of curiosity, like when Ralph and I found some flower or bug we had never seen before. We wanted to know what it was and how it worked. I naively (but probably in their eyes, flirtatiously) wanted to know how boys worked. Real simple.

I knew things were serious when Mother informed me that Sarah was going to have a baby. She and Bobby were going to get married and they would both have to leave school—he already had a job washing cars at the Chevrolet Agency.

My sexual forays at Union High were initially not even sexual from my wide-eyed perspective. It was like living next to the same person for years, but never meeting them, then running into them at a party and realizing you should have got to know each other much earlier. Boys had been my neighbors forever, but I had never got to know them. Thus, when we were first really introduced, while sex was undoubtedly on their minds, I was still trying to figure out what kind of house my neighbor lived in. I was attempting to define the opposite sex to my own satisfaction. To me, this was a prerequisite to sharing any more of myself or my life with them.

It was not that I did not know about sex. I had, in fact, a better basis than many of my classmates, having taken both health and advanced biology. I had been exposed to vivid graphics of coitus, as well as tales of the huge risks of syphilis, and learned the entire cycle from zygote to fully formed embryo. Intellectually, I understood well. Socially, I was on shakier ground.

By the time I put on my cap and gown to receive my diploma, I had managed to have a relatively good exposure to the male of my species—although, not nearly as expansive as some of my schoolmates. I had had dates—quite a few. Starting with a movie and a stolen kiss in the shadows, going forward to going all the way in the back seat of a 1962 Galaxie with Henry Fisher, and then comparing his performance some months later with that of Jerry Olson.

By the standards of the time, I was not a prude and certainly not saving myself. But I was also not easy. I was, whether I realized it or not, still deciding what I thought of boys as I learned firsthand that they likely had more weaknesses than strengths.

Moreover, in spite of Mr. Corrigan's efforts, I was still undecided as to my future—undecided except that I knew I did not automatically want to jump from high school into the role of wife and mother. There was more to life and I wanted more. I did not want to wait.

As arguably incomplete as I felt my grasp of inter-gender socializing was, this did not stop me from being the prime reference and definitive guide for Susan. I possessed seemingly endless wisdom and sure-fire solutions to any and all of her problems.

Susan never questioned my abilities—even when time and again they fell short of expectations. Sibling devotion apparently covered for a multitude of ills.

We were, in our own way, devoted siblings. Susan relied on me for advice, seeing me as the trail blazer for her. She always would be, in some ways, Paula's little sister. But this relationship was almost transactional rather than familial. She saw advantages in using to her own benefit the knowledge gained by those who had gone before. Not too novel a concept.

This was pragmatic. This was logical. Susan was a case study in pragmatism and logic. When she would be introduced to Mr. Corrigan's career planning, she would be ready to go. Completely independent of any parental influence, she knew the lens through which she was looking. My sister was sure of exactly what she was (not wanted) going to be: a lawyer.

She was ecstatic Mr. Corrigan had a brochure specifically for her choice.

She understood at an early age there were expected roles for women. She understood equally that these were unjust in many ways. But, for her, more importantly, she understood that her best tactic was not to rail against these inequities, but to simply set her sights on a laudable task and achieve it—thereby demonstrating by doing that she had the right of access.

She knew the feminine place in the law profession was to be a clerk, or maybe even a legal secretary. However, she knew as well that if she were in the top of her class, she would be able to knock on closed doors—even if she needed to do so loudly.

As strange as it seemed, at least to me, my little sister had grasped all these elements of her future by the time she left seventh grade, while I was still trying to decide what classes to take in my sophomore year at Union High.

She was focused. She was driven. She was only getting on to fourteen.

She was my sister; I imagine I loved her. Certainly, in those days of our youth we always said we loved each other. We loved all our family. We even said we loved our friends. Sometimes we loved milkshakes. Nonetheless, we were not well versed in love. We had no concept of levels of affection. Of loving or liking? We were family and families loved each other. It was enough.

Yet, even being joined by love or some other emotion, we were very different.

Susan was driven, but she was also ready to wait—patiently and succinctly planning her next step as she recognized her ultimate goal and never vacillated in her efforts to achieve it. At an early age, she proved she was a skillful architect of her future, devoted to achieving her ends.

While my sister strategically built her road forward, I thrashed about in waves of perplexity—everything, then nothing, seemed a good option. If childhood is defined as the period between birth and full growth, and we assume this growth is both mental and physical, then my sister left childhood well before I did.

Transition

At times our own light goes out and is rekindled by a spark from another person. Each of us has cause to think with deep gratitude of those who have lighted the flame within us.

—ALBERT SCHWEITZER

MY FAMILY, MY CHILDHOOD, my schooling—it all seemed pretty typical. But like the dog-eared old proverb, I couldn't walk in another's shoes, so I really don't know if these core parts of my life were typical at all. Looking again through the filter of time, I imagine my life as seen by outsiders was generally similar to that of my schoolmates and neighbors.

At home, things had always seemed normal. As far as I knew, my father did not beat my mother (or the reverse), we had food on the table, and clothes on our backs (even if patched and faded). It all seemed normal.

Now, as I look through my filter, as I am able to have deeper insight into the lives of at least a few others, I realize I have no idea of what normal should have been. With age, able to contrast things a bit better and decades of living to perfect my views, I would now classify my childhood as comfortable and safe—not overly warm nor loving.

As I grew to learn, my father was more than an insurance salesman. He was the key person for most of the investments of the Carlyle Family—the town's time-honored robber-barons who were by far the wealthiest and most politically dominating. He did sell insurance and oversee a small staff that served much of the community with all kinds of coverage.

What I learned as time went by was that the entire five-story building (the tallest in town) where my father had his office was owned by the Carlyles. My father was also the manager of this structure as well as having managerial responsibilities in a number of other businesses housed in this local sky-rise.

The net result of all these tangled webs was that my father was rarely at home. He left early, came home late, and was at the office many Saturdays—leaving us to the yard work.

What I also learned later was that my father had a serious heart condition. Stress, overwork, being overweight, and bad genes, all combined to make him very susceptible to a coronary. This was the burden my mother carried.

Mother cared for us, but she incessantly worried and fretted and lost sleep over the health of her spouse. She only had so much energy to divide among us and (perhaps justifiably) my father sucked up the lion's share.

This, in part, may have explained why Susan and I were so different. We did not have a strong common denominator in our parents. They were, overtly or covertly, fighting what they saw as a battle for life and death. They kept their offspring healthy but were not able to provide other spiritual support that may have been useful, or even necessary, to have a more cohesive and emotionally attached family.

Through my life, I have witnessed the ironclad bonds some have with their families—wondering what it would be like. Similar to the argument for nature or nurture, one school of thought would certainly maintain that strong family ties are an important asset for a successful life—whatever success may be. Whether or not these attachments are critical components of success, I cannot say. Nevertheless, they do seem to be an elixir that helps mitigate many of life's personal challenges.

Keeping focused in the mirror, suffice it to say that my sentimental links to my family and my youth are somewhat limited. I blow off the dust and look at the now pale pictures we proudly took with our Polaroid, realizing we did, in our own ways, love each other. My parents truly tried their best to provide and cope.

With rather shallow roots at home and in the community, it was not long after taking off my cap and gown that I was looking to the other side of the hills that surrounded our valley—wanting to see more, wanting to feel more.

The first step in this process seemed to be college. I had good grades from Union High. With my parents' blessings, I had spent much of my final months in the hallowed, if rather tawdry, halls of this school that had shepherded me from childhood to near adulthood, applying to colleges near and far.

While there were some negative replies, by far the majority of colleges welcomed me; quite a number were offering financial support for a good female student from a middle-class home. The choice became a problem.

Gratefully, if uninvitedly, my aunt offered good advice that swayed my decision and my parents' support. She had been a rarity: a female officer in the infantry at the frontline. In fact, she had been with the first troops to liberate Paris in World War II. She had returned, at least physically, un-wounded from the war; she went on to get her Masters, becoming a re-spected expert in her field of nutrition.

She said, "A girl should be free to follow her aspirations. A girl should live up to her talent and not have to wait for acceptance—not have to wait for 'her time'. But to do this, a girl must go to school and study hard."

This met with acceptance from all, so for her big brother's (my father) benefit, she added, "A girl should also get far enough away from home to be able to let her talent shine and get her feet on the pathway leading to her aspirations."

Following my aunt's guidance, with the perhaps reluctant acquies-cence from my mother and father, less than three months after receiving my diploma, and after sorting through the various possibilities, I found myself at St. Mary's College of Maryland, in St. Mary's City. It was eighty miles southeast of our nation's capital and 2,500 miles east of home. I had a pro-visional major in education—Mr. Corrigan's plan still haunting me—and a room in Whitcomb Hall that I shared with Caroline Newcastle from, as she quickly and emphatically informed me, a good Virginia family.

Caroline and I quickly established a working relationship. I was an ear-ly riser, often studying before sunrise, but in my bed and, hopefully, sound asleep well before midnight. At an organic level, my roommate's academic scheduling was upside down to mine. Rising as late as possible, she would rush out to her first class in a jumble, but then was clear-eyed and astute studying (or otherwise engaged) into the wee hours of the morning.

My bunkmate also had a totally different set of priorities from mine. While I was serious about expanding my horizons in all directions, I was also serious about my education. My eighth-grade career explorations had made me keenly aware of the importance of good educators, even if I was less sure that I had the makings to become one of the members of this cru-cial team. Whether to teach or otherwise use my intellect, I knew I wanted to learn.

Caroline had a very different priority: find a husband. As we shared our lives, it became apparent her family was as well off as she had initially espoused. She would never have to worry about money or have to get a job. But her family wanted her to marry, to marry a good college-educated boy to bring home to the family business. While engaged in this search, Caroline was also determined to set her hooks into whatever was seen as the St. Mary's upper crust. She frequented the most prestigious student societies, went to the most fashionable gatherings, circulated with the *beau monde*, and effectively made sure she was seen where necessary, when necessary, and by whomever necessary.

Two people, two worlds.

It all worked out well. In the morning, I was up and out well before she was awake. I was asleep well before she returned in the evening. We barely saw each other. On weekends, I had the whole room to myself as she was either at home in Virginia or at one or another social function for the privileged.

As my first semester of college drew to a close, I found myself motivated—even excited. In addition to the boilerplate undergraduate classes, I took some introductory education classes, since I still maintained at least the facade of one day becoming a teacher. This occupied the majority of my schedule. However, for the second semester there were a few hours left over and I began to investigate other academic areas of which I had heretofore absolutely no knowledge at all. Subjects that held my attention included areas that dealt with people like sociology, anthropology, comparative religions, and international studies. I could only take a small bite of the apple at any point in my curriculum, but I slowly began to let my imagination run free.

I had tried to do the best I could when selecting my college. St. Mary's had a lot of pluses. It was ranked in the top 100 best colleges in the country. It had a small student body, less than 2,000, and an equally low student to professor ratio. It had been putting out high quality graduates for 140 years. It seemed a good choice and a unique opportunity.

Happily, my initial experiences were positive and motivating.

I was also impressed by St. Mary's City. Coming from the West, old to me was something that had been around for a century. St. Mary's City, the first colonial settlement and first capital of Maryland, had been around for more than 340 years. It amazed me. It also tantalized me. I was curious. No, I was almost infatuated. How did the lives of those early settlers affect us today? How had they managed to do all they had done with so little, when today we seem to be able to do nothing without ten thousand dollars' worth of equipment? They truly did so much with so little. Was this a model or simply the random fortuitous hand of chance?

Although long-established, the city and surrounding county sharing the same name with the college, were rural and, by East Coast standards, not heavily populated—the city having fewer residents than the college had students.

Located, of course, on the St. Mary's River, the county was effectively the confluence of this smaller watercourse with the Potomac and the great Chesapeake Bay. For a girl from the landlocked hinterland, these waters opened up nearly as many mysteries as the founders of St. Mary's City.

Bottom line: I was satisfied with my choices and, at the ripe age of nineteen, felt I was moving ahead without delay—albeit, I would have been hard-pressed to indicate where I was heading.

Caroline had so wanted to experience Greek life. She had so wanted to become a member of Kappa Kappa Gamma. Her mother had been a Kappa. Her grandmother had been a Kappa. She should be a Kappa.

However, St. Mary's did not have any fraternal or sororal social Greek letter organizations. Apparently, the college's leadership felt these detracted from the ambiance of a common academic family they wanted to promote. This was a problem for Caroline. She had to weigh what she saw as the pre-eminence of coming from an honors college with high standing and going home without her Kappa pin, against going to another school where she could be cubby-holed as having attended a humdrum school but where she could wave the Kappa flag. She chose, feeling she was making the ultimate sacrifice, academia. She chose St. Mary's.

Nevertheless, being forced to cast aside sororal life did not mean being forced to live one's life in a public residence hall. When Caroline returned for her sophomore year, after a summer in France, she did not return to Whitcomb Hall. She, and a few of her genteel sisters from the Young Republicans Club rented a luxury home with a swimming pool at Ancient Oaks.

My new roommate, Sheila, was a year ahead of me—a biology major who had hopes of becoming a medical researcher one day. Our paths had never crossed before even though she was in her third year at St. Mary's—happy in her studies and with her boyfriend Stewart.

Sheila had been born and raised on a 600-acre corn and soy farm seventy miles north of Dubuque, Iowa—about seven miles north of the small town of McGregor. This township of about 800, as I was to learn, located on the shores of the Mississippi and initially settled by descendants of the famed Rob Roy, had been the epicenter of Sheila's life before coming east to the shores of the Chesapeake.

A farm girl at heart, Sheila's and my daily routines were much more in sync than they had been with Caroline. We both followed the adage of early to bed and early to rise—crossing our fingers that we would, as promised, at least become wealthy and stay healthy, even if wisdom evaded us. Our harmony went beyond our daily schedules—we just seemed to get along well.

Sheila, literally coming from the land, was additionally a big influence on me. In my sophomore year I was still formally seeking a career in teaching. Privately, I was even more uncertain of following this channel. In fact, I was increasingly certain I should not.

It was not because of any diminished prioritization of education—not at all. Every year I remained in school, the more I was convinced of the importance of having dedicated and qualified teachers for all students. After fourteen years of pedagogy on the learning side of the equation, I had benefited from excellent instructors and suffered through painful months with others who could kindly be classified as mediocre. Teaching, good teaching, was both a science and an art. At its best, it required a unique mixture of academic skills and empathetic personality. I was now convinced I did not have the needed temperament to be a good teacher—not to mention to be a great teacher. I was sure I could master the curriculum laid out before me and once again wear a cap and gown, but I was deluding myself if I thought I would really excel at my teaching profession—not excel for my clients nor myself.

As my self-doubt peaked, Sheila subtly introduced me into the natural world—her world of biology. While I could not manage to share her fervor for the inner workings of a cell or the metamorphosis of a tiger swallowtail, I was able to—with her help—see things in a much larger, integrated context.

Like the founders of St. Mary's City who had had to fight so diligently against so many odds to succeed, life for most, even those of us today, is not monolithic. We are part of a much bigger whole that impacts on us and upon which we impact. Education is an important—I would say a critical—tool in this back-and-forth world we share with so much else. But there are many tools. My interests, as they began to distill from the vapors of my inner space, seemed to be much more in the results of people using these tools, rather than in how to use the tools themselves. How were we as humans doing? Where could we do better?

This felt overly grandiose—arrogant. This seemed ignorant. This appeared misguided. How could a twenty-year-old girl be so silly, or just plain stupid, to have such exalted thoughts? But I was, I guess, too naive to be worried about such practical considerations.

As I moved through my studies and found more and more hours to investigate other domains—other careers—I began taking classes that delved into the human condition: philosophy, psychology, sociology, economics, international languages, religious studies. Yet, what really held my attention, as it had from the first time I was introduced to it, was anthropology. By the second semester of my junior year I had changed my major to anthropology with a minor in international studies.

A year later, I was well immersed in cultural anthropology, studying the cultural variation among humans. My mentors took me down the road of cultural relativism, which basically stated that to understand a person you needed to understand well his or her culture. Humans, they maintained, acquired their culture through a process of enculturation—different locales, different situations leading to different cultures. To gain knowledge, to gain insight, significant time in the field was necessary to understand as well as possible the impacts of time and place on the cultures that arose.

I seemed to have, I hoped I had, found my sweet spot.

As I look back at my college life through frosted glass, there is no nostalgia nor distress. To me, this was part of a process—the process of growing-up and being trained to do something somewhere.

I often hear others of my generation wax about the wonderful years of high school and college. Some wishing they could go back and relive those terrific times. Perhaps this cohort is well represented by one of my former classmates when, fifty years after leaving secondary school, she was asked about her best school-time moments. She replied, "There were so many, I could never count them all!"

As most things, reflections on school days occur along a spectrum. A world full of wonderful days is contrasted by others who feel these were the most godawful years. Years where decisions were made that have been unwelcome baggage for the remainder of one's life.

On this sentimental bell curve, I am smack dab in the middle. I am neither effusive nor cavillous. These were neither the best of times nor the worst of times. This was time invested in me. Effort devoted to being able to do what I wanted to do quickly, without waiting, without waste.

Given my matter-of-fact views, once I had found an objective with which I was satisfied, my goal was to get done as quickly as possible.

Following the suggestions of my advisor, the summers after my freshman and sophomore years I had profited from my proximity to Washington to participate in the Department of Education's Student Volunteer in Federal Government Program. I had learned a lot about the management side of education as well as about the goings-on in our Capital. Once I had changed my major, I had classes to make up and, to keep to my schedule, decided to go to summer school after my junior year.

The upshot of all this was that I did not get home much. The fact that I lived on the other side of the continent made it easy to justify staying put. Nevertheless, I could have found ways to get home more often—it just didn't seem necessary. I believed in making a decision and not looking back. I did go home for two Christmases, and met my parents in New York for a third, so I had not shut myself off from my family.

I was also not so absorbed in my way forward as to totally neglect leisure time. I went home with Sheila one Thanksgiving and over one spring break. I had a number of liaisons with boys, actually going home with one to meet his parents, which, for me, was more of an opportunity to see New England in the fall, but for him, I guess, it was more of an attempt to get his folks' greenlight as to a potential candidate for spouse.

I did not date a lot but did manage to keep socially active. No student organizations, no clubs, no special events—just old-fashioned boy-girl get-togethers. There were some extended hot and heavy relationships and some one-night stands. There were some real nice guys and some real nut cases. However, there was no room in my plans for a significant other. Short-term gratification or longer-term camaraderie were fine, but this was always without any thought of commitment.

In spite of my academic vacillations and variegated social life, my senior year went by in the blink of an eye. Sheila had graduated and with joy accepted a graduate studies position at the University of Ohio's School of Allied Health Professions. I stayed in Whitcomb Hall, finally getting a much sought-after single room that allowed me to completely immerse myself in my senior project—comparing the rates of acculturation in two immigrant communities in the DC area. I focused on arrivals from Ethiopia and Guatemala with whom I had managed to have entrées through local community service organizations dealing with adult education.

I became totally absorbed in my research, spending days and weeks on the sidewalks and alleyways of the Capital. Nonetheless, I managed to graduate as planned—not top of my class, having to settle for the number three slot. This was, however, good enough for me to consider a move ahead to my next step, a MSc in anthropology. Strong GRE scores added to my undergraduate record from an honors college allowed me to have considerable latitude when considering a graduate school. Everyone I asked had praise for a different university, so I applied to nearly a dozen carefully selected institutions.

However, I was less certain than my professors that a jump straight away into graduate studies was the best choice. I was, after all, tired of school. I very much enjoyed my academic work, but very rigid scholastic calendars for years had, in my view, limited my ability to do what I wanted to do. Although, I was the first to admit, I didn't know exactly what I wanted to do. I just knew I didn't want to wait.

My family was, to no surprise (at least to me), lobbying for a totally different course: Come home, settle down, meet a nice guy.

Settling down was the last thing on my list. I'd already met some nice guys. But I tried to mollify my parents while I looked at the road ahead. As often, I tried to split the difference between graduate school and going home. I looked for a third pathway.

I found my compromise through someone with whom I had volunteered at the Department of Education. A few years earlier, she had volunteered at a museum in the UK and had had a wonderful experience.

Following this tip, with my not-too-shabby record (as Sheila had called my scholarly transcripts), I was able to gain admittance into a volunteer program with the group responsible for the archeological collection at the Museum of London. As part of the museum's overall mandate, this group obtained and classified a wide variety of archeological items relating to the city's history.

This was a great opportunity.

It did not, however, come without a catch.

I had to pay my travel and maintenance costs with the exception of lodging which was covered by the museum. For a typical six-month volunteer period, this required considerably more than I, a new graduate, had in my now exhausted bank account.

I had to find a solution.

I bid a fond farewell to St. Mary's—sure I'd miss my professors more than most of my fellow students. I first spent a week in DC to thank those who had helped me with my project as well as renew contacts with those with whom I had worked during by volunteer period. I felt lucky to have known St. Mary's, unsure of where I was going, but in a hurry to get there.

I was worried that if I went home, I would get snared into the family routine—sucked in, never to leave again. So, I poured over newspapers looking for the best I could find in the area of help wanted.

I found a slot as an associate at a big hardware store across the river in Fredericksburg, Virginia. I quickly learned an associate was really a title that combined the tasks of clerk, shelf stocker, and custodian. Nevertheless, the job offered considerable overtime for those willing to work weekends and off hours.

I found a real cheap apartment. I did nothing but go to and fro from work, trying gallantly to keep a smile on my face in spite of self-righteous supervisors and intolerant customers.

It took me a little less than a year to save enough for my six-month excursion to England. During this period, I spent my free hours following up on graduate school admissions. A break in my formal studies was welcome, but I was definitely not ready to abandon my hopes for a graduate degree.

My time at the Museum of London was rewarding. I had a real hands-on entrée into archeology and my first taste of another country with new customs and norms—a country that had very open opinions about Americans in general, and very quickly, about me in particular.

It was time well spent. It made all the hours grinning at fatigued hardware shoppers and pushing heavy boxes onto unbelievably high shelves worthwhile.

Intercontinental mail coming through the museum had been intermittent at best. Upon returning to American shores, the first thing I did, therefore, was to check up on my status as a hopeful graduate student. The news was terrific. I was being offered a fully paid graduate assistantship and master's program at Harvard—the top school in anthropology in the US year after year.

I had a few months before registration.

Somewhat apprehensively, I headed west to spend some time with my family—unsure of how they would see my now clearer future route to more studies and less family life.

They accepted my plans with unexpected nonchalance. We spent an enjoyable, if at times tepid, time together before I retraced my steps east, getting to Cambridge before the leaves began to turn to get ready for my first term as a graduate student at Harvard.

It was amazing. It was scary. To think that I was actually at Harvard. Never should have happened—or at least I am sure this is what many people in my hometown thought when they heard that that crazy Paula was going to go to an Ivy League school. Somebody who was a comic book fanatic now at Harvard? Impossible!

While I won't digress into the comic book story lines that I found were so often offered by real people in real lives. I will agree that earlier I, too, would have never thought it possible to do what I was now doing.

But here I was.

I was eager. I was ready.

I was soon enveloped in my studies, defining my research, oblivious to all else. Building on my senior project with clarity and steering from my major professor, Dr. Jeffries, I began to examine and outline an innovative inquiry looking at critical triggers in the parent cultural population that resisted acculturation and, even if latent, could be re-lit in later life.

Undertaking this exploration in depth was beyond the scope of a MSc program. Nevertheless, it was seen as so progressive by my advisor and his colleagues that we were able to sketch an ambitious master's project that did not identify the specific triggers and the potential for re-sparking, but rather described and defended the process without defining precisely the methodology to ultimately undertake the modeling.

Everything seemed to come together effortlessly. Luckily, given my distain for the doldrums (having to wait), under Dr. Jeffries' watchful eyes, my studies and my work moved seamlessly forward. All too soon, I found myself the proud owner of a brand-new master's degree.

It was great, but it should have been more.

It was somehow as though my bubble had broken and I didn't know where I had fallen. It was a strange landscape with many familiar figures.

It was like when my father had helped me use a test tube, some nails, and a bunch of wire to make a simple electric motor for the science fair, or when I had worked so hard on my biology project for a research methods class as an undergraduate (today, to my surprise, remembering exactly the title of my effort and little else—the soon-to-be-forgotten mini treatise on "protease activity in herbivorous and carnivorous echinoderms")—many points along a twisting pathway. Seemingly important tasks that captured my energies and then were gone. Separate disconnected events, pieces of a riddle, or integral parts of the blueprint of my life?

Throughout, I'd worked hard, I got to where I needed to go, but what was next? Were the pieces coming together or still floating in space in random motion?

It wasn't that I had a vibrant social life with a June wedding planned after I got my degree. It wasn't that I had the job-of-a-lifetime lined up. It wasn't that I was going with a bunch of mates on a boat trip around the world, or even a train trip to Canada. I now had my master's and I had no idea of what to do with it.

Navigating the Waters

Constant kindness can accomplish much. As the sun makes ice melt, kindness causes misunderstanding, mistrust, and hostility to evaporate.

—ALBERT SCHWEITZER

BACK IN MY SAM Jackson days, I'd already begun to feel unsure—unsure of far too many things for a girl of my age.

Like in that old Doris Day song, I'd ask my mother, "What will I be?"

With a tolerant mien, Mother always told me, "Just use the gifts God's given you."

I didn't know exactly what gifts I'd been given by God (I didn't know if Mother knew). I was not sure, but I hoped I was on the right track. The keyword here was hope. For someone who hated waiting, this hesitancy was uncomfortable. I wanted to know. I wanted to do.

In retrospect, I now wonder if I have been following my heart or my brain?

Was this what Mother would have considered as using God's gifts well?

What did someone do with a graduate degree in cultural anthropology? How harebrained was it to follow this path? I could have been a teacher.

Dr. Jeffries' suggestion was simple, if simply shortsighted: Get a PhD.

I felt it was time to leave the shelter of academia. I figured, if I didn't know what to do with my Master's, I still wouldn't know what to do with a doctoral degree.

Awash in my own overactive imagination, I paid a visit to the Office of Career Services to see if a neutral third party could help. I encountered a Career Services Officer who looked like she had been as awash as I felt. Frumpy and lethargic, she looked more like someone who had just spent the night in a bus station rather than the dynamo for someone else's career.

Impassively half listening to my situation, she fumbled under her desk for some papers. She extracted a sheaf of printouts that looked like fleshed out, updated versions of Mr. Corrigan's brochures (so I wanted to be an anthropologist!).

In addition to the omnipresent forms to fill out, there was some general guidance about job hunting and then a checklist of specific targets given my area of specialization. My stodgy guide took the nub of a pencil and ticked off the list of positions for anthropology graduates: social worker, public relations officer, museum curator, human resource officer, equity and diversity officer, or college lecturer.

Handing me the bundle, she wished me luck, indicating I could get more details on specific employers at the library, and, as an afterthought, threw in, "Don't forget about corporate cleanup."

As I reviewed my career options, I was underwhelmed. I did like museums and being a curator had kind of a special flair. But, none of the highlighted jobs really piqued my curiosity. I seemed to still be seeking some sort of divine street sign to point-out my route.

As visions of life spent as a corporate personnel or PR officer swirled about in my brain, I recalled the parting advice about corporate cleanup. More grasping at straws than serious targeting, I contacted faculty members to enquire about how anthropology could be somehow linked to reparations made by big business.

My colleagues were able to connect dots that now seemed so obvious: disasters. When there were disasters or major mishaps and messes that effected a community, the government or the ostensible malefactors often engaged people with anthropological training to monitor how the community was adjusting—healing. By chance—one dare not call it good luck—they pointed me to the recent catastrophe at Three Mile Island.

With plenty of free time and the wealth of resources at Harvard at my disposal, I looked into Three Mile Island. I really only knew what little I had retained from the news. A year or so ago, a nuclear power plant in Pennsylvania had had an accident that could have been terrible and, in spite of its modest negative impact, had strongly reinforced anti-nuclear energy sentiments across the country.

As I dug deeper in the library, I learned the accident had happened in March of last year, the cleanup starting in August. The facility was located along the Susquehanna River, about fifteen miles southeast of Harrisburg and five miles, as the crow flies, south of the Pennsylvania Turnpike. Through a series of mechanical and human errors the plant had released radioactive gas into the environment. It was estimated that somewhere around two-and-one-half megacuries were dumped into the surrounding neighborhood that included Dauphin, Lancaster, York, Lebanon, and Cumberland counties—reportedly two million people were affected to some degree. The accident, considered the worst commercial nuclear accident in US history, was rated five out of seven on the International Nuclear Event Scale (I would learn years later that the Chernobyl disaster had been graded seven out of seven).

There were obvious concerns in local communities about increased cancer and the risk of birth defects. Many court cases had been initiated, but the underlying problem was that people were afraid. They did not want to live next to a nuclear plant. The state of Pennsylvania and her partners had started a community support program to document and follow up on health issues while educating people about nuclear energy and trying to help them adjust to going home. This, like the overall cleanup campaign, was a work in progress.

The community support program was still recruiting people. According to the article I found, amazingly, anthropology was among the skills they were seeking. There was an 800-number for the state's Bureau of Human Resources listed.

Thinking dubiously of a career as a member of the Pennsylvania community support program, I, nonetheless, called to enquire.

I was informed that, given the scope of the problem, there were still a number of posts available. I would, however, have to fill in the standard application forms and, if I was shortlisted (and, I was assured I would be as they needed people), I would have to go for an interview in Harrisburg. The whole process, albeit expedited due to the urgency, would take six to ten weeks. I needed to be patient, my usher informed me, as she laid out the steps required in minute detail—underscoring, in my mind, the need for a focus on minutia in that line of work.

Anxious to do something, and not wanting to do just anything, nuclear disaster cleanup work seemed like the best thing (honestly, the only thing) on my plate. After all, who wouldn't want to go and work somewhere contaminated by radioactive waste?

The paperwork was the same old stuff and within a week I had received and returned my stack of documents. My efficiency notwithstanding, it was another three weeks before I got a call from the Harrisonburg bureau saying there had been a problem processing my submission. I had indicated I was single, but I had not indicated how many children I had.

Damn. This was my rural West upbringing. In the eyes of the conservative society of my youth, married people had children—if you were single, obviously you had no children. I had been duped by my past.

I apologized for the omission. I confirmed I had no children. My contactor assured me he had checked the box accordingly—the dossier would now be resubmitted. I would hear from them soon.

Soon turned out to be a month!

Waiting was not only a lifelong aggravation to me—it was a downright inconvenience. As typical, university housing was scheduled around the academic year. With my diploma came an understanding that I would be leaving campus—moving on to make room for others. Now, instead of moving on, I was hanging on. I had to make special arrangements to stay in my studio apartment. I had to find ways to occupy my time. Moreover, my research assistantship now complete, I had no source of income and had to really count my pennies.

As I had already started spending long hours in the library researching the recent US nuclear catastrophe, I decided, while waiting for the office gnomes in Pennsylvania to do their thing, I would continue my research. I started looking into other avenues of employment, figuring the Three Mile Island work, even if I got it, would be relatively short-term.

I was starting to look through a different prism. I knew, of course, that my particular specialty was a branch of anthropology that focused on diverse human cultures. It was founded on the principle that culture was composed of a variety of elements including, among others, knowledge, beliefs, and practices. Hence, in my domain, populations reacted to circumstances—different situations derived different cultures. Cultures were learned through enculturation. People like me tried to learn about the learning through what was called "participant observation." This just meant getting out and talking to folks.

Moving from the cerebral to the practical, I began to see how my training could allow me to examine how shocks affected people—how changes brought about by external factors brought about long-term shifts in cultural norms. Basically, how people coped.

With an overabundance of free time, I began to wonder if I could turn my new skill set inside and see how I coped?

Eventually things worked out—or I guess they did. I reputably had qualified, at least to take the next step. A task force had been set up by the Pennsylvania

Department of Environmental Protection—a subset charged with recruiting temporary staff to assist with the aftermath of what was called by some "the meltdown."

This recruitment team paid my expenses to come to Harrisburg to meet with them. It was all very impersonal. I was met at the airport, taken to a hotel where I was picked up the next day, accompanied to a spartan conference room where I was questioned by three people for fifty-seven minutes. My hand was then shaken, I was told to stay tuned, and was dropped off at the airport. Slam, bam, thank you ma'am.

It took another two weeks before I was in fact able to tune back in. After a fortnight of frustratingly digging in the library and generally moping, I got a late afternoon call asking how soon I could be in Pennsylvania.

Thankfully, there followed a bit more of an explanation, sketchy as it was. The interview had been a success and they were offering me a job—a one-year contract. To save time, the paperwork could be taken care of when I arrived in Harrisburg. The work itself would be to join a four-person support party that covered a three-township zone within the high alert area circumscribed by the mishap. The other members of the group would represent public health, environmental monitoring, and economic development. To my surprise, the anthropologist was slated to be the team leader.

Seeing this offer as really the only avenue currently open to me, I accepted.

Within a week I had extricated myself from all my university obligations, said goodbye to my colleagues, got a small U-Haul hooked up to my 1975 Opel Rekord, and was en route to Harrisburg.

I got a room at the same hotel where I had stayed for my interview—the only place I knew—and reported to the DEP office attired in shined shoes, pressed slacks, and a starched blouse.

I was welcomed kind of as though I had been the undertaker—someone you really would rather not need, but when you did need them, you were glad they were there. There were cursory introductions, then I was shepherded into a small cubbyhole to complete the prerequisite paperwork.

As I filled in the accustomed, if tedious, information about date of birth, social security number, address, gender, and all the same stuff I provided scores of times over recent years, I read in detail the job description. This was the first time I'd seen the fully fleshed narrative. The prime area of concern for radiation-caused ill-effects was found in a circle with a ten-mile radius, with a locus at the nuclear plant. DEP had then divided this into six slices like cutting an apple pie. My slice was on the west side of the Susquehanna River, directly across from Three Mile Island, in York County, covering the townships of Newberry, East Manchester, and Conewago, regrouping over a score of communities and approximately 30,000 people.

The hiring formalities were handled promptly, DEP making it very clear they wanted me out of the office and in the communities as quickly as possible—the least they saw of me, the better from their perspective.

On my second day, I met with the leaders of the other five teams: Christy Brinks, Henrietta Vander Berg, Ralph Osborn, Cecelia Brown, and Bob Henshaw. Bob covered other townships in York County—my nearest neighbor. The quintuplet spent six hours with me in the same spartan conference room where I had been interviewed, going over their work, setting forth the smallest pieces of a very complex puzzle. They reviewed the accident itself, analyzed the real known impact, enumerated the perceived impacts, and described the affected communities. It was concise and comprehensive.

On the third day, my team met me in the same room. Alice Nash was the health person. Ted Rathburg handled the environmental part, while Emma Gaines dealt with economic issues. All three were natives of the Keystone State. They were correct, guardedly friendly, and clearly uncertain why I was their team leader instead of one of them.

I was briefed thoroughly. Town by town, hamlet by hamlet. The challenges facing my team were highlighted. If, as I believe, first impressions are critical, my first impressions were that the distressed people were driven by fear. They saw the accident not as a rare, one-off mistake, but as the harbinger of a major failure that would, next time, take them with it.

Such a reaction was not unexpected. Reversing this course was extremely difficult, to say the least. We had our hands full. We could, in a succinct and straightforward way, report on the social, cultural, ecological, health, and economic impacts—to the extent these could be measured and analyzed. It seemed already quite probable that luckily most, if not all, of these analyses would show minimal tangible long-term effects. Like any disaster, natural or man-made, there would be lingering repercussions. However, in spite of the scare factor, there was no physical damage to homes or businesses. So far, there were no known documented extreme health issues nor greater environmental problems. It was far from benign, but the real concerns were hidden in people's minds.

With this cheery thought, I bid my team goodbye—agreeing we all meet in two days in vestry of the Goldsboro Church of God where the team had some temporary working space.

My immediate task was lodging. Following the advice of my coworkers, I rather easily found an apartment on Blue Barberry Street in Goldsboro, east of I-83, the VFW Memorial Highway, and west of Three Mile Island, on the opposite side of the river. The town of about 900 people was the closest to ground zero on our side of the river. In some ways, I felt uncomfortable living in what could be tainted ground—this magnifying my understanding of how the residents must feel.

I was standing in front of the church when the team pulled up in the state-owned white 1980 Ford Econovan. The team typically tried to visit the same community as a group, using the van, collecting any useful aggregate data then splitting up to work directly with different community associations as well as individual interested parties. Overall, the work grossly fell into two categories. There was hard data. Water, soil, and air quality tests were run, and samples sent to labs for more in-depth analyses. Hospital, clinic, and doctors' offices records were consulted (within the limits of confidentially) to document any radiation-related illnesses. Businesses, real estate agencies, and chambers of commerce were contacted to garner specific data on any investment changes that could be linked to the disaster.

Then there was less-easily quantifiable data relating to how people felt, to gain an understanding of the before and after scenarios regarding the lives of those living along this stretch of the Susquehanna River. This was more my domain. Others collected anecdotal bits and pieces that were folded into my more comprehensive examination as to how life had changed due to the mishap at Three Mile Island. Trying, as well as I could, to document the scars that had formed around the terror of being consumed by a nuclear inferno.

Across the affected region, it was becoming increasingly clear that the hard data was not identifying any massive issues—albeit a number of potentially serious problematic matters had been flagged. As everyone knew from the onset, the real tricky part was how people were reacting. Were they able to just go back and pick up the pieces? Many were not. Some moved away. Others could not sleep. Others became activists. A few felt so overcome by what they believed to be their inevitable demise that they even went off the rails—drinking excessively or otherwise attempting to deal with the pain.

The team leaders would meet in the DEP offices once a month to assess progress. The picture appearing in my area seemed very similar to what was being depicted for other parts of the impacted zone. DEP was able to put together PR and educational programs using the hard data to try and assuage the communities' concerns. But really calming the overactive nerves of those who could still clearly see the stacks of the nuclear power plant from their front porch was a much more challenging task.

The team leaders reflected a divergent group of highly qualified professionals, all coming from outside the state. Christy came from the University of Chicago Department of Economics while Cecelia had previously been affiliated with Princeton's Department of Sociology before working with the United Nations Atomic Energy Commission. Both were married, Cecelia having a five-year-old daughter. They had each moved here with their families, their spouses finding employment in Harrisburg. Christy's husband was a lawyer who had just passed the Pennsylvania Bar, Cecelia's better half was a chemist who had landed a good job at BAZF Corporation. Henrietta was a public health doctor, engaged to a surgeon in Denver. Ralph was a tenured faculty member of the MIT Department of Nuclear Science & Engineering who traveled east as often as he could to check on his students and family (in that order). Bill had been a professor at UCLA in the Institute of Environment and Sustainability. He was a native Californian with a spacey surfer demeanor that hid a razor-sharp intellect.

Our monthly gatherings were extremely helpful—serving to underscore common denominators across the affected area as well as indicate areas of exploration that might be red herrings. These meetings were generally a two-day affair—starting early afternoon of the first day and finishing before noon on the second, unless urgent or unusual factors had arisen. Although we were all close enough to home to not make this an overnight event, we would go out for a drink after our first session to reinforce the feelings of camaraderie that were already prevalent. The other ladies would generally leave after a glass of wine, Ralph following soon thereafter, after a couple of highballs. Bill and I were the only beer drinkers—also, the only ones unattached. We would generally dawdle. The first few times not lingering too long. Then, as familiarity set in, we stayed for extended periods, sometimes throwing in a late dinner together.

It was probably inevitable. Maybe it was even subliminally planned.

One evening we went farther astray, in more ways than one.

Seeking some history with our meal, we ventured across the river, taking Wright's Ferry Bridge on Highway 30 to the Revere Tavern, the building dating back to 1740. Reportedly, the site was where Stephen Foster wrote "Swanee River" and the premises had once been owned by President James Buchanan. We had a superb meal of beef Wellington, exceptionally accompanied by a more than generous quantity of excellent red wine. Heading back with that warm feeling of having eaten well, we appeared to be retracing our steps to our side of the river. However, we found ourselves on a king-size bed in the Lancaster County Comfort Inn, tumbling about like a pair of Mexican jumping beans. It was curl-your-toes, take-your-breath-away sex.

By the time I reached my six-month anniversary, I was feeling spiritually and professionally fulfilled. The work had an evident gravitas. This was accentuated by working with a group of truly exceptional and dedicated people. It was demanding. It was rewarding. It could, however, also be disheartening (but, I reconciled myself, such is life).

Free moments, and in retrospect it seemed these were only moments—almost disjointed moments like the frames of old 16-millimeter film—were increasingly shared with Bill. We developed a close, in some ways deep relationship. Yet, it was not a relationship with any anticipated long-term outcome. It was somewhere between living for the here and now and building the foundation for a lifelong pairing. There was commitment to a good friendship, but nothing more.

When Thanksgiving came around, DEP decided to give the entire operation a holiday break—fortunately, with pay. There was a backlog of administrative work in the department, and they felt the best thing to do was process all the data, reports, and ledgers outstanding before moving forward in a new year. Bill invited me to California to spend the holidays. This was not to "meet the parents"—his folks were dead, and he had no other close relatives in the state. This was just to enjoy warmer weather and a different ambiance for a few weeks before jumping full force into the Pennsylvania nuclear winter.

We agreed on a hybrid arrangement. I was not willing to spend the entire six weeks from the end of November to the middle of January with him in Hollywood. This felt imprudent. I knew I was teetering on the edge. I liked Bill—I liked him a lot. He was not my first beau. But he was the steamiest. While our personalities seemed to complement each other, in bed our connection was much stronger than a complement—it was almost seismic. We connected on so many levels. It would have been so easy to just jump in with both feet, say "to hell with it," and bond with him for eternity (or until our liaison wore itself out). I could not let myself slide down this slope—I had too much to do. I could not wait for a conjugal bond to pass before getting on with whatever lay beyond the next hill.

My skittishness was magnified by the fact that I knew—or at least thought I knew—that Bill was ready to take the leap. He was worried to bring up the subject for fear of cooling our relationship. Nonetheless, he was ready.

I was not.

I was also not ready to spend all my holidays in sunny southern California with one of the beach boys.

I decided—we agreed—that I would start my break in DC where I would pay a brief visit to old contacts, making sure the links were still strong (knowing one never knew when one needed to know someone). I would then spend Christmas with my family before traveling south to LA to spend

New Year's with Bill. I'd limit my time in the sunshine to ten days with my inamorato—hoping we even made it outside into the sunshine between trysts in the big waterbed he had so often described as being the centerpiece of his LA apartment (which I had no idea why he kept).

Everything went as planned. No major surprises. Overall an enjoyable break in what had been a hectic few years.

Bill and I shared one last slobbery kiss at LAX before I boarded the redeye to DC. On the plane, I got settled in my spacious first-class seat—the upgrade a gift from Bill—in his words, "A first-class seat for my first-class girl"—a bit trite for my tastes. As usual around holidays, the plane was full. I had, by choice, an aisle seat. My neighbor at the window was a fiftyish black man with an impeccably tailored three-piece suit and a closely coiffed beard. As the seatbelt sign extinguished and the first drinks were served, my co-traveler introduced himself as Anthony Brown, the Executive Director of The African Foundation.

I was elated. The gods had smiled.

I had first come across the foundation when doing my work on refugees at St. Mary's—much of the background information about the Ethiopian group I studied came from the foundation's archives. Much more to the point, Africa was the source of much of the cutting-edge cultural anthropological work. This was one of the few parts of the world where cause-and-effect data could relatively quickly be incorporated into policies and the impacts measured over the short-term. It was a region offering tremendous opportunity to develop, test, and then operationalize tools that could have immediate application and hopefully derive long-term benefits.

As the drinks kept coming, I had a chance to review my work on acculturation and my research at Harvard on critical triggers in parent cultural populations. My neighbor seemed most interested—apparently really seriously engrossed and not simply feigning engagement.

As the pilot announced that our decent was beginning, Anthony Brown passed me his business card with a private telephone number, saying he had enjoyed our discussions and thought he might have something for me. He asked me to give him a call after Valentine's Day.

I reined-in my imagination, put the date for the call on my calendar, and concentrated on getting back to Harrisburg and back into the field with my team.

The hiatus had been good for everyone. We resumed our work with renewed energy, if not with fully renewed enthusiasm. From my seat, and I think this pretty well described most of us working on what was sometimes almost callously called the cleanup, we had grown into our job with a bag of mixed emotions and impressions—I dare not say truths, as these managed ever to elude us.

The event had been and continued to be frightening. The drama and potential destruction from nuclear missteps loomed high. Anyone who had gone to school when there were regular Cold War drills and test evacuations organized by the federal Office of Civil and Defense Mobilization (I learned from Bill, who evidently had an endless supply of knowledge, this office had been operational from 1958 to 1973), had nearly a built-in nuclear fear factor.

This could not, we ultimately concluded, be overcome—it could only be modulated.

But there were hitchhikers on this could-have-been-a-frenzy problem. First, preliminary indications suggested massive repercussions may well have been avoided. This led to a communal thank-God moment from managers in the government and the nuclear industry alike. The aftermath of this we-almost-really-did-the-worst-of-it shock was an anti-shock—a push back in the opposite direction. An unspoken but practically tactile feeling that we got away with it. The least we said, the better.

It was like someone who, while driving, realized they narrowly missed having a severe accident. The rebound was to take a deep breath, say a prayer, do nothing, be thankful, and hope it never happened again.

Had the worst happened, probably no one would have been adequately prepared. No one wanted to shine a light on this fact.

And then, of course, as in all significant activities, there was the question of money. Nuclear energy and the energy sector in general formed a huge political and economic net that ensnarled the entire country. It touched virtually each and every household. It was also rife with a multitude of questionable and down-right improper or unsafe acts. It wanted to operate under the radar. It wanted high publicity mistakes like Three Mile Island off the evening news as quickly as possible. It applied pressure to officials—at local, state, and federal levels—to wrap up and return to the status quo as soon as possible—even sooner, if a few extra dollars could help accelerate the processes.

The result of all this was that we all developed tremendous empathy for the affected communities (and really for us all as one community), but realized we were an unwelcome irritant to the powerful. Any meaningful measures to better safeguard the nuclear plants, or the wider basket of energy sector facilities, was improbable. The impetus was on closing the book as fast as one could—if this meant big cash settlements or half-hearted promises, so be it.

Thus, academically and intellectually, each of us saw the present activities as a way to put our disciplines into action—often, to the test. It was challenging and it could be professionally rewarding. Nonetheless, in the bigger picture of really having a positive impact on the lives of potentially damaged families or potentially troubling industrial practices, our meaningfulness was less than we would have liked.

This was frustrating.

I recalled, at times such as these, my mother would have again told me to put my faith in God. I wasn't all that pious—much to my mother's chagrin and in no way due to a lack of effort on her part. Sadly (I guess), my spirituality was mostly to question the human spirit.

Mother would have added, "All comes in God's time."

I really couldn't wait.

The reality of our efforts notwithstanding, we kept at it. Bill and I kept at it too—still conspicuously wanton in our carnal unions, but reservedly demure in the workplace. We had a particularly rapacious feast of Saint Valentines— satiating ourselves in many ways.

After a bawdy celebration of Valentinus, we resumed our routine with the addition that I called Anthony Brown.

He was cordial, even warm, saying he was glad I was following up—he had made all the arrangements. He had a place for me!

This was great news.

Anthony further explained there were some formalities—underscoring these were purely routine matters to address (after all, he was the boss). But it was a done deal—my job was waiting for me.

The hoops to jump through involved making a personal appearance at the foundation offices in DC—having relaxed discussions (a.k.a. interviews) with some key staff, filling out some forms, and submitting a CV. Nothing to be worried about, he assured me.

He had already set a date for these formalities—next week.

This was fast—more so than expected. This was also, from all appearances, a tremendous opportunity.

This was a must-do.

I was able to arrange for a few days off, driving over to DC on the eve of my appointment.

After about four hours chatting with various affable foundation staff, I found myself seated in front of Anthony's large desk in his large corner office on the seventeenth floor, discussing where I wanted to live when I moved to DC to work for the foundation—would it be Maryland or Virginia?

I left Anthony's office with a warm handshake and more assurances that all was in readiness.

I needed to make a final stop at the personnel office to fill the prerequisite forms and drop off my CV. The cheerful personnel clerk with whom I dealt affirmed this was all nearly ritualistic (I found this an interesting choice of words) as the boss had given the go-ahead several days ago. My interlocutor further advised that the processing of the documents could take three to four weeks—I should call back in two weeks to check the status and make sure there were no outstanding questions that could delay the final processing and preparation of a contract (more waiting, ugh).

I got back to my hotel by five, had a welcomed drink at the bar before going to my room and calling Bill—to brag, I guess. I was planning on calling some of my old contacts from my volunteering period while at St. Mary's—letting them know I was coming back to DC. When I mentioned this to Bill, he recommended I, uncharacteristically, go slowly. While he professed to share my happiness at my new job (I'm not sure this was really the case, I doubt it), he recalled our daily lesson: the only certainty is uncertainty. Maybe I should hold off on advising too many people of my arrival in Washington until the contract was signed?

Begrudgingly, I agreed.

We chatted a little longer, then I went across the street to an Ethiopian restaurant for dinner before an early bedtime.

The next morning, I took Highway 270 northwest to Frederick, then switched to Highway 15, which guided me north to Harrisburg. About three-quarters of an hour outside my destination, I crossed Gettysburg. I could almost hear the battle cries from three days of bloodshed nearly 120 years ago that led to an estimated 50,000 casualties on both sides. Totally different from Three Mile Island, I thought, but with one common denominator: casualties. The combat produced thousands of dead and wounded. The accident produced thousands of scared and paranoid. Do we ever learn? If people adapt—acculturate—what of societies?

With these thoughts, I reached home and prepared to rejoin my team the next day.

In two weeks, as arranged, I called the foundation. I spoke to the same person who had helped me in the personnel office—finally learning her name was Amy. She said all was on track—I should expect a contract within two weeks. She added, critically, that the contract had already been drafted, but was not yet finalize nor signed. The final touches aside, reportedly senior management (Anthony?) had insisted on stipulating an immediate start-up. This meant that I would have to report to work within two weeks of signing. If the contract arrived, as planned, in a fortnight, within a month I could conceivably be working at the foundation.

On one hand, this was very exciting.

On the other hand, it was problematic.

My current contract with DEP required a month's notice when terminating. I had to resign now.

I was very uncomfortable with this glaring perplexity—I had to quit before I was sure I had my new job in hand. Not ideal. Not at all.

Bill strongly advised me to find an alternative solution. However, I was convinced he had ulterior motives. While I emphasized that DC was not that far away, he was patently unhappy with me being more than one county away.

Visions of roaming the African Savannah in the footsteps of Louis Leakey, finding my own Olduvai Gorge, twisted about in my head. I could not be deterred by the practicalities, possibly the realities, of my situation. I resigned.

I submitted a final report, bid my colleagues and team goodbye, took a painful (but promised to be brief—or at least so we hoped) separation from Bill, paid up and left my Blue Barberry Street apartment, and moved to a long-term studio apartment in the greater DC metro area—close enough to my new job to get there on short notice. My new temporary lodging was just off Route 66, in Bull Run, Prince William County Virginia (near the battleground of the same name)—only thirty-three miles west of our nation's capital.

After settling as comfortably as possible in my new and cramped space (available only for an outlandish price), I called Amy at the foundation to give her my new address for mailing the contract. When no one picked up on her extension, I called the main switchboard. The operator told me Amy was no longer in the personnel office, connecting me with someone else in that branch. The new nameless person with whom I was now talking seemed to have no knowledge of me nor my pending employment. She (and this was all I knew about my new insider: she was a she) said there was no imminent hiring. After a brief pause to check the records, she added that the most recent job posting had recently been pulled down because management wanted to revise it before re-announcing. If I wanted, my contact would happily fax me the old announcement as a now defunct reference and then send the new posting once it had come out of the boss' office.

I gave the fax number of the office of the complex where I was staying.

An hour later, full of questions, I went by to pick up my document.

It was, indeed, a job announcement for a portion of anthropologist at the foundation. All the requirements seemed to fit. In fact, they seemed to be tailor-made for me.

I didn't know what to do. So, I did nothing.

I did call Bill that evening.

"That really sucks," he tried to commiserate. "But, my impatient friend, don't become a pain in the ass."

I hemmed and hawed.

"This is probably just the same old bureaucratic bullshit we're all too familiar with. Someone got the wrong code or something on the announcement and they just caught it. They'll get a new one up in no time and then you'll be all set."

He nearly said this last with noticeable sadness in his voice, accenting the fact that satisfactory resolution for me meant we'd still be separated—at least for the moment.

I started, "But—"

"No but's," Bill cut me off, "if you get all in a rush and start calling them and digging into what's going on, they're gonna figure you're a troublemaker and not worth the effort. You gotta just sit this one out and it will, I'm sure, turn out well."

"That's a lot of wishful thinking," I said, reminded of Mother's admonition to trust in God.

"What else you gonna do?" Bill concluded.

I didn't have a good answer.

Bill did manage to quell the waves that were building in my stomach. I knew I had to wait. Boy, did I hate to wait!

The arduous days rolled on, one into another, before I got a call from the apartment's office that I had a fax. Trying to show control I did not feel, I forced myself to slowly walk to collect my new message.

Back in my room, I sat at the miniature dining table and put the two faxes side by side. There were no codes. There were no substantive changes in the job description nor the benefits package. There were only two very small additions. First, the job title was now anthropologist/socio-economist. Second, under requirements, it was stipulated the need to have fluency in Xhosa—one of the official languages of South Africa. A language, that I did not know.

I called Bill.

"Well," he said, trying to keep any gratification out of his tone, "they damn well seem to have sunk your ship."

I didn't see it.

"They've added a requirement of speaking a language that very, very few Americans speak—certainly not you, I believe."

"Uh-huh."

"Someone came out of the woodwork, or some powerful political somebody flushed someone out of the woodwork, to pick up a cherry salary at the foundation. They stole your spot."

"But—"

"Nope. Nothing to say. You'd better look elsewhere. Sorry. This isn't fair or right, but it is not going to change—you're back in the unemployment line."

I couldn't tell if he was gloating or trying to help—it sure didn't feel like help. I lied, saying there was someone at the door, and hung up.

I then called the foundation—calling Anthony's private number. He didn't pick up. Bill was right. I was screwed.

Another one of Mother's favorite counsels was, "Let go and let God."

I am not very good at letting go—especially when I think I have been wronged. Nevertheless, there was nothing I could do. What had started as pure good luck due to airplane seating now reverted back to shoddy reality. And, to add to my gloom, I had really lost two jobs.

I might have been able to go back to DEP and explain there had been a major miscommunication that had resulted in my erroneous resignation. But I couldn't do that. I had to turn the page.

I could manage to stay in my far-too-expensive studio for a few months. And, I was ever so close to the Capital of the United States. I should be able to get something going.

I didn't have to look too far.

George Mason University was located less than twenty miles down Route 66. They had a Department of Sociology and Anthropology with a focus on sociocultural anthropology and bioarcheology. They taught ethnographic methods with an emphasis on gender roles, conflict analysis, human rights, and public policy. These were all areas of my interest, several touching on work I had recently been doing with DEP.

I spoke with several of the faculty. They were happy to make arrangements for me to audit some classes with the proviso that I, already a master's graduate with some experience, actively engage in classroom discussions. This was fine by me.

While on campus, I made it a habit to regularly pass by Career Services. After three months back in academia, I learned that Career Services was organizing a job fair. This seemed like a good opportunity—I attended with no expectations, but with an open mind.

With the tech industries competing for the limelight, there were not a lot of stand-out options for anthropologists. There was, however, in one corner, nearly in the shadows, a small table occupied by a Peace Corps recruiter.

Feeling a bit lost, I sat down at the Peace Corps' table, more to rest than to seriously consider volunteering. It was a slow moment, with no one else close by. The recruiter—Kathy, I learned, a former English teacher in Mali—appeared to sense that I was really not a candidate, but more simply someone who needed a few minutes of random chatting to take a respite from the hard work of looking for work.

Kathy and I chatted about traffic to get into the center of town, the need for rain, and the rising price of fuel—everything and nothing. After about ten minutes, I got up to mine the employment resources of the fair once again. As I was leaving, Kathy handed me a few documents, merely to browse if I needed something to do.

These papers somehow made their way onto my dining table. Weeks later, as I was cleaning up the detritus that was accumulating in every cranny of my tiny space, I came across the Peace Corps handouts, including a stamped postcard to send for more information.

Not wanting to throw anything out, without really reading the accompanying pages, I put my name and address on the card and dropped it in a mailbox. Four or five weeks later, having completely forgotten about the card, I received a manila envelope with an application form. Inexplicably and atypically considering the way I generally deal with such unsolicited paperwork; I did fill the forms—again mailing in the stamped self-addressed envelope provided.

It was a rerun of my previous experience. I totally forgot anything and everything about Peace Corps as I got more and more engaged in my studies (even if informal) at George Mason. Then one evening, there was a knock at the door and a courier with an express mail envelope. It was from Peace Corps. I was being offered a position in an agricultural outreach program in Guinea.

Misguided or Not

The purpose of human life is to serve, and to show compassion and the will to help others.

—ALBERT SCHWEITZER

THERE WAS EVERY REASON to ignore Peace Corps. This was for younger people—folks who had recently left school and not yet had a real job or gone to graduate school. This was for novices, tree-huggers, and touchy-feely youth in search of finding themselves. This was not for me.

All these factors aside, the fact of the matter was that, at this moment in my life, this was the only opportunity I had. What could it hurt to look a little more closely?

There was an 800-number listed in the offer, so I called.

The gentleman with whom I spoke introduced himself as an RPCV (Returned Peace Corps Volunteer, I was to learn) from India. He worked in recruitment at the organization's headquarters in downtown DC. He then very politely, and very slowly, introduced me to the process. It took time (damn). The offer was not an offer to immediately become a volunteer, but an offer to begin the process. There was more paperwork; including security and medical check-ups. If everything went well, in about two months' time there would be a staging (evidentially Peace Corps' term for a well-orchestrated no commitment on either side event) in Chicago where all the invitees would gather with Peace Corps officials and consultants. The aim here was to have each side evaluate the situation and determine if Peace Corps was the right match for the individual, and if the project being offered was the best fit. If all was deemed as a good pairing, there would be a three-week gap for the person to go home, pack, say goodbye, and get to the US training site. In regard to the specific project in question—agriculture outreach in Guinea—the training site was at the University of Florida in Gainesville.

My chaperon into the intricacies of Peace Corps then asked if I wanted him to send me the full recruitment package. I quickly calculated. It looked like the process here would require at least three months. In that amount of time, I should be able to find something that was really better aligned to my current point in life. But, if this didn't happen, having a fallback was not the worst idea. I could go through the motions, while devoting most of my efforts to finding a real job—a paying job.

Agreeing to three months of bureaucracy seemed the prudent choice.

When the package arrived, it was over 300 pages of stuff: forms requiring biographical details of my life since birth, medical forms covering every pimple I ever had, forms for the police station to initiate a security check, a history of Peace Corps, a history of Guinea, a history of agricultural outreach, a sketch of volunteer life, an outline of what happens after Peace Corps, and more and more. I was swamped in bureaucracy.

I guess it was a good thing I didn't have a job. I dedicated my full attention to Peace Corps and its sticky red tape. Within ten days of talking with the Indian RPCV I had assembled all those bits of the package that needed to be returned in the mail in the large, stamped, addressed envelope kindly provided by the taxpayers.

There had been absolutely no joy in tackling the Peace Corps' assignment. But I felt great joy in dropping the big envelope in the mailbox. Gone!

I had thought I would now have ample free time to jump back into my search for true gainful employment with the generous assistance of George Mason University's Career Services. But, no sooner had I refocused my mind on these vocational concerns than I got a call from Peace Corps. I guess maybe being close to their office helped—for what ever inexplicable reason, my processing appeared to have catapulted ahead.

My new contact started, after underscoring she had been a volunteer in Panama, by almost gushing how happy she was to inform me that I had been chosen to move forward in the process. She would be sending me roundtrip tickets to Chicago. The staging, requiring three full days in the city, was to take place the week after next at the Wyndham Grand Chicago Riverfront Hotel.

I could feel the current sucking me in.

Before I lose track, I should not forget Bill.

Bill had demonstrated true friendship in addition to much-appreciated love-making skills. He had helped tremendously as I struggled to leave DEP gracefully.

I believe he secretly hoped I would find a way to come back to the clean-up. Nonetheless, he knew me well enough to know that this was unlikely. Not only had I burned my own bridges, but it was, in an objective analysis, not a job that I really enjoyed—not a job where I thought I was making good use of my energies. Bill understood.

Bill did not, however, understand my staying in Bull Run after being sandbagged by the foundation. I think he saw me going into academia full-time—either as a PhD student or as an instructor. He thought, or hoped, that somehow through this avenue our liaison could be maintained.

He questioned my strategy of ferreting out a career at George Mason. But, he stoically stuck with me—making the almost three-hour drive from Harrisburg to Bull Run several times a month—not so much to visit the battlefield or relive the country's history as to create new memories bordering on the lascivious as we thrashed about most of the surfaces of my confined space.

Our ardor— and true friendship— aside, Bill could not get his head around Peace Corps. He recited my initial misgivings, ending always with, "You're too old."

While I didn't like his argument, I did appreciate the spirit with which it was made—he wanted me somehow close—accessible.

When I seemed to be only flirting with Peace Corps, Bill attributed this to my overactive imagination and kept up his amorous visits. Then, when I told him I was going to go to Chicago for a staging, he suddenly realized this could be for real. He knew better than to openly try to oppose the possibility, and he had used up most of his soft-sale options, so he just sucked it up into himself—like a sea anemone closing around a morsel of food, Bill closed up about us. He came to Bull Run one final time before I went to Chicago. After an unusually energetic workout (even for us), he hugged me, tearily asked me to write when I got where I was going and said goodbye.

The Wyndham's grand view of the river and the metropole was lost on the invitees.

The staging was kind of like the first day of school for twenty-year-olds. On the eve of the event, there were a lot of twenty-somethings roaming the hotel's corridors and making good use of the hotel's bar. There were some spontaneous introductions, but mostly everyone seemed to be scanning the horizon to get a good set of bearings—acting more like cats checking out a new home.

We were lodged two to a room. My roommate, Ruth, was from Colorado. This didn't seem like the time for long presentations. After all, we didn't know if we'd ever see each other again. We had little idea of what would happen after the staging. Thus, we just shared the basics. Ruth had come from a small town probably similar to where I had grown up, but in the southeast of the state. She had gone to Colorado State in Fort Collins, graduating with a BS in biology. She was twenty-two.

The next morning, after breakfast, Ruth and I went to the hotel's big meeting room at nine o'clock for the startup of the ritual. The room was about two-thirds full—straight-backed chairs occupied by mostly white young males sitting as upright as the chairs, looking taut as though awaiting the results of their girlfriend's pregnancy test.

The dais was occupied by over a dozen people. At the appointed hour, a middle-aged man with a paunch and a microphone stood up and welcomed us all to the staging. He introduced himself as the Peace Corps Director for Guinea. He briefly outlined the agriculture outreach project as one of the most important activities in his portfolio and the country's program. He informed us that we, the lucky recruits to be, were forty-two of our country's prime youth. However, the project in Guinea could accommodate sixteen new volunteers. Hence, through the next three days, we would interact with a team of high-level experts to make sure that those of us who continued and flew to Conakry in a few weeks would be those who could bring the most and the best to Guinean farmers who so counted on Peace Corps Volunteers for support in growing the food they so needed to feed their families.

At the mention of a triage process—more candidates than posts—there was an audible gasp. Obviously, everyone, including myself, had thought that this was a laissez-faire event—anyone who wanted to go could. After all, how many people really wanted to go to Guinea? How many people even knew where Guinea was?

While I was more than a little skeptical, the next seventy-two hours were quite exceptional.

There was, beginning at the first lunch when everyone was together for the first time, a rapid and strong bonding among candidates. Perhaps it was a connection catalyzed by facing a common enemy: deselection. Perhaps it was an attachment founded on the promise of sharing a unique future: Guinea. Possibly it was simply fear of the unknown. For whatever reasons, we quickly linked together. Age seemed a nonissue. I was older than most, but there were others who were older than I. There was a Vietnam vet and a woman who had been a high school teacher in Poughkeepsie for fifteen years. While most of the group were indeed young, white, Anglo-Saxon, protestant males, there were nine females including two Asian and three black women.

Here in Chicago, I found a rare opportunity to participate in a unique and nearly an unprecedented experience (at least for me). The staging was singular. It was intense. It was in many ways unpleasant. It was a period of naked self-analysis as well as a period of equally naked analyses by others—complete strangers delving into the most hidden parts of my psyche. There was a crew of psychologists, psychiatrists, sociologists, developmentalists, civil servants, and even one Guinean extension agent—all of whom apparently had the sole task of tearing open the corporeal housing to bare the inner workings of our souls.

Why did I want to be a Peace Corps volunteer? Why did I want to go to Africa? Why did I want to work with farmers? Had I worked with people of other races and cultures? What did I think about Africans? What did I think about people who were not Christians? Could I live alone, isolated, for extended periods? What would I do if I lived in the bush and got really sick? Would I happily eat strange foods? Would I learn French, Fula, and/or Malinké? I was a woman (yes!) and I would, by American standards, quite possibly be harassed by men—what would I do? I was a woman (obviously!), could I, if I needed to, urinate in public and have my period where there were no off-the-shelf sanitary pads? Could I manage to not get pregnant? Did I realize that if I did get pregnant, I would be sent home? Did I realize the rampant STDs in Guinea? Could I cook on an open hearth? Could I wash my own cloths by hand, with a block of soap in a stream? Could I live in a mud-block house? Could I ride a bicycle long distances every day? Did I like children? What did I think about cockroaches and rats? Could I survive?

Every evening Ruth and I moved through a different drama as we reviewed the day's adventures. The first night we were concentrating on merely getting through the night, sharing a bedroom with someone we scarcely knew. The next night we were overcome with anxiety: would we make the cut? We had had the position in Guinea skillfully dangled before us—possibly embellished—like a bright shiny object. It definitely had caught our attention and was now an objective we wished with all our hearts to attain. Everyone knew the best psychology was to let people know they might lose something they didn't even have—everyone, of course, desperately wanted it then. There was keen—even cutting—competition.

Then on the third night, the feeling of needing to fight was replaced by a feeling of, "Oh my God! Can we really do that?" after the full day had been devoted to describing in detail the country and the work.

The last night was characterized by an immense feeling of gratification—for better or worse, Ruth and I had both made the cut. We were going to Florida for training.

As had been indicated by the Indian RPCV, with the go-ahead coming out of the staging, it was now time to commit, to move to the next step—training. But first, there was a stint at home. Although I was living nearly at Peace Corps' doorstep, and had not been home for a long time, they agreed to provide me with a ticket home and then a flight back east—not to DC but to Florida.

As I flew west across the Mississippi and the Rockies, I stared out into the void. My mind roamed the nothingness—questioning. Just like Ruth and I had wondered that night in our hotel room, I speculated on whether or not I had been sucked into volunteering for fear of losing something I didn't have? Was I so happy to have one of the slots for which so many competed so aggressively that I lost track of my main job in going to the staging—determining if this was the right move for me? Had peer pressure (from a group I had really grown to like in a very short time) and institutional machinations shoved me where I otherwise would not have gone?

Or, as the Conakry Director had proclaimed, was I simply lucky and finally, more or less by chance, on the right path to my own Olduvai?

When I got home, I had no answers. And, to my surprise, my family had few questions for which I had to concoct replies. I guess they had merely become inured to my shenanigans (as they probably saw them), or this was such an off-the-wall choice that they did not even try to understand. For whatever reason, it was as though I had just come back from summer camp. There were shallow and perfunctory questions about my health, my social life, and my work—those questions folks ask out of politeness, but in which they have already lost interest before the responses are even given. It seemed my parents were simply content to have me around for a while.

Since moving east, I had been living modestly—not wanting to invest in very much material incumbrance until I was stable. Now I was limited to one suitcase of personal effects to carry me over the next two years. Therefore, I had sold my car and boxed up all my stuff from my Bull Run studio—sending it to my folks—knowing it would arrive well after my departure, but who cared? Thus, while home, I took great pains in selecting just the right things to accompany me to Guinea.

Surprisingly quickly, I was back on the move. After a rather bizarre homecoming when no one really seemed to know why I had come home, I was soon flying back across the Rockies and the Mississippi, this time to Gainesville, home of the University of Florida.

However, our training site was not on the main campus. It was situated at the University's Suwannee Valley Agricultural Extension Center-Farm, about sixty-five miles north of Gainesville. Here, like a modern-day version of an old Conestoga camp, Peace Corps and her contractors had circled five seventy-two-foot mobile homes—four for trainees and one for trainers.

Beyond Peace Corps' temporary structures, the Center had a variety of facilities. The nucleus was a multipurpose hub housing classrooms, offices, and meeting areas. For the trainees, the core was a large hall, probably intended to assemble local Florida farmers—now the rallying point for a Guinea-bound covey of would-be Peace Corps Volunteers.

Peace Corps had arranged the hall to accommodate daily gatherings of the trainees, the trainers, and any other individuals who might have a part in the day's activities. While possibly functional, the furnishings of the hall were unusual.

It looked like Peace Corps had scoured the nearby dumps for any old armchairs or sofas. The quarters were filled with such a curious assortment of bedraggled furniture as to be almost comical. There were overstuffed items, with the stuffing coming out. There were hardwood seats that mashed your sacrum into your pelvis. There were tweed sofas that looked as if they had been declined by the Salvation Army.

At seven o'clock on the morning of day one, we were all convened in this big room, each choosing a seat that seemed the best for them. Once we were all settled, a rather large middle-aged man in khaki trousers, a plaid shirt, loafers, thick glasses, and gray hair appeared before us. He introduced himself as Dr. Clark.

After a quick generic welcome, Dr. Clark challenged us, "Look at you. Look around. The easy chairs for the easy goers!"

There was a uniform reaction of shock and surprise, but no one said anything.

Dr. Clark continued, in a rather high, nearly piercing voice, "Those worn-out old couches and club chairs seem pretty disgusting, don't they?

Your folks would never have them in their homes, would they? But, ya know, they might look pretty good when you've lived in a village in Guinea for a year?"

No reaction.

"So," the good doctor continued in the same tone, "those of you on the comfy furniture—are you the easy goers? Are you looking for the good life—the life of luxuries? If so, let me tell ya, you're in the wrong place."

Still, no reaction from a now entranced and stone-faced audience.

"Let me tell you." He went on, "I can't teach you how to do your job. Now I'm a pretty damn good agronomist, but I can't tell you what to do, how to do it, or when to do it. You're gonna have to figure all that out yourselves. You're gonna be there—face-to-face with the farmers—your farmers—and you're the expert. But I can't tell you how to be an expert. You've got to figure it out yourselves. That's why you're here."

Dr. Clark then introduced Steve and Frank, two RPCVs, now his graduate students, and the spearheads of the training team—in effect, our personal trainers under Dr. Clark's obviously stern supervision.

Our trainers, in a more relaxed fashion, then explained the training.

Here at the Center, each of us would have our own garden plot. The underlying axiom was that we each needed to grow a crop ourselves before we could teach others how to do the same—we were going to do that here.

It was not simply any crop any way. There were core principles underpinning the Guinea project: water and soil conservation with nutrient recycling. Our own gardens needed to incorporate these principles.

Now, our trainers added, if we had not already noticed it, we should be advised that none of us had degrees in agriculture. None of us had been farmers. We were all more or less generalists—certainly not agronomy specialists.

This was by design. Helping smallholder farmers grow a relatively limited number of crops using a relatively limited number of technologies can, if you already know too much, quickly become monotonous. Monotony was the enemy of volunteers. Once things lost their flair, volunteers tended to think about going home. No one wanted anyone leaving early to go home. Hence, it had been found that recruiting people with a different skill sets, so that they too are learning as they teach others, was the best way to maintain high levels of interest throughout the volunteer's two-year assignment.

At the end of the day, our trainers assured us, based on their own experiences, it is not learning the exact technologies that was important in doing the job well—it was learning how to solve problems—how to solve problems using available resources—that was the key.

We would need to follow a strict schedule if we were to be able to find this key.

In addition to daily seven o'clock meetings here with the whole group, there would be trips to the main campus. For the first week of the eight-week program, there would be two trips to campus—thereafter, only on Fridays. On campus, we would have access to all the University had to offer—libraries, staff, laboratories, anything. But, before we could go to campus, we needed to have a plan. We needed to write down how we were going to use our gardens—what crops we would grow and why, what techniques we would use and why, and how all this would meet the principles of soil and water conservation and nutrient recycling.

Once we had a plan outline approved by our personal trainer (Steve and Frank dividing the group in two), we would be able to get on the bus and go to campus to collect information and data that made our plans complete—implementable. By the beginning of week three, we had to have an approved full-blown plan and begin work on our plots.

We would manage our plots through week seven when we would take a tour of selected farms in Florida where we could talk to farmers and see operations firsthand. Then, on week eight, we would harvest our own plots and calculate if we had made a profit while adhering to the core principles.

That was it—the whole deal laid out in front of us.

No one knew what to think.

We were then each given an extra-large three-ring notebook and a huge stack of punched paper along with a pair of pens—our trainers telling us to snap to it—write our plan.

It was hard work. It was hectic. It was frustrating. It was even threatening. One day, a trainee, Sam, whose garden was close to mine, just didn't show up at the seven o'clock meeting. We never knew what had happened. There weren't even any rumors. He was just gone. Could others vanish? It simply added to the stress.

Then it was over. We had four days to ourselves before meeting up in New York at JFK for the flight to Paris and then on to Conakry—the capital of Guinea about which we had all been dreaming.

We left Dr. Clark, unsure if we were thankful for what we had accomplished or just thankful to be leaving. Each of us left with our three-ring binders jammed full of all sorts of papers, reports, and notes. What we didn't know was if any of these were true. Did these riches mined from eight weeks toiling over our gardens in Florida really constitute a guide for two years as a volunteer in Guinea? Or, were they merely a foil? No one knew. No one had ever told us, not even at the end of training, how we should do our jobs. We hoped we knew now how to solve this problem once in our villages.

I spent an enjoyable, if tumultuous few days in DC before going on up to JFK to join my group. I had tried to get Bill to come over. Although he answered my call, he said he was too busy, and wished me well. Accordingly, I vented all my bottled-up training exasperations and uncertainties on the bars and nightclubs of our nation's capital, reconnecting with folks from my days at St. Mary's when I had been a different kind of volunteer in this city.

I must have had a good time, because one morning I woke up in a bed in a Holiday Inn next to Stu. He assured me he and I had worked together way back when, when we were both participating as student volunteers at the Department of Education. I hadn't a clue. No clue about Stu—it made me giggle.

But the amusements of the short furlough were fleeting. I was truly en route to Africa and this was a serious undertaking of protracted preparation.

The flight to Africa was the longest of my life—providing more than enough time to stare again into the void.

As I peered out, in addition to being bathed in the saffron nightlights of the sleeping cabin, I was also bathed in that kind of melancholy I still get on long flights, when gazing out into the blackness, my mind racing to try and understand why. Why I was where I was? Why life was the way it was? Why I was I thinking about "why?"

I was sitting next to Ruth, but she was dozing. I decided to shake her awake and push the call button for more drinks—that might help. As we emptied more of those little bottles, we verbally cried on each other's shoulders as we had done so often over recent months. This was a big thing. It was wrapped in bipolar feelings of dread and trepidation countered by glee and anticipation.

When we touched down at Conakry, the overriding thought was, "What the hell am I doing here?" There was a torrential downpour as we had to walk from the plane, sitting far off on the tarmac, to the mildew-covered terminal which seemed to radiate fumes of jet fuel, stale urine, cigarettes, and mushrooms. Although we were met by a Peace Corp official, once inside, all of us drenched to the skin, we were confronted by a throng of men and women in drab uniforms, billed hats, and all variety of bobbles—all yelling at us in a language or languages we could not understand. It was chaos.

It took several hours with much shouting and handwringing before the fifteen trainees, including myself, were successfully seated in the old school bus rented by Peace Corps; our sopping luggage for our two-year stay on the roof rack, the Peace Corps welcoming committee seated in the front, guiding the driver to a hotel in the Matoto neighborhood of the city, not far from the airport. We reached the hotel parking to the blare of generators, as there was a general electricity cut across the capital.

The hotel room, I again shared with Ruth, smelled of insect spray and bleach. We sloshed in with our oozing bags—but we were too tired to do anything but fall in a heap on our beds. We slept unaffected by the perfume from the malodorous linen and the shaking of the generator outside our window. Our first night in Africa was spent in exhausted sleep.

The next morning, after a breakfast of bitter instant coffee and tasty fresh-baked bread, the bus took us to the Peace Corps training site in Kindia, seventy miles east of the capital. Here we would undergo intensive language training, mostly French, but with an introduction to Fula and Malinké. We also had cross-cultural training, training in bicycle repairs, training in First Aide, and how to stay healthy. At the end of six weeks of this assorted schooling, we were assigned a post and sworn in. We were now officially Peace Corps volunteers (PCVs in the parlance of Peace Corps).

I was posted to the village of Fomi, roughly in the middle of the country, about halfway between the administrative centers of Babila (a town of 16,000 on the banks of the Niger River) and Kiniéro (a town of about 22,000 near the boundary of the Upper Niger National Park). My post was almost 400 miles east of Conakry, making the trip thirteen to fifteen hours if things went well.

A Peace Corps Land Rover and driver took me to my new home along with my now very old-looking suitcase, a box of books accumulated during training, and my new bicycle with a bag of parts and a tire pump. We took the N-1, one of country's major highways, all the way to the Niger River, to the crossing at Koumana, 360 miles and about twelve hours from Con-akry—a commercial and government hub having a role similar to a county seat. We spent the night in a small hotel catering to truck drivers running up and down the N-1.

Soon after sunrise the next morning we continued on to Babila. As a bird flies, this hub was less than five miles upriver. However, given the roads we had to travel, the trip required making a big loop four times this distance— frequently over very difficult terrain.

Here we had a lot to do. I was introduced to the local administrators as well as the agricultural staff in this zone roughly equal to a township (using Pennsylvania's local government structures as a reference). We shopped for staples I would not be able to find at my post and stayed the night in a small guesthouse on the edge of town with no electricity or running water.

On day three, with great anticipation, we drove to my new home: Fomi.

Here to my surprise, Peace Corps and the government had already prepared a house for my accommodation. It was a mud block cubicle affair with, according to Peace Corps standards, a tin roof and a cement floor. There was even a kerosene fridge, a locally made bamboo bed with a straw mattress, and a freshly dug latrine in the back. I had purchased bedding, kerosene lamps, tin plates, and toilet paper in Babila—so I was set to go.

Nonetheless, we spent only one night at my new home—the driver sleeping in the vehicle and me in my new bed. The next day we continued on to Kiniéro, this requiring another circuitous routing of forty-five miles and over two hours driving. This was my second government administrative precinct of assignment; a second township where I was to work. My post sat astride the two districts of Babila and Kiniéro. Accordingly, it was important to go through the same formalities at each center since I could be working with extensionists and farmers from either area.

We got back to Fomi that evening and the driver left very early the next morning for the long haul back to Conakry. I was alone in the heart of Guinea.

This solitude was for real, but it was also peculiar. I was alone in regard to my bevy of friends, family, and colleagues for the first time in a long time. For the past fourteen plus weeks I had literally been immersed in collegiality. Now I was alone in a strange house in a strange village in a strange country. But I wasn't really alone at all. There was a whole village at my doorstep. Somehow, I had to integrate.

When I thought about it, it seemed easy. When I planned it (and I had become a pretty good planner thanks to Dr. Clark), it didn't seem that difficult. But when I set about doing it, it seemed impossible. That first step simply would not come—it was like I was paralyzed.

It was all candidly too much.

I'd told the guys in Chicago I could do all these things, but when it came right down to it, I had my doubts. Cooking using charcoal, bathing in a bucket, taking a dump in a hole—it was too much. No electricity, no running water, and no way to get out. It was overpowering.

Then I got screaming dysentery—my bowels opened and streamed like Niagara Falls. It was terrible. It was traumatic.

Frothing taffy-colored slop surged and leaked from me onto the bed, the floor, and some even into the pit whose margins were now encrusted with a fly-attracting glaze.

I would lie on my bed and wonder, when I died, how long would it take Peace Corps to find me?

Ironically, it was this shitstorm that precipitated the needed first step. The villagers were not going to let that new white girl die on their turf—what would it do for their reputation? They rallied around and soon showed real affection, not simply concern about avoiding an unpleasant problem. They were wonderful and they pulled me through.

One day, it was honestly like the sun rose for the first time—I felt well. I felt good. It was amazing.

Moreover, when I got up and got going, I found I was somehow already a member of the community. I was accepted. They now had a vested interest in me.

People helped me with everything: cleaning, cooking, laundry, fetching water. All the overwhelming realities were now just part of daily life. I was soon on my bicycle, visiting farmers and trying to literally get the lay of the land to lay out my plans which I would then discuss with the authorities in both administrative centers.

Most of the adults in my villages spoke Mandé, with only a smattering of French. I was still pretty much a novice in French but was a toddler in terms of trying to communicate even minimally in Mandé. I often had to rely on school children, who had a better grasp of French, to be my interpreters.

One exception was Ramatou. She had actually lived for a while in Conakry (a place that now seemed far, far away), but had returned to take care of her ailing parents. She spoke much better French than I, but was patient, and we were able to communicate well—doing so often.

One day Ramatou asked me, "Have you seen your brother lately?"

This took me totally aback. My brother? I realized by now all whites would be considered as my brothers and sisters—but I had not seen any whites for some time and was certainly unaware of any specific male who could even be considered as my brother.

When I pursued the topic, Ramatou expanded, "You know, the guy who teaches in Morinimaya."

I knew neither the place nor the person but decided to ask around. It turned out this somewhat larger village, amazingly only three miles due south of me, at the junction of three important, if unmaintained secondary roads, had a high school and, at this high school there was a white, possibly Peace Corps teacher.

At the earliest occasion, I set off for Morinimaya on my bike. I found the school and I found the teacher. Joel, indeed a PCV, was a math-science instructor.

While he appeared to be glad to see me, Joel was starting his second year and he had somewhat of a don't-pull-me-down air (been there, done that). He'd gone through his adjustments and was enjoying, at least according to him, his life and his work.

Nevertheless, once we'd made contact, we kept in touch. We weren't that far away from each other after all.

October 2, 1958, Guinea had attained independence from France. This day was annually commemorated with big celebrations all across the country—it was a big deal. There was an extended school holiday and Joel came to Fomi to memorialize, or probably to carouse, with me. One thing led to another and Joel and I ended up observing the festivities in my bamboo bed.

This was the epitome of a relationship based on convenience. Joel admitted he was concerned about having any type of relationship with anyone in Morinimaya. There had been too many scandals of teachers sleeping with their students. He did not want any smidgen of doubt in that direction. So I was, in a manner of speaking, his port in a storm.

We were frank with each other and accepted this for what it was—pragmatism.

I didn't know where this could have led. I guessed the casualness, nearly insignificance, with which we saw our union could have transformed into something more meaningful. It certainly was not the mind-boggling sex I had had with Bill. But it was a release.

Joel and I did more than share a bed. Ironically, our other activities seemed to spawn more guilt than our random intimacies.

Part of the volunteer experience which we both took very seriously was integrating as much as possible into local communities—learning new ways and new customs. As Joel said, "I didn't come all this way to hang out with Americans!"

So, we didn't stick together—weren't stuck together. Each in his or her own way, I believe we tried our best to join the greater non-American world that surrounded us. Our serious commitment to globalism notwithstanding, at times it was a nice respite to revert to our mother tongue and rehash more common lifestyles. To accomplish this without appearing to shun those with whom we should be bonding, we decided only to rendezvous in nearby bigger cities where we had the freedom of the wanderer and none of the surveillance of the village.

Our posts were about equidistant from the two biggest market and political centers in this part of the country. Kankan and Kouroussa were each about one hour away by car when the roads were in good shape. Every so often, Joel and I would go to have a time on the town. We'd take a bush taxi—a Peugeot 404 station wagon that carried nine to ten passengers (not counting the driver) along with a great heap of luggage on the roof that might include bunches of bananas, sacks of cassava, a goat, and a basket of chickens.

We'd go to see Chinese or Indian films with scratchy soundtracks in languages we could not understand and robotic actors who skipped about more than intended due to the missing sprocket on the projector. We'd go to Lebanese or Senegalese restaurants for fare we found to be truly excellent. We would walk the byways—totally unknown, unlike in our own villages—enjoying the scenes of mosques and markets, breathing in the scents of dust and detritus, savoring life in Guinea.

Then things changed. Then I met Abduli.

Abduli was the Deputy Administrator from Babila. He would, I learned, come to our village at least twice a year to talk with the headman, to see how his people were doing. He came in a shiny white Pajero, accompanied by an assistant and a Gendarme. He would spend a night at the headman's house before moving on to the next village on his list.

During his first visit after my arrival, the headman brought him to meet the new PCV now living in the village—now one of his people. He invited me to the local cabaret—our one kind of public space where one could get some roasted meat (at times), a plate of millet porridge (at times), or a cup of tea (all the time).

As we sipped our tea, he enquired about me, my background, and my hopes. I was taken aback. It might be too much to say I was swept off my feet, but I was really impressed by this man not too much older than myself.

After I had told my tale, I had the presence of mind to ask him about himself. He was unexpectedly poised and comfortable in sharing his life with a complete stranger.

His father had been a herdsman—raising goats and cattle. He had grown up running free over the grasslands, herding animals, carrying water, and fighting with his many brothers—he had grown up as a normal kid. He had been born in Doko, not far from the Mali border. In fact, he had attended secondary school in Bameko before going to university in France. He had always been a good student—a quick learner. When he had returned from his studies, he easily got a mid-level job in the civil service. Babila was his second post.

He smiled a wonderful, welcoming smile, leaned back, and said very slowly in French, to make sure I could understand, "There you have it. Not much. Merely the life of a local guy—someone like so many others."

Maybe he was like so many others, but to me he was spectacular—charming, lithe, and appealing.

I would think of him after he had left. I would think of him fondly. But I would think of him abstractly. He was not part of my world; he was a passerby.

Then, only a few months later, obviously too soon for a biannual stopover, he showed up at my door. He apologized profusely. He regretted not contacting me before he arrived. But this was really a last-minute assignment. He needed to visit the Upper Niger National Park (apparently without his assistant or the Gendarme, as he was driving the Pajero and alone) and it occurred to him that, if I had not seen the park, I might enjoy profiting from the opportunity to go with him. It would, he cautioned, be roughing it—camping in the bush.

I was enthralled. I was titillated. I was also excited to see the park.

I asked him to check with the headman, because I really did not know what to do.

He affirmed he had arranged everything pending only my acceptance. We were off.

The park was impressive. Over 2,000 square miles of forest and savannah—a key conservation area that protected much of the highland hydrology of the Niger River system.

But the park was not as impressive as Abduli.

He was smart. He was funny. He knew all the plants, all the places, all the histories. He filled the car with beautiful legends as we bounced from stone to stone.

That night, it seemed only natural that we share the same tent—the same sleeping bag. It wasn't the same fireworks as with Bill, but in many ways, it was more moving.

As I got to know Abduli in the familial as well as the biblical sense, I learned (he was completely forthcoming) he had two wives and three children. He was a devout Muslim. He was a devoted worker for his country. He loved his family—and he loved me.

We saw each other at least once a month. I am not sure how Abduli cleared this with his boss, but he seemed to be able to arrange for regular trips to Fomi which not only brought him to my door, but also brought the village to greater prominence.

I had the difficult task of telling Joel that we could still be friends, but that I had developed a serious relationship that would impact on the level of our friendship. He didn't like it. However, he knew he couldn't change it (rumors of my ties to Abduli spread rapidly and, although he said nothing, Joel already undoubtedly knew the whole story).

I knew Abduli really cared for me. I wasn't sure if it was love, as I wasn't sure my own sentiments were love. Yet, whatever we had, we had something important—I think unique.

It wasn't only physical. It was in many ways deeply intellectual. Abduli was extremely interested in how a single American female adjusted to a village in Guinea—my acculturation. He also shared frankly and thoroughly his own similar transcultural challenges as he had adapted and acclimatized to life in Europe as a student.

He freely recounted how people would call him a chimpanzee to his face, how so many felt Africa was principally the home to elephants and lions (the rare uncivilized savage possibly thrown in on the side). How people would ask, "Do people in your home have shoes?" "Do you know what electricity is?" Laughingly, he added, "The only thing missing was for them to ask me to drop my drawers to see my tail."

But we both knew it was not a laughing matter.

Prejudices and ignorance were major factors affecting all our daily lives.

We both had dreams of a better place—but knew these were dreams.

We had something special.

We kept, each in his or her own way, trying to see how we could imagine a longer-term solution. There didn't appear to be one—and we racked our brains, that's for sure.

He knew I was not going to become his third wife (although, he didn't know how seriously I considered this option). I had no life to offer him. After a year of passion and frustration, we decided it was in everyone's best interests to break things off.

We would still see each other in the course of our normal activities. We even occasionally had a cup of tea together. But what had been was gone.

Before moving too far down the road, it may be of interest to note that over recent years, a project to build a dam in Fomi has become a hot topic.

The planned site, on the Niandan River in the Niger Basin, would inundate nearly 200 square miles, produce roughly 100 megawatts of power, while providing water for irrigation, aquaculture, and transportation.

The project would, if undertaken, displace 48,000 people and affect another 70,000. Most ominously, it was also predicted to adversely affect the hydrology and sustainability of the 15,000 square mile Inner Niger Delta in Mali which had a major economic and social impact on the entire region.

I do not know if my work with farmers around Fomi, farmers in need of reliable water supplies, had in any way impacted on the efforts to create an impoundment in that area. I do not know if Abduli's frequent visits to Fomi, often officially, had in any way influenced the decisions on how to plan impoundments in Guinea. I do know that this was a very contentious subject and remains so up to today. It may, moreover, be a tangible indication of how a little stone can cause a big ripple.

After two lengthy dry seasons and two smaller rainy seasons at my post, I had to begin to think about leaving—the end of my contract was approaching. It was time to go. I had no idea where.

I also had no idea of what was happening around me.

While my microcosm seemed in perpetual movement—adjusting, adapting, growing—I had very little contact with, nor news of, the world outside my bubble.

During my first six months at my post, I listened to the BBC and the Voice of America religiously. In fact, my transistor radio was almost my tabernacle. While the news in special English was monotonous, and the BBC really said little about francophone countries, I would have had to listen to France Inter to get better coverage, but my French simply wasn't up to that of the Parisian radio journalists.

Then, as I grew into my village and my job, these gaps in outside updates became less and less noticeable. Soon my transistor was just collecting dust on the corner of my one rickety bookshelf.

With the cyclical nature of events, as I began thinking of life after Fomi, I dusted off my radio, got fresh batteries, and began trying to understand what had happened during my absence.

To all appearances, my dropping-out had in no way affected the messes we were all wading through. Havoc, sadly, as so often, seemed prevalent— Africa having particular problems as the afterglow of independence waned in many parts of the continent.

My own sub-region was a case in point.

The neighboring country of Liberia had been established by freed American slaves. There had been growing friction between the ruling Americano-Liberians and the people from the indigenous ethic groups who were effectively taken over by the freed slaves when they declared Liberia to be a country, their country, in 1847.

Things boiled over in 1980 when Samuel Doe, the first non-Americano-Liberian leader, took control of government through a coup. Much remained in disarray, and there had recently been an attempt by an army officer to overthrow Doe through a second coup. Elections were now scheduled for next year, but many people were worried about the outcome—worried about their survival.

Some of the most affected areas were in the forest zone, in the north of Liberia where she shared her borders with Guinea and Sierra Leone. This area was not only remote and more easily affected by unsettled governance, but this area was an area rich in diamonds—sought after by all. This area, called the "Parrot's Beak" by some, was frequently in turmoil, as leaders cared much more about shiny stones than the wellbeing of local populations.

When the fragile balloon of false security burst and everything whirled about harum-scarum, these local people moved to avoid being crushed—seeking refuge where they could. Right now, there was a rapidly expanding movement of Liberian refugees into southern Guinea, the region of Nzérékoré, from Lola to Guekedou.

While I had been totally unaware of any of these goings-on in the southern part of the country, when I went to Conakry to begin the lengthy process of checking out, this was the topic of the day. It was, indeed, more than a topic. NGOs like OXFAM and Save the Children, who were assisting the Liberian evacuees coming in waves into Guinea, were looking for help. They needed feet on the ground. They were looking at Peace Corps—offering contracts to PCVs completing their service.

Having become used to blowing in the wind, and with nothing else on my calendar, I signed on. Within a month, I found myself at a refugee camp outside Nzérékoré.

My intent has not been to compose an autobiography of my life in Peace Corps. Many PCVs and RPCVs have done so admirably—certainly better than I could and with more substantive and arresting subject matter.

My intent is purely to attempt to show how my life, and perhaps many lives, were affected by serendipity. And, how through this serendipity, I ended up in Peace Corps—a fact that may have been the tipping point of my life.

I may have already written too much, gone into too much excruciating minutiae and abstruse detail. Try as I might, I am not able to encapsulate my Peace Corps experiences as I would like. I am not able to spread them out on a table as objective cause and effect data gathered in my studies or work. I am only able to appreciate that I would not have ended up as I have if I had not entered Peace Corps.

Self-determination

Do something wonderful, people may imitate it.

—ALBERT SCHWEITZER

NZÉRÉKORÉ WAS IN THE forest, far from everywhere. From the capital, the quickest way, if time were the only factor, to try and get there was on an internal flight in an old Russian-built, plywood-constructed, prop-plane.

I had signed a one-year contract with Global Refugee Assistance (GRA) who had offered me a considerably better deal than other NGOs working in southern Guinea. I felt like a mercenary. I really wasn't planning on offering myself to the highest bidder. It was simply that the salaries and benefits were so variable among the different actors, it only made sense to go where the arrangements were the best. This was certainly GRA.

As a local hire, they gave me a stipend to buy what otherwise might have been classified as necessities. As a PCV, I hadn't had much. As a GRA employee (local hire, or not), I was entitled to more. I wasn't sure I wanted more, but it was there for the taking.

Conakry is not a world-class shopping center, but I was able to get a lot (in my eyes) of personal and household items that, along with my original Peace Corps suitcase, would be trucked down to Nzérékoré while I flew in the plywood box.

Nzérékoré was a big city by Guinea standards. A commercial crossroads, it reached out to parts of the hinterlands of Liberia, Sierra Leone, and Côte d'Ivoire. There was a human ebb and flow—different ethnicities, different religions. It was probably as close to an ideal study area as a cultural anthropologist could hope to find.

But I was not there as an anthropologist. I was not even there as an RPCV. I was there to try and see how best to help people caught up in the changes when the typical ebb and flow turned into tides nearing tsunami size.

There was what might be considered as a normal resident refugee population coming from all the neighbors—people moving when local conditions became too difficult to tolerate. Then the political upheavals in Liberia shocked the system, overlaying the normal levels with large influxes that the existing facilities could not accommodate.

The United Nations had overall oversight for the refugee situation, in close collaboration with the government of Guinea. Specific clusters of refugees were then catered for by different NGOs. Some of these clusters were far in the forest, exacerbating the constraints on providing real services to people in need. The groups under GRA's care were in the area surrounding Nzérékoré—in what could be considered the city suburbs.

GRA's sites, like most of the others, were, in effect, tent settlements: camps. Sturdy canvas and plywood structures lodged hundreds of families—these residents (temporary or not) requiring support facilities including sanitary stations, kitchens, schools, and clinics. The camps were mini-cities next to a city. They were self-contained encampments, even with their own security forces.

I was initially surprised by the high level of security. After all, the security problems for most of those fleeing Liberia seemed to be back in Liberia.

My new colleagues quickly set the record straight. Refugees received a standard minimum of care that included adequate accommodation that protected them from the elements, adequate nutrition that maintained their health, adequate healthcare in the case there were health issues, and adequate schooling for the children. These were all provided in the camp.

Outside the camp, many of the residents of Nzérékoré found it difficult, if not impossible, to provide such an adequate life for their families. In short, those outside were, by many measures, having a significantly more difficult time coping with life than those inside the fence-line.

This led to jealousy. This led to antipathy. This, at times, led to outright violence—especially at times like when the government teachers were on strike to try and increase their pittance of a salary, but kids in the camps still could go to school because their education was guaranteed by the NGOs managing the camps (not by the government of Guinea).

It was the reverse of the roles we often see in Europe or the US, where refugees or immigrants are marginalized—frequently living in sub-standard conditions. Here, many Guineans felt they'd be better off if they lived in the camp—if they too were refugees.

I was a gofer. I, with my RPCV label, was a grunt. Although I, and all the RPCVs working on the refugee program (I'd guess there were about a score of us scattered throughout the Forest Zone), had a lot more practical knowhow in terms of getting things done, in terms of understanding local cultures, in terms of communicating with stakeholders, in terms of just about everything—the camps and their related activities were all supervised by NGO professionals coming from outside the country. These people had little regard for Peace Corps.

So often, these bosses tried to the breaking point to get a round peg to fit into a square hole. So often, they simply didn't get it. But I was one of the silent—or, so I was told to be—fixtures who were there to do what we were told—full stop. It was common knowledge (or perception) that the NGOs paid "big bucks" compared to a PCV's living allowance.

We were encouraged to be grateful for the windfall provided by the more than generous NGOs. The sweat of our brows and not the subjects of our thoughts were what was needed.

It was far from ideal from my vantage point. Yet, in some ways it didn't matter. The out of touch (or, don't-give-a-damn) managers were generally found in their air-conditioned offices near the city center. They rarely directly engaged the refugees—only making irregular visits to the camps, and then often not getting out of their comfy Toyota Land Cruisers.

If you were willing to get out into the muck, crying children, heat, flies, and odors of the camp quarters, you could do a lot with virtually no oversight. You could, I could, anyone could really help if one got off his or her backside. There definitely was a job to be done. In retrospect, Dr. Clark had provided many of the tools needed to do it.

The bosses, those who many in the local vernacular called the *mawbe*, had assigned a nomenclature to the camps. Each camp had the name of an animal (primates thoughtfully excluded)—a kind zoo-a-rama mixture of African and European critters ranging from the hedgehog and the lion to the sparrow and the zebra.

My camp was ANTELOPE.

The camps were, in turn, divided into numerical sectors.

In spite of the seeming almost arrogant disregard for experience and skills at the highest levels, at the interface with the refugees, there was a latent awareness that these things mattered. This was nearly begrudgingly acknowledged. My own case as an example, with my anthropological and PCV experience, I was assigned mainly to ANTELOPE-2 and ANTE-LOPE-7—the first being the screening section for new arrivals and the latter being the group that dealt with unanticipated problems as they arose (and these were many and varied).

This whole taxonomical nonsense of assigning names to places was much more practical than I had first realized. As the overseer, the UN had set up a two-way radio network covering the whole refugee area. But we all used the same frequency—we had to share. Therefore, when someone coming from the central station yelled, "Break for ANTELOPE-7, Break for ANTELOPE-7," others would leave the airwaves free so someone from ANTELOPE-7 could pick up the mic for an important communication. It worked.

I was able to forge, as were many at the bottom rung of the ladder, a very busy schedule dealing with newcomers one-on-one. It was demanding and rewarding. In spite of the bumbling efforts of many of those making decisions, I found the work gratifying. My interactions with those relying on me to help them, hopefully not only provided some modicum of assistance, but also provided me with considerable insight into people and people problems.

Outside the camp, I was now facing two new challenges, however. The first was omnipresent for all in what might be called a caring profession—it was so hard not to get too involved. Everyone had a story. Everyone had needs. It was hard not to be overwhelmed by these needs, just as it was hard to not become overly emotionally engaged with those having such acute needs.

The second challenge was more personal: my social life. In Fomi, while I wouldn't say I had been tremendously socially active, my own needs had initially been fulfilled by Joel and then by Abduli. After the painful separation from Abduli, I had had occasional flings with a few people—more often than not, when someone transited through my sphere or I transited through theirs. These were spontaneous and short-lived—as a rule, one-night stands. And, these casual couplings notwithstanding, my social life was sparse by most yardsticks.

Now, in Nzérékoré I was basically surrounded by randy males. It was like an all-you-can-eat buffet. I could choose almost any physiognomy and find a candidate.

But it wasn't that easy. Not only did I not want to attract a label of a wanton tramp, but, irrespective of some of my less-than-discerning choices in bed mates, I was not interested in just anyone anyhow.

As often in my life, when finding no quick solution, without waiting, I went to one extreme—I became effectively celibate.

Life in the forest continued. It was a mixture of ups and downs, good and bad, fun and sadness—like life anywhere. Most of my time was spent dealing directly with refugees—this provided the highest highs and the lowest lows. These were people sometimes with horrific stories to tell. These were people who were suffering. These were, at times, people who were wounded or ill. These were people, nevertheless, who always tried to smile. These were also people of great warmth and generosity (with the little they had)—they gave of themselves to say thank you for the assistance offered.

There was no question about the justifiable concern for these people's safety and the obligation of society as a whole to intervene to offer a helping hand. Sadly, it was the helping hand part that led to many of my harshest frustrations—especially those matters that went outside the bounds of the human suffering that was bathing the camps.

The hands that were extended to comfort and nourish ultimately came from international organizations driven by politics and edacity. At the apex of each organization were those attempting to gain political ground while they accumulated wealth.

At the most basic level, this was all part of the contracting processes where NGOs competed aggressively for contracts to undertake the management of one or more camps or assume other refugee-related functions outside the wire (such as dealing with logistics, communications, and the like). In total, this involved a large group of disparate firms and associations—each lobbying for a bigger slice of the pie.

At a higher level, this was all about the pie itself. Quick resolution of infrequent major events led to reductions in budgets for such things as humanitarian relief and catastrophic assistance. While the snarl of international politics and conflicts did not truly bode well for any significant reduction in problems, it was more the perception of the problems than the problems themselves that drove the money allocation processes. It was the failures and not the successes that brought in more support.

In the ultimate analysis, it was unclear how much pressure there was to really succeed—to sustainably resolve issues and help people lead their own lives.

I guess in some ways I was disillusioned. I felt jaded. I really felt more flummoxed than deluded.

Things seemed to be driven by external and internal interests that were sometimes self-motivated, sometimes ignorant, sometimes both. In the end, the vulnerable seemed often to only be steppingstones—a means to an end—an end being more riches, often from unbridled exploitation of seemingly endless mineral and forest resources.

More confounding was the web of those engaged in these actions. One day, when coming back from a border crossing quite far in the bush, we had to get off the narrow path to let an unmarked Jeep pass—an unmarked Jeep full of US military—the flag clearly visible on the uniform sleeves. What were they doing here?

The endless crises—hour by hour, day by day—were so all-absorbing, they clouded many thoughts of the overarching actions. When literally engaged in life and death struggles, it was hard to see the bigger picture. I was not sure I was really able to get a complete view of the theater in which we were all actors.

When there were rare lulls in the pandemonium, I would ask myself, "Why do I do it?"

At times I would lie in my bunk and impugn my own motives. Was I a vagabond? Was I a thrill seeker? Was I simply looking for a high from the next thunderous excitement, often caused by others being closer to death?

I didn't know.

Then, other nights, falling on my mattress after hours and hours in the camp, remembering the smile of a child and the laugh of her mother, I would know why. I wanted, I hoped to make a difference. It was more. I thought I made a difference.

Regardless of the corruption, in spite of the inhumanity, even in the face of a ruthless system, I managed to help. I guess it was that simple.

At the end of a year, I had saved some money, lost six pounds, and added ten years to my psychological age (maybe, five years to my physiological age, too). Over this period, the camps had grown. The Liberian situation had only worsened. The government was threatening populations of Gio and Mano ethnic groups in Nimba County. Charles Taylor left the government and fled to Côte d'Ivoire from where he had mounted an armed opposition. Every day, when people thought things could not get worse, they did.

The conflict spread.

I also became conflicted. I became conflicted with myself. Yes, there were personal gratifications in helping—in making a difference. Yes, it was a two-way street—I was learning a lot of real-life odds and ends that I could wrap in the ample packaging of anthropology. Yes, the way things were evolving, I could probably spend years with GRA.

Yet, was this the right choice? Could I even choose what was right for me? I did choose. Looking back through the yellowed lenses of time, I think I chose correctly.

I chose to look for a change. Initially, I was unsure of what change, but intuitively felt a change was required.

I went to Conakry to complete my service termination. Unlike in Pennsylvania at the DEP, there were no goodbyes in Nzérékoré. My life there had been in a constant state of flux. It was like watching a horse race from the far end of the field—a blur. When things went well, refugees moved through the system at a quick pace and, at nearly the same speed, so did the senior and junior staff. The refugees left hoping to find a safe place for their families. The staff left hoping to find a better job. I guess I was no different.

I abandoned the plywood plane for the much longer and more jarring (not to say that little plane couldn't be jarring) road-trip, profiting from a GRA Land Rover making the normal biweekly run between Nzérékoré and the coast.

I bounced about in the Land Rover from Nzérékoré, all the way to the Novotel, in the borough of Kaloum, where GRA had booked a room for me. We followed the N-1 throughout, from the musty and somehow crowded forest all the way out the little finger from the city of Conakry that is Kaloum—a digit of ancient land that somehow sticks into the belly of Sangareya Bay.

My room overlooked the bay—the sea and even the hotel feeling calm by comparison to the camps of Nzérékoré.

There wasn't much involved in leaving GRA—a snap compared to all the bureaucracy I had faced when leaving Peace Corps. Then, for the first time in quite some time, I was free. I had nothing to do and I wanted to do nothing.

Looking at Conakry on a map, it reminded me of a Twinkie—the city was long and narrow (and, after a fashion, soft), ending at the digit that was home to my hotel. A little way inland from the hotel was the Sovereignty Nightclub.

I had never been much of a nightclub person—but now seemed like a good time to see about changing this custom. After a few days of simply lying by the hotel pool and vegetating, I put on a chic, kind of translucent, white shift (that I had bought at a used clothes stand in Nzérékoré market—what they call the *fripperie*), dabbed on a wee bit of makeup (which I never wore, but had a small amount tucked away in my now tattered Peace Corps suitcase), combed my hair, and went to the Sovereignty after the encouragement of a pair of Scotch on the rocks at the hotel bar.

It was loud. It was smelly. It was full of cigarette smoke. It was full of wreathing bodies. I almost left.

Then a stunning man—tall and muscular—asked me to dance. We danced and we danced. He was gorgeous. I knew his name was André. The next morning, after he had demonstrated how truly athletic he was, we had coffee and croissants in my room and he explained he was a rather junior officer at the BIAM—the French-owned International Bank of Coastal Africa.

André and I spent nearly every night and much of the afternoons together for the next six days—practically nonstop. Then he had to go for an extended work-related visit to Dakar and it was over.

There was no regret. There was no hollowness. It merely was what it was.

I went back to the Sovereignty a few days after André left. Guilelessly curious, I guess.

It wasn't really like fishing—but I imagined it was. I quickly caught Frederik—this time learning a bit more about him before we shared morning coffee and croissants. He was South African. South Africa had the deepest mines in the world and Frederik was a mining engineer. He was advising, on behalf of major South African mining firms, several Guinean operations—potential gold exploitation northeast of Conakry as well as three large bauxite companies (he informed me Guinea had one quarter of the world's reserves of bauxite—I had no idea). He came to visit Guinea three or four times a year—staying two to three weeks at each stay. He candidly proclaimed that, although he loved his work, he hated coming here—it sure wasn't South Africa.

Our relationship was relatively short and purely physical. However, as Frederik was an Afrikaner, it was through him that I met his fellow Dutch-speaker (and Dutch native) Martha, who worked for the International Justice Bureau, the IJB, in the Netherlands.

Martha was delving into Guinea's recent past on behalf of the IJB.

Not surprisingly, much of the disorder that seeped from the coast into the forests of Nzérékoré was political. The long-time president of Guinea, who had ruled the country since independence in 1958, Sékou Touré, had died a little over a year ago (an event that had dumbfounded most of the country, but that I had scarcely felt in Fomi).

Sékou Touré had been an important personage in West Africa in the sixties. The trade unionist and Marxist turned president had begun his political career staunchly anti-colonial—stifling all in his way, chalking up a long list of human rights accusations. When foreign politicians and other leaders of his ilk encountered difficulties at home, he readily offered them refuge in Conakry. This included giving a home to Kwame Nkrumah when the first Afro-centric president of Ghana was driven out by a coup as well as welcoming the US civil rights organizer Stokely Carmichael and his wife, South African singer, Miriam Makeba. This also included opening his borders to a number of lesser-known personages—principally coming from across Francophone Africa.

As Sékou Touré's presidency matured through successive mandates, he became more open—even encouraging the United States to invest in his country. When he died in the US in 1984, he left a country in transition.

Before Sékou Touré's successor could be elected, there was a military coup—Lansana Conté taking over the presidency. He was of the Susu ethnic group while Touré had been a Malinké. This change in leadership, not only led to political transformations, but also to new ethnic frictions.

With all this as background, Martha was here to dig through the archives to document those political leaders—particularly those with poor human rights records—who may have transited through Guinea. Her organization tried to keep tabs on such individuals, closing files when the individuals were deceased.

The hotel was expensive, and Martha was nice. I liked her; I think we liked each other. Martha was also considerate. IJB was renting a small apartment for her during her one-year stint (now in its fifth month) and she asked me to move in.

We got along well. I was still indolent. Furthermore, I felt no inner motive to be otherwise. So, while Martha was arguing with ministerial civil servants about access to records, then spending hours trying to find her way through years of dusty archives, I enjoyed the modest but tidy apartment. I did the cooking and cleaning. I did the shopping and errand running.

We lived in a three-story building in the borough of Lambanji, about halfway between the Polytechnic and a small but much-appreciated seaside cove called Azure Beach. We were close to shops, restaurants, banks, and bars. Martha's favorite local was Racing Bar—where they televised horse races from France. Martha liked horses.

I think initially there may have been some sexual tension between Martha and me. I was never sure of her sexual orientation and, in hindsight, think if she had made the right overtures, we might have had some exploratory adventures. As it was, we just were amical flatmates.

On weekends we would often wander over to Azure Beach to try and find a semi-private spot among the tourists and Conakry elite who constituted the majority of partakers of this once pristine cove. During these relatively quiet one-on-one periods, I enjoyed listening to Martha talk about her work, her findings—prompting her to go into detail, as her natural reaction was to be taciturn when discussing her job.

Martha's work—what amounted to a review of the historical evolution of a new political system—was interesting, but it also was tangential to my core professional (and, to a large extent personal) interests. The post-independence uses, and abuses of power cloaked in the name of democracy were instructive and, in some ways, a foible common to most human communities. However, this was an idiosyncrasy that formed fundamentally the base and not the essence of my interests. My inclination, from the cheap seats, would be to couch the subject as an analysis of how these high-profile evolutionary social adjustments (from relatively minor modernization impacts to major political shifts) jolted the management and functions of a community.

My interests were not the policies themselves per se, but their effects. How these issues affected the grassroots cultures of those living under these emerging and transitioning neo-political systems; these new systems that forged a variety of social changes—some anticipated, others not.

The corollary I drew in my mind was, naturally, with my recent work in Nzérékoré. While there were many evident afflictions (and probably many more not-so-evident messes) with the system's overarching efforts, on the ground someone could nearly ignore these and make significant progress. It was apparently a case of pragmatism overcoming imperfect policies. More simply put, it was an acknowledgement that some high-level induced changes touched everyone while others seemed to fly above the heads of most, like a jet flying high over my folks' home—they knew it was there, but it had no real immediate impact unless it came crashing down.

Overlaying these questions of impact was the question of how the drivers of these impacts were seen—how and by whom. Certainly, the same impactful, or even shocking actions were seen differently by different people.

The true influences of externally promoted change on the full spectrum of society's actors were seldom completely known in advance. Moreover, they were infrequently examined after the fact.

This was a subject that inspired me: what were the immediate and longer-term consequences of actions that were perceived by wider society as good, but may have been seen by those most directly involved as bad or corrupt?

There was an old adage: no pain, no gain. Were difficult first steps really transitioning to hoped-for, longer-term benefits? Was the gain worth the pain? Were, alternatively, these painful acts, driven often by distant elites, simply processes that benefited the elites to the detriment of the community? Or, were, in fact, these potentially painful steps, so far removed from the reality of the intended communities that there was a complete disconnect—decisions of the decisionmakers never filtering down to the intended beneficiaries?

Could cultural transformation lead to more homogenous multitiered society, or did it reinforce a feudal structure of nobility and peasants?

More questions than answers.

Post-cold-war global political processes, particularly in what was referred to as the developing world, were real-time laboratories where cultural change was unfolding. Martha and I were at the epicenter.

As Martha and I grew more comfortable with each other, understanding each's perspectives more clearly, Martha and I would discuss at length these possibly esoteric issues. The subjects were arcane but familiar—in many ways—similar to the time-honored nature or nurture arguments. Were the ultimate results (and the longer-term outcomes) chiefly an effect of government's good or bad management, or an effect of the ability or inability to assimilate changing social and cultural norms? We often got way far off in the weeds.

Our intellectual bemusement aside, as my inertness waned, I began to think more earnestly about my next steps. I could not hibernate permanently on Azure Beach. Nonetheless, to my consternation, I really did not know which way to turn.

The answer came from Martha. IJB was preparing a project in Namibia in collaboration with UN partners. It was anticipated that the upheaval that had virtually become a way of life in this country since independence might soon be coming to an end. Martha added needed background.

Southwest Africa (now Namibia) had been a German colony from 1884 until 1915 when, under the League of Nations, it was mandated to South Africa. German was still an official language (about two-thirds of the population speaking Afrikaans). At the end of the Second World War, when thousands of Nazis wanted for war crimes fled to South America, it was reported hundreds escaped to Southwest Africa—chiefly the coastal city of Swakopmund.

In 1968 the UN approved the name change to Namibia, the following year declaring the South African occupation illegal. This set the stage for one of the hotspots of the Cold War. In opposition to a continued South African presence, the new leadership of the new country accepted assistance from the Soviet Union and Cuba. The ensuing conflict (known by several names: The South African Border War, the Namibian War of Independence, or the Angolan Bush War—this latter probably because, through time, fighting shifted from Namibia to Angola) engulfed much of southern Africa.

As of now, at least in Namibia, things were settling down, there was, in IJB's view, a need to quickly document actions and wrongdoings. One part of this multifaceted examination was to determine, if possible, the impact on social stratification of the German versus the South African influences. In other words, if present, how were foreign-driven socioeconomic imbalances incorporated into local cultures?

Martha thought this might interest me.

It did.

With her facilitation, I was able to get an invitation for an interview in the Netherlands.

This was the ideal end to my listless period. First, the all-expense-paid trip to Holland was a wonderful change of pace. Then the job (initially as described by Martha, and then when more fully explained by IJB staff) was compelling. Finally, the interview went so well they were willing to put me on an open-ended contract (minimum of twelve months with an automatic renewal for a minimum of three months) with a start-up in one month's time.

My work was kind of fuzzy. It was fuzzy both in terms of the subject matter and in regard to the arrangements. From all indications, I was seen as contributing a small piece to a much more expansive tableau. The major theme—establish baselines for the wellbeing of rural populations in Namibia—was undertaken by a large and well-funded team completely outside the sphere of my activities. I was providing a different lens through which to look at vulnerable populations. To what extent could their vulnerability be explained by historical interactions with external cultures? To what extent could it be expected their traditional cultural values could counteract (or be exacerbated by) any negative residues from the past? The answers for these questions needed to be excavated from a country that was complex politically, historically, ecologically, and socially.

The country was big—bigger than Texas. However, it was reportedly the seventh least densely populated country in the world. The average concentration of humans was seven per square mile (the range from less than one to almost sixty).

Geographically, the country was shaped kind of like an ax stuck in a chopping block. The head of the ax, on an axis along the Atlantic seaboard, covered an area from the Cunene, Okavango, and Zambezi River basins in the north, across the Kalahari Desert to the drainage of the Orange River in the south. The ax handle followed the Zambezi eastward, in what some call the Caprivi Strip. These different ecozones had, naturally, led to very different coping strategies for native populations.

These same populations had been greatly affected by outside influences—some much more than others. In 1904 the Herero and Namaqua (also called the Hottentots) ethnic groups waged a three-year war against the colonial Germans that resulted in at least 75,000 deaths among those indigenous communities the Germans saw as the aggressors. What became acknowledged as an attempt to massacre native peoples—a genocide—reportedly killed eighty percent of the warrior tribes; survivors were relegated to concentration camps (of the type used by the British to contain hostile Afrikaners next door in South Africa) or assigned as slave labor in mines or other German-run enterprises.

While the bellicose groups received the brunt of German wrath, none of the country's ethnicities were exempt. Since 1886, the colony had had a policy of segregation—separate laws for Africans and whites. Most Africans were confined to "native territories" (later called "homelands" when under South African rule).

The outsiders came in search of wealth—farming along with diamond and copper mining among the principal targets. By the end of the German occupation in 1914, of an overall population that numbered more than 200,000, there were almost 12,000 Germans and about 2,000 other whites. Interracial marriage had been illegal since 1912.

Race relations did not improve under South African leadership.

Zipping forward to the present, as so often, it was a tale of two worlds. The capital and port—Windhoek and Walvis Bay—respectively (the population of the former, five times that of the latter), were modern, European-like (in Africa, Namibia was second only to South Africa in terms of the percent of the population being of European ancestry) cities that were clean, efficient, and comfortable by any standards. These centers were moving along what some might call the high-end of the scale of socioeconomic development—the antitheses of these municipalities were found in the hinterland.

There were many traditional communities. The 50,000-strong Ova-Himba in the north were a good example. They still lived in mud and manure plastered homes and engaged in subsistence farming and animal husbandry as they had for generations. Most had never been to Windhoek or Walvis Bay. In many ways, these two worlds occupied parallel tracks—each almost pretending the other did not exist.

Yet, as had often been said, "Reality was a bitch."

The two tracks did indeed manage to cross and even collide. This was why I had a job. When cultures separated by centuries slammed into each other, could the result be positive—advancing the overall progress (however perceived) of the country? Could this be done while protecting the vulnerable?

To answer these queries, getting back to the fuzziness, I had to try and understand the situation holistically. Any large development scheme would run headlong into communities who, at best, felt marginalized. If precedent was prologue, these communities might well react not by attempting to understand well the pros and cons of the proposed activity, but rather out of emotions fired by historical misdeeds. My job was not to redress this possible position, but rather to provide insight into its sources. This required being nearly as nomadic as the people with whom I was hoping to work.

Once again, my intent in this storytelling is not to dive deeply into the inscrutable work that occupied my time during fifteen months in Namibia those years ago. It is enough to say that, unsurprisingly, the case was much more complicated than many had foreseen. Traditional roots ran deeply into the hard-sunbaked soil. Nonetheless, I was, to my own dismay, able to be accepted by most communities with whom I was in contact. I was able, with their open and honest help, to compile a great deal of information which I spent my last five months analyzing. I do not know, in the end, if my work made any difference.

One footnote that I did not put in my final report was that, in my meandering, I came across a project supported by The African Foundation. In East Caprivi, they had a water supply and sanitation activity. They were digging wells for livestock and people with the aim of providing the local populations with a supply of five gallons of potable water per person per day. Through access to better water supplies and improved hygiene, they also hoped to reduce the frequency of water-borne diseases that were affecting families—especially in young children.

I guess it was a good project. I was happy I was doing what I was doing. Thus, I concluded, it was good I did not get that job at the foundation.

My work in Namibia had greatly expanded my professional vistas. It had also expanded my bank account. For over a year, I really hadn't been able to spend any money on anything. My living and travel costs were paid, and all I did was travel.

When it came time to go, I decided it was also time to spend some of my savings—I wouldn't want to become too affluent. I decided, since I had been a constant traveler, to keep up the forward momentum and travel northward, ultimately (I guess) on my way home (wherever that might be).

My route was not something that could be charted by a travel agent in Windhoek. It was a plan in my mind.

I crossed the Caprivi strip into Zambia. Slowly crossing the country, I traveled up Lake Tanganyika to Burundi, thence crossing over into Tanzania. From there, I moved, frequently slothfully, through Kenya and into Ethiopia, ending this leg in Addis Ababa. I then had to revert to the skies, flying southwest to Gabon, visiting, among other locales, Lambaréné. I then followed the teeming coast through Cameroon, Nigeria, Benin, Togo, and Ghana. I endured endless police check points, armpit-drenching muggy weather, and frequent diarrhea induced by delicious, but sometimes suspect foods.

At that point, I was very tempted to continue on to Côte d'Ivoire and across the border to Nzérékoré. I was also very tired. In my travels, I had concluded the obvious: this was a really, really big place. This was a really, really big and complex place. For things to work, one truly had to have a bigger picture than most of us were ever able to absorb. So much was done only to be eaten by the forest or covered by the desert sands. Much was needed, but we really needed to take our work to a higher plain.

I think I also confirmed to my own satisfaction that the old adage—you can't go back— was true.

Hence, although I had decided I needed to go to see my parents—go to what was ultimately my home, I would not go back to Guinea. Therefore, I flew again—this time from Accra to Dakar.

After roaming about Senegal for a few weeks, I mustered by inner forces and bought one more ticket—a ticket home.

I should add for all those who don't already know (and, I'm sure nearly everyone does), traveling is hard work. I had covered a good portion of the continent—a distance the equivalent to over four thousand miles by air and easily twice that on land. Surprisingly, I had accomplished this relatively unscathed. That is, until I boarded my flight in Dakar.

The roll-up staircase to enter the plane had definitely seen better days. When the flight was called and the waiting room doors opened, the throng, pushing and shoving, flowed all the way to the unsteady stairs.

I nearly had my foot on the bottom step when some three-hundred-pound bulldozer whammed into me, sending me sprawling on the tarmac. Others kindly helped me up and I hobbled up the wobbly staircase and gained my seat with a bruised knee and a swollen ankle. I was a little worse for wear, but ready for takeoff.

The flight to New York was uneventful, if a bit painful. I immediately changed planes for my voyage westward to my parents and home.

My parents were old. But they were happy—really tickled—to see me. We spent hours sipping coffee then wine, talking about what I had been doing. They were interested. They feigned understanding. I think they hoped it was over.

When I got to the part about my travels north from Namibia, Mother nearly went apoplectic. Then she seemed to shake herself, like a spaniel getting out of a duck pond. She nearly stammered, "You could have been raped!"

I just nodded.

"You could have been killed! Maimed!"

I guess to save face, my father chimed in, "What the hell were you thinking?"

I tried to smile—imagining myself as the Sphinx.

In unison, they added, "You silly, silly girl. Do you know how lucky you are? Did you thank God?"

It wasn't going too well.

"What the hell did you think you were doing?" Dad seemed to need to repeat himself.

I felt compelled to answer. I didn't want to say too much—it seemed useless. I only replied, "It seemed like the right thing to do."

"What?" they again reacted in harmony.

"Yeah," I concluded, "I couldn't wait."

Bigger Picture

Ethics is nothing else than reverence for life.

—ALBERT SCHWEITZER

MY PARENTS DIDN'T SEE things through my eyes. It truly wasn't their fault. We just saw things differently—everything differently. They had spent their adult lives in our hometown. They had friends. They had PEO and Elks. They had their grocer and their plumber. They had their barber and hair-dresser. And, they had their family. Their family was Susan.

Susan had ultimately not become a lawyer. In fact, she seemed to have forgotten she ever had thought of becoming one (so much for being driven and succinct planning). She was now a primary school teacher (not at Sam Jackson, but at another school about five miles away). She was married and had two children of her own—her homegrown husband worked for his father in a contracting business.

Susan had gone to college at a state school 150 miles from home, at that time, the furthest she'd been from her birthplace. Her junior year (now an education major with no more aspirations for the law), she took a six-week US History study tour to the East Coast, to see the world. She then met her husband-to-be at a New Year's party hosted by our parents' across-the-street neighbors that same year. They were married the June after she graduated—the reception was held in Mother's garden. Twenty-eight weeks later Susan gave birth to a baby boy she named after our father.

Susan and her family had Sunday lunch every week with our parents. My folks had their family. It was great.

I was an outlier.

Mother and Father had settled into the rhythm of grandparenting and getting old.

What I at least see as ironical is the fact that, as I tell this tale, I am two decades older than my parents were when I returned from Namibia. I know

I surely am not young—but I feel younger than my parents felt during those blasé days of my homecoming.

If my parents didn't see things the way I did, it was safe to say most people did not see things the way I now did. I do not want to exaggerate nor, most definitely, appear as though I'm patting myself on my back. I simply looked at things differently (and still do).

It wasn't really that I had had an epiphany. It was, I guess, a convergence of two factors: chance and observation. Before my fortieth birthday, I had been fortunate enough to have seen a great deal—not generally through precise and disciplined planning, but through pure luck. Then, when offered these unique experiences, I had been able to observe people and events that had made a lasting imprint on me.

I was a product of all those hardworking, outgoing, thoughtful, and hospitable women, men, and children with whom I had been fortunate enough to cross paths. The laughing child on her mother's lap in a taxi, the fired once high-level and still fierce civil servant working his farm in the bush in his underwear, the secretary who sat at the same empty desk for three years waiting for a typewriter, the smithy who made farm implements from old car parts, the herdsman who lived with his cows along the two-hundred-and-fifty mile trek to market, the lady serving plate upon plate of rice and beans at a smoky chophouse, the nurse whose once white garments were covered with the soil of sorrow—all helped me become who I now was.

I didn't believe I was special—I believed I had had special opportunities.

Needless to say, I didn't last too long at home. After about ten days of biting my tongue (as well as my nails) and being overpowered by monotony, I made plans to make plans. The first step was to get somewhere where I could burrow back into the subjects that had so entrapped my imagination.

I needed to be able to climb the hill to see the bigger picture. I knew this panorama would be more than anyone could fully digest. Yet, the magnitude of a controversy (indeed, much of what was on the table was controversial to at least some) should not crush us. The immensity of the issues should not detract from their importance nor from our efforts to redress those matters needing urgent attention. One should not be overwhelmed by the enormity of the problems.

Still, it wasn't enough to know there was more out there. It wasn't enough to want to counteract the tunnel vision that could be a common result of everyday life. It wasn't enough to want to redress intolerance. Becoming a vehicle of positive cultural transformation required being at the nexus of time and place—it demanded opportunity.

The logical place for me to start was back in DC. However, this was not going back to what had been, but going to what could be. There would be no Bill, no foundation, none of the old episodes. I had to find a new direction.

I wasn't going to go back, but I didn't want to exclude those few contacts I still had from my volunteer days while at St. Mary's. Indeed, one of these old-hands was able to find me a reasonable short-term apartment in Beltsville, snuggled between I-95 and Highway 1, not far from the local branch of the Prince George County Library.

I flew back east to my latest abode, seeing the slightest inklings of smiles cross my parents' faces when they bid me goodbye from the stoop as I got into my taxi to the airport (they had a conflict and couldn't drop me off).

There wasn't much to do in terms of settling in. The apartment was furnished with the essentials. I had replaced my bedraggled Peace Corps suitcase with a new facsimile. A stop at Walmart filled any gaps, and I was ready to go.

A combination of bus and subway took me wherever I wanted to go. I began to canvas the Capital, having coffee with all my contacts, making new links with the contacts' contacts. Not job hunting and not proselytizing, I was exploring.

After a week, the lay of the land became pretty clear. After another week, it was confirmed. If I was looking for a seat in the theater of the big picture, I wouldn't find it in DC. Here it was a peepshow where the aperture was controlled by US policies and priorities—by economics and influence.

The view from this hill was important, but it was unquestionably not all-encompassing. It was biased. It was slanted. At times, it was even tainted.

These detractions did not make the American view any less exceptional. These possible weaknesses did not make it unimportant. After all, every actor on the stage had an agenda. Every actor had vested interests. The shortcomings from my current viewing station were more pragmatic. I needed to see more. The curtains on the DC stage were not fully pulled back—the full, be it partisan, stage was not visible. The US took on only parts of the puzzle.

I needed another vantage point.

❖❖❖

I began foraging closer to home—spending a lot of my time at the County Library—an outpost bridged to a much larger and formidable information network. If it hadn't been before, it now became evident that I needed to be hooked up to multinational groups to be able to get the scope I felt was required for any type of long-term sustainability (on my part).

The UN system was certainly an option. However, it was a big—a very big—bureaucracy. I had had ample expose in Nzérékoré. It was frequently saddled with traditions and processes that ultimately hampered forward movement. It was frequently nepotistic and enmeshed in archaic practices. It was, at times, bridled by pompous and self-serving leadership—regularly at the beck and call of member countries with the biggest budgets. It was, nonetheless, often very effective—representing a much wider point of view reflecting the consensus of some of the finest experts around the globe.

Looking closely at all sides, it seemed other options would be better choices. There were quasi-governmental groups like IJB. Alas, these shared many of the constraints common to the UN. The more governments and national politics were interlaced in attempts to help vulnerable populations, those being targeted all too often found themselves in second place (or not even placing) when balanced against the pulls of hegemony and wealth.

I needed to look on the margins. I needed to find a place whose pre-eminence and independence allowed for as clear a view as possible of the horizon and the approaching storms.

It was a tall order. It seemed nearly impossible.

Then, by chance, I stumbled across the Ecumenical Humanitarian Trust—EHT—in Geneva. This group had been working around the world to try and give a louder voice to those needing to be heard. The trust had been established in 1946 with private funds coming from the estates of three venerable Italian families and with the mandate to help those who had lost everything in the War. The founding families had been Venetian merchants trading with Marco Polo in the thirteenth century. They had done very well by any criterion. However, in the 1600s they encountered the displeasures of several powerful Italian politicians and moved their businesses across the border into Switzerland, near the Umbrail Pass. They built three separate estates around what was now Santa Maria in the Swiss National Park, roughly forty miles southeast of Davos. Today, their substantial fortunes were still active in several modern economies, but they also maintained EHT in good standing.

EHT undertook a variety of interventions around the globe—spotlighting assistance to poor countries (what some now called LDCs, lesser developed countries). They really had no specific area of focus other than hoping to optimize positive impact. They dealt with the full gamut of concerns from education and the environment to HIV/AIDS and infrastructure.

It was EHT's methodology and not their subject matter that stood out to me. One of the core principles was that the problems afflicting peoples in need were frequently common—or at least shared a high degree of commonality around our planet. Hence, EHT worked in specific communities in different parts of the world to attack a common problem. They then distilled the results from these diverse test cases into a toolbox to address the targeted concerns on a much wider geographic scale. Results were impressive.

However, I was an outsider looking in. I knew no one in EHT. I knew no one in Switzerland. It seemed a long shot that an RPCV from Guinea would be of any interest to them at all.

Not being deterred by reality, I wrote a letter to EHT's chief executive, appending my CV. I then went back to grubbing through files in the library, seeking other options.

I was stunned when, three weeks later, I got a reply from EHT. I was even more stunned when I read it and realized they were offering me a position. I was moving to Geneva.

This was much like previous relocations—rather unpleasant, but not harrowing. EHT had offices squeezed between downtown Geneva and the lake, directly on Quai de Mont-Blanc. For the first two weeks of orientation, I had a room in another Novotel—this time Centre Ville Genève.

Geneva, the source of the Rhône River, was one of the more expensive cities in the world. I fortunately found a most delightful and affordable apartment in nearby Satigny Commune, commuting to work by trâin into Cornavin Station, followed by a nice walk across downtown to the EHT offices.

This was, as could have been expected, in many ways a rerun of starting previous positions—getting to know people and processes. It soon became clear that this in and of itself, would be a process. EHT occupied three floors of a high-rise—different segments of their space designated to different tasks. I had been hired as a member of the Mixed Assessment Team. As always, there was an acronym in use, and I was part of MAT.

MAT was a quasi-permanent structure that reviewed global EHT actions. It was what some might call an interdisciplinary unit. There were two economists, a sociologist, a demographer, an ecologist, an environmental engineer, a legal/institutional counsel, and now, with my addition, a cultural anthropologist. Our MAT octet added technical subject-matter specialists depending on the area of review for a total effective size of ten to twelve experts.

It was a big and powerful squad.

We were located at the end of a corridor on the third EHT level—I have no idea if this was seen as a prime spot or a place relegated to the shadows. But the encapsulation of different groups of EHT staff meant that it was hard to know coworkers very well. Across the hall from us was a water resources group, next to them a soil conversation contingent. Beyond these two neighbors, I was pretty much in the dark as to who did what and where. I guessed this would become clearer with time.

In the immediate, I had no time to ponder the overall staffing of EHT. MAT was actively engaged in reviewing projects in Bangladesh and Mozambique, so I had to hit the ground at full speed. This meant spending hours and hours outside our normal office times in the impressive library that occupied a full third of the first level. I reviewed historical MAT files and then probed deeply into the projects in the two current target countries. It took a lot of time.

Educating myself was doubly challenging as the office was bilingual. Switzerland's official four languages were divided geographically, Geneva in the francophone part of the country—actually, almost imbedded in France. Much of the daily routine and reporting was, accordingly, done in French (forcing me to do all I could to really beef up my Guinean Peace Corps French).

French, however, did not travel too well outside the zones of the "francophony." English was a necessary transnational communication tool. This helped. Nonetheless, as I combed through the archives, I needed to have my French/English dictionary at the ready.

It took about four months. But by then, going to work in Geneva felt just like going to work anywhere else. I enjoyed the city, I enjoyed my colleagues, and I enjoyed our assignments.

Things were OK.

It appeared to me that I was finally being able to see the bigger picture—at least through the ocular of specific projects. MAT tried to examine from the highest common denominator—studying specific project outcomes and seeing how these could be folded into wider regional and global programs.

We got into some very deep, some would say, egg-headed assessments.

I had wanted to see what it looked like from the stratosphere and here I was, looking down on the efforts of people scattered about the globe. It soon became very easy to use a telescope instead of a microscope to look at actions and reactions.

This ease of long-distance viewing was nearly enough to plant a seed of disquiet in my psyche. Were we really seeing what we thought we were seeing? Were we observing pragmatism, populism, or escapism? Questions began to live within me like a constant ringing in the ear.

Sitting on the shores of Lake Geneva, how much could I really ascertain about the impact of a new charcoal brazier on the lives of women in Nepal, women in Asia, and women around the world? My mind began to roam far, too far.

Then I met François. He was an ag engineer—a member of the water resources group. He was also handsome, witty, and in amazing shape (thanks, as I would learn, to being a member in very good standing of the Lake Geneva Swimming Club).

We literally ran into each other as the elevator door closed upon us one evening when I had been studying late in the library. There was an electric pulse as the heavy automatic doors pushed my breasts into his chest and we squeezed together into the elevator compartment.

"Well," he said, affecting hyperventilation, and speaking melodic French, "after that we should have a drink, if not a cigarette."

That was that.

We had a drink. We had several, finishing in his apartment, with Swiss Alpenbitter (an aperitif some call the Swiss national drink that is purported to promote good blood flow and make you feel good). Since going home, it had been a long run of self-imposed celibacy and I was ready for some bracing sex. I got what I needed, several times over.

Between EHT-MAT and François, I found myself totally exhausted—in a good way. From the meeting room to the bedroom, I was hard-pressed to find a free moment. Life was stimulating.

The comparative studies of MAT remained enthralling. From my outlook, this was a real and unique chance to dig into those possibly abstruse topics Martha and I had so deeply examined. Furthermore, within EHT's domain, this analysis cut across countries and continents. Looking intensely into the political and social remnants of times gone by as they affected the cultures of today, looking to see common denominators as contrasted to *sui generis* factors was right on target in regard to my professional interests—as my younger colleagues said, this was right in my wheelhouse.

François also seemed to be in my wheelhouse. He was intelligent, curious, and most athletic. He was honestly interested in my past—honestly wanting to share my present.

As our relationship matured from solely sensuous to somewhat intellectual, François shared some of his history to complement my tales from life as a PCV. He was French. He was also, by birth, a *pied-noir*, a Frenchman born in Algeria. His great-great grandfather had migrated to Algeria in 1847. This ancestor had greatly benefited from the colonialists' takeover of much of the country's lands. He obtained a large tract in the Dahra Hills (in western Algeria, fourteen miles south of the Mediterranean Coast and six miles west of the administrative center of Taougrite), where he started growing grapes—laying the foundation for a very successful winery that was passed to his children and his children's children. Then in 1960, when François was only five and the Algerian war for independence was six years old, the family fled back to mainland France as the colonial regime crumbled (leading to independence in 1962).

Although he had only spent a tiny fraction of his life surrounded by the family's vineyards, François attributed this period to the time when his future had seeped into his blood (like the family's good red wine, he would add)—a future derived from his infatuation with agriculture, his advanced studies in this field, and his ultimate good luck at finding a dream job at EHT after a brief stint working on irrigation schemes in Burkina Faso.

My jampacked schedule—personal and professional—became the norm. It was only broken by the moments of quasi-isolation as I commuted back and forth from Satigny Commune. With what seemed to be incredible rapidity, I was approaching my second anniversary with EHT and nearly eighteen months with François. This would soon be the longest I had ever spent in one job and already was the longest I had spent with one partner.

Things seemed to be getting comfortable. Life seemed to be becoming routine (in a good way). There was a growing normalcy.

Then, as is wont to happen, EHT got a new Director General. The new man (it seems they're always men) wanted to write on a clean slate. He decided we needed to be doubly sure we were drawing the right conclusions and giving our clients the best advice.

Sharing some of my initial concerns, he queried whether or not we could deliver the authoritative products we were reputed to produce if we relied solely on desk studies, modeling, and hypotheses from our comfy offices in Geneva. We needed to get our feet dirty.

I concurred to a point. I believed additional ground-truthing of our conclusions was needed. I did not think, however, this required that we revisit all the ground-level processes we were using for our base material. We needed to have acceptable levels of confidence in the data we crunched, but we did not need to know the exact origin of every data point nor every census taker.

The DG disagreed. We needed much more direct engagement in the field. Thus, after six months on the job, he announced he had established the framework for joint collaboration with a number of the major national and multinational development agencies and NGOs. Under the new arrangements, EHT staff would, on a rotational basis, spend up to one year in the field working directly with EHT's development partners and the direct beneficiaries of their assistance.

My hectic but predictable life changed forthwith.

It was amazing how much impact one person could have.

The DG's vision was that fifteen percent of EHT staff would be in the field at any point in time. Of course, this did not mean there would be an overall increase in total staffing by fifteen percent. This simply meant that those in Geneva had to find the ways and means to absorb the tasks of those rotating into the field.

It was a mess.

First two MAT members were among the initial cohort to go into the field. Within a month, François followed.

Back at the office, we had to pick up the slack for our departed colleagues. While at home, I was overcome with free and solitary time—my partner now helping out on a DFID irrigation project in Niger for the next ten to twelve months.

Things were moving. Then my time came. Whether through the luck of the draw or not, I was outposted to a UNDP/UN Women project in Nigeria aiming to promote gender equality through economic empowerment of women. In simple terms: help market-women make more profits.

On one side of the equation, the issue was providing market-women access to larger quantities of high-quality foodstuffs. This would allow the vendors to sell better products for better prices as well as selling larger quantities—offering what the market could bear and not what their suppliers could provide.

On the other side, this was a question of trying to reinforce the role of women in the family without disrupting traditional standards. If women could make more money, they could theoretically become more independent—even more influential. But this evolution could only happen if it could take place within existing cultural guardrails—bending but not breaking prevailing patterns.

This was my role: how far could things bend before they broke?

As my work, well and good in the field, was more of a study than a longer-term intervention, my secondment was for six months. Although François and I were more or less neighbors, we only met once in Ouagadougou. Given our different schedules, it seemed as though we would be back together again in Geneva at about the same time.

However, as I was wrapping up my work and submitting my findings to the UN offices in Abuja, I got a brief letter from François. His star had risen. He had been offered a senior post as Liaison Officer at the African Development Bank with L'Agence Française de Développement—AFD being the major French international development agency.

I was happy for him. It was a good move for which he had had to wait a long time.

Back in Geneva, there was once again a new normal for me. There was no François. There was no pending outposting. Since I was just getting back from my secondment assignment, I was momentarily at the end of the queue. There were no upcoming big events—for work or pleasure. There was simply immersion in MAT and riding the train.

But it wasn't only the train I was riding. With EHT's restructuring, not only did we, the Geneva team (what the DG called the Headquarters crew), rotate into the field every five to seven years, but we were now (strongly) recommended to spend twenty percent of our time visiting the sites where we had, heretofore, only been doing long-distance work.

The advantages of *in situ* examination and data collection had been long recognized. It was all about money. Travel was expensive. Travel to remote areas could be very expensive. Nonetheless, our new DG would not be deterred.

He could be persuasive and was certainly persistent. He was ultimately able to secure a surprising amount of supplemental funding, whereby all staff were expected to travel at least fifty-five days a year.

I welcomed the change. I travelled. I was even able to augment my own travel budget by getting funds from MAT coworkers who had DG-justifiable excuses for leaving town less frequently.

I went to Piso Firme, Bolivia. I visited Yogyakarta, Indonesia. I made it to Gorna Oryakhivistea, Bulgaria. I even arrived in Madelena, São Tomé. I departed and arrived so often; I could almost navigate Geneva's Cointrin Airport with my eyes closed. I had to add pages to my passport to accommodate all the ornate visas from out-of-the-way places.

Not only did my passport swell. My files grew and grew. I soon had two walls of my modest office fully occupied with floor to ceiling shelves of box files containing data on countries, communities, and policies—each individual box file identified by a postcard I had carefully selected to reflect the contents. There was a picture of a Tuareg women and a Lebanese mother wearing a hijab on the files containing my work on gender issues in Muslim communities. There was a picture of a Tsonga girl under a baobab tree on the file with the reports detailing my efforts to examine the long-term impacts for communities displaced by hydroelectric dam construction in Mozambique. There was a snapshot of a Tamil family on the spine of the file holding my analysis of the subsequent cultural impacts in Sri Lanka when the country shifted from dominion status to that of a full republic in 1972. I had files on everything.

Partially, I suppose, as a result of this body of work—but very likely also due to simple good luck (although, good luck is rarely simple)—as I traveled and filled box files, I moved up in the ranks of EHT.

In the case of EHT, moving up literally meant moving down. Just over a year after returning from my rotation to Nigeria, I was first promoted out of MAT into a slot as an advisor to the director of TAG—the Transnational Advisory Group. TAG's offices were on the second floor. Then, after only six months in TAG, I was promoted down to the first floor as coordinator of CSTF—the Cultural Stability Task Force—rumored to be an elite service reporting directly to the Assistant DG.

As I moved down while my professional level moved up, I felt I was truly achieving my hoped-for vantage point to see the big picture. The scope of my work increased significantly with each move. By the time I reached the first floor, ironically, I felt I could now clearly see the expansive vista reaching to the far horizon. I was on track.

When I had moved to the second floor, I adopted the encouraged practice of having morning coffee with other midlevel staff to reinforce a sense of camaraderie as well as to informally exchange ideas and experiences. EHT had thoughtfully provided a very comfortable, almost homey, space where a contractor offered the best of Swiss coffee and sweets at a subsidized price for honored second-floor officers—of which I was one.

We would assemble at ten o'clock each morning to sip our coffees, nibble our pastries, and effuse about our work. One morning, soon after I was installed on the second floor, over an aromatic cup of arabica, I was introduced to Samuel Mooketsi. He was presented as a former Minister of Local Government from Botswana who was now, similar to me, a special advisor; he advising the director of EIN—the Educational Impact Node.

I almost choked on my coffee. Samuel was beautiful.

Men in my life had been charming, funny, and athletic. While there had been some real losers, the keepers had had many admirable attributes— I had thought of them with glowing adjectives. They had been handsome. Some had been hot. But Samuel was beautiful.

He reminded me of a statue in bronze from the Benin Kingdom I had seen years ago in the National Museum of African Art at the Smithsonian. His skin had the sheen of polished bronze—although I could not immediately reach out and caress it (as much as would have liked to), it seemed also to have a metallic smoothness. Furthermore, his body had the statuesque form and curves of a perfect Benin bronze. He was beautiful.

As the constrictions in my throat loosened and I stabilized my coffee cup, I shook his hand. It was velvety—the grip firm. Both his eyes and his full lips smiled as he released my fingers, saying, "enchanté de faire votre connaissance" with a very unmelodic southern African accent.

It was I who was enchanted.

Smitten!

I felt like I was back in the Smithsonian, admiring the Benin bronze— admiring, somehow, from afar.

That day, Samuel joined our table for coffee. He was convivial—convivial in almost a regal way. He followed the lead of others, not being the centerpiece but contributing thoughtfully on a regular basis—soft-spoken and jocular.

Thereafter, I would see Samuel frequently at coffee time—not every day, but frequently. At times, he would join my table, at others, he would be seated with other colleagues. Yet, wherever and with whomever he was settled, he would always greet me with that smile that moved up from the corners of his mouth to embrace his eyes.

One afternoon, several days after we had first met, I was surprised to see Samuel at my door—with him, another gentleman whom I did not know—both men dressed in impeccably tailored suits with matching red and blue striped ties.

We sat in the corner of my office where there were three captain's chairs for just such an occasion. Samuel introduced his companion as João Carlo, an advisor to the Minister of the Interior of Angola (Samuel seemed to handle the Portuguese pronunciation of the name very well). Pointing to his tie, he added, "João and I were students together at the University of Stellenbosch."

João then picked up the discussion, in very good English. He explained there were—thank God—hopes that the lengthy Angolan civil war would be ending soon. For years, the violence had severely limited access to many parts of the country. With a ceasefire, areas that had been closed off would become accessible—accessible to investment and very possibly exploitation. He added, almost as an afterthought, access pivoting on how quickly areas could be cleared of the multitude of mines planted across the country by all parties—mines most happily supplied by a hoard of arms dealers.

Yet, mines or no mines, the country had rich mineral resources—the harvesting of which had been affected by the war. In the aftermath of the conflict, it was anticipated there would be a rush to stake claims to a variety of underdeveloped mining options. With a surge of outsiders and outsiders' money, local communities would be stressed—very stressed.

His minister wanted to be preemptive—doing the needful before the doors opened with a peace agreement (who knew when this might come).

Samuel had told him of some work I had done in Botswana, looking at the impact of the diamond mines on the cultural changes in local communities. João was interested in seeing my work, discussing the Angolan situation, and examining possible efforts needed on the ground in his country.

I was a bit taken aback that Samuel knew of my work in his country and honored that João was interested in my assessment of the possible pending contentions in his country.

I was able to provide João with a full briefing—in sufficient depth for him to be able to go back to Luanda and talk with his superiors about the need to plunge even deeper into this topic as the real possibilities of peace hopefully approached. While I was going over technological impacts on traditional cultures with João, my mind was really going over and over Samuel.

I was infatuated with Samuel. I would imagine us in the steamy throws of ardor that put my trysts with Bill to shame. But then, I would apply the brakes. I was older, if not wiser—far too far down life's path, I'd guess, for a teen romance.

Teen romance or not, I seemed to have slipped into this man's grip—even if totally unbeknownst to he himself.

Was I approaching a midlife crisis as I approached middle age?

Was Samuel some sort of youthful elixir (if only in my mind) that I was seeking?

Was Samuel an object of my fantasies, surreptitiously viewed as a fresh catalyst to reinvigorate my life that was growing monotonous?

I really did not know how old Samuel was. He seemed timeless—truly ageless and flawless like that Benin bronze. Nonetheless, to my encouragement, he was not a youngster. He clearly had been around and knew how to handle himself—in the bedroom too, I imagined.

My increasing responsibilities at TAG quickly forced me to discipline myself—to push lascivious thoughts to the sidelines and concentrate on the complex jobs at hand. Nevertheless, I frequently shared my coffee with Samuel and, in my spare moments, in my imagination, also shared with him my bed. Yet, as I approached the end of my first quarter at TAG, although we seemed to have established a reasonably close friendship, the most intimate thing I had done with Samuel was divvying up a croissant over coffee.

Near the midpoint of my assignment to TAG, I was asked to attend an in-house seminar given by a former Secretary General of the UN. The intent of the event was to underscore the importance of cross-pollination work of the type prioritized by EHT to try and better understand and positively address the crises that seemed to be overtaking the world.

Things across the globe were indeed in turmoil. I don't know if things were particularly in greater turmoil than unusual—but things were in turmoil. The US had invaded Panama. Soviet troops had occupied Azerbaijan. Nelson Mandela had been released from prison. President Mobutu Sese Seko had allowed opposition political parties in Zaïre for the first time in two decades. Tamil Tigers had killed more than 600 people, while an earthquake in the Philippines had killed more than 1,600. Samuel Doe had been killed in Liberia. Iraq had invaded Kuwait. WHO had even managed to provoke animosity from some factions when it had removed homosexuality from its list of diseases.

Were there common denominators to reduce, mitigate, or even stop these malicious acts and crises of man and nature? This was much of the focus of EHT and the topic that assembled us to hear the ex-Secretary General's words.

EHT had a rather plush (rather too plush for my liking) auditorium that could seat over 500. I slipped into a seat in one of the back rows just minutes before our DG started his introductory remarks. As the lights dimmed and the DG started with a grating clearing of his throat, I was startled to feel someone grip my right forearm. Looking in that direction, I may have gasped; it was Samuel.

I did force myself to listen to the ex-Secretary General, although, as I knew full well in advance, it was just a jumble of words emphasizing why our interdisciplinary, broad-spectrum approach to problem solving was critical. It was music to our DG's ears to hear accolades heaped on EHT and the former head of the UN strongly espousing that the "EHT Model" (as he called it) should be widely adopted.

There were no revelations. There was just reinforcement.

After a seventy-five-minute allocution and thirty-seven minutes of rather watered-down discussion, the lights came up and it was time to go. As we stood, I felt Samuel's hand on my shoulder. Turning back, he asked me, "How about a drink after work to discuss these illustrious words in more depth?"

Unsure of how much his statement had been tongue in cheek, but totally sure I wanted to have a drink with this man, I (hopefully not too quickly) accepted.

This was the pivot point.

We met, by prearrangement, at Le Bistrot de Charlotte, not far from Four Seasons Hôtel des Bergues Gèneve—about four blocks from our offices and more or less on my route to the train station.

I don't really know how to describe this—the first time I had had anything even approximating a date with this Benin bronze that I had been amorously contemplating for so long. It certainly wasn't amorous. Maybe it was contemplative?

Completely opposed to my (and their) introductory maneuvers with my other beaus, this did not lead to us being in the sack within eight hours. For better or worse, this was just what it was: a drink.

When I arrived at Charlotte's, Samuel was already seated at a quiet corner table. As I approached the table, he stood—shaking my hand warmly and kissing me on both cheeks before I was seated.

We ordered drinks (I had a Scotch on the rocks, he had a gin and tonic). Then I had no idea what to do.

Fortunately, Samuel charmingly and unassumingly began. With that smile that so captivated me, he asked, "What did you think of the magnificent (with a twinkle in his eyes) show in the auditorium?"

Not really prepared for an analysis of the ex-UN Secretary General's homily, I was a little shaky on the uptake, "Always good to tell people what they want to hear."

"Exactly." He silently applauded. "Keep the troops at it."

"Uh-huh. As long as the troops are following the right battle plan."

"Are they?"

"I hope so." Where was this going? If this was a professional postmortem, I might as well jump in with both feet. "I certainly believe in the holistic approach."

"The view from above?"

"Yes and no. I think the DG was right we need to pull on our boots and get into the field. Nevertheless, at the end of the day, any meaningful problem solving—and, that's what we're all about—solving problems—will require addressing a whole basketful of issues at the same time."

"OK. But realistically, can it work?"

This seemed almost like an interrogation or a third-degree interview. I wondered if this libation was business or personal. "I don't really know," I honestly replied. "I do know that fighting fires doesn't work in terms of addressing the root causes of the problems. These are, after all, all people-problems and, to have any hopes of succeeding, we need to understand people—others—as well as we can."

"Agreed. Agreed in principle. But, can we do it?"

Feeling pushed, I had to double down, "I hope so. I really don't know. Yet, I do feel we're making progress."

"Really?"

"Yes."

"It truly isn't easy. I often feel overwhelmed."

"I know. We all do. It's all so chaotic. However, thoughtful, well-researched options are the best strategy to finding sustainable solutions. I wholeheartedly believe this."

"I'm sorry. I kind of got off the deep end. While I was sitting here waiting for you, I was looking out the window at all the opulence of Geneva and thinking back to my village. We live in a world of extremes and can only survive if we find the necessary bridges."

This was a shift—a change of tack—a welcome change of tack. We moved from an intense, almost tense, discussion of the pillars upon which we built our work, to a more benign exchange about on-the-job frustrations. "I do understand. We all want to do more—see greater impact—actually see things improve."

"Sometimes it is tough. I know from your work; you know villages in Africa well. There's so much to do."

I tried to push a bit further out of what could have been a rut, "But in spite of all the massive challenges, some are doing better. I think *chez toi* in Botswana is often touted as a success?"

"Success? No, I don't think so—but, maybe less of a failure. Maybe there I would give a 'yes.'"

"The longest journey . . ."

"I know," he laughed, "the first step . . ."

"So, tell me, it's been some time since I was in Botswana, are things still on a positive trajectory?"

"I guess so. I don't get home very often."

"What of your family?"

Shift made. Samuel seemed to unstick his thoughts from the pressures of EHT like someone pulling his feet out of heavy clay. His family lived a few miles outside Kanye, the capital of the Southern District, and about fifty miles southwest of Botswana's capital Gaborone.His father raised cows. His father was also the Chief of the Ngwaketse people—a subset of the Tswana people who accounted for eighty percent of the country's population. His ancestor, Makeba, had moved into this area in 1790.

My Benin bronze was nobility. It was no surprise.

He added a few additional personal details, apparently feeling he somehow needed to complete the picture he had begun painting. He was unmarried. However, his father had two wives—one married under customary law and the other married under civil law—a common practice for traditional leaders. From this threesome, Samuel had three sisters and four brothers. He was the firstborn from the (second) civil marriage. He had one older confrere from his father's first marriage who managed the family cattle business. After graduating with honors from Stellenbosch, he had been admitted to Cambridge, ultimately obtaining a doctorate in economics. He had started his career at the African Development Bank and then returned to Botswana to become Minister of Local Government before joining EHT.

With the mention of EHT, the conversation then seemed to magically slip back to more work-related matters. Picking up on my accolades for Botswana's development since throwing off the moniker of Bechuanaland and English rule in 1965, he asked almost rhetorically, "Could a country with less than two million inhabitants and rich diamond mines and cattle ranches really be a prototype? Gaborone, a relatively modern city the size of Geneva (both cities of roughly 200,000 inhabitants), was less than two percent the size of London—as world capitals go, one of the sleepiest. Were there really teachable lessons here?"

I ordered another round, realizing we were probably going to discuss the transferability of economic options for the next several hours.

Looking back, I guess it was a rather unusual first date.

But it was the first. Before we parted, we agreed to pay Charlotte's a visit in two weeks' time. Forewarned, I made a personal commitment to prepare well to be able to drive the conversation in a softer, more intimate direction.

I apparently succeeded because we were soon having dinner together every Tuesday. On the fifth Tuesday— just as Bill and I had once taken Wrights Ferry Bridge across the Susquehanna—Samuel and I crossed the Rhone to his apartment on Rue Saint-Ours, near the Université de Gèneve— a roomy but functional flat befitting (and affordable for) the son of a chief.

I was soon spending three or four nights a week in these (in many ways) comfortable surroundings.

Fortunately, we worked for different directorates. It was easy to limit our in-office interactions to coffee and chitchat. Evenings at Samuel's were far less chitchat and far more action. He lived up to all expectations.

Then, unexpectedly, a few weeks after Samuel's and my bonds were growing, I was promoted to CSTF. Moving down to the first floor limited my coffee time to special trips back to my old haunts. By the end of my first year on the first floor, I seemed rarely to make it up the stairs to share coffee with my old mates—there weren't enough hours in the day.

Nonetheless, there were hours in the night and Samuel, and I put these to good use.

EHT was, in many ways, a generous employer. We benefited from thirty days a year annual leave (not counting public holidays) and a home leave every two years—this latter provided in the form of cash to purchase a ticket to our official residence. In my own case, although I had been recruited from DC, my parents' home was considered as my formal stateside base.

This was a real advantage—the cost of a ticket for a nearly 5,500-mile trip was considerable. What's more, the vacation days and the ticket funds rolled over from year to year—it was not a question of use-it-or-lose-it.

My first anniversary in the CSTF team marked my fifth year at EHT. Over this time, I had been allocated 150 leave days and three home-leave tickets. Of this, I had used forty-five days and one ticket.

The year before, possibly to celebrate my fourth anniversary being em-ployed (never having lasted this long elsewhere), I had gone home to see my parents. They were, of course, older. They were, naturally, tied hand and foot to Susan's family. In short, it was nearly a rerun of my visit home before joining EHT. We were just on different plains. It was good to see them. It fulfilled a feeling of responsibility and even provided a little bit of a warm, cuddly feeling. But it felt even better getting back on the plane and returning to Geneva.

The upshot of my vacationless lifestyle was a growing account of benefits that really needed attention. Samuel began pestering me; he advised me not to take the risk of losing what I had worked hard to amass.

I figured turnabout was fair play, so I challenged him (he who also had only been home once since coming to Geneva) to go on vacation with me. I had it all planned out. We would discover Switzerland together. After all, neither of us had been more than a hundred miles away from Geneva to see the country where we lived.

I had a great trip planned. We'd fly to Zürich and rent a car. We'd drive to St. Gallen and then take a quick tour though Liechtenstein, spending a night or two in Vaduz. Then we'd go south to Chur, turn in the car and take the cogged train over the Alps to Brig from where we'd go to Zermatt—home of the Matterhorn. Finally, back in Brig, we'd rent a car and follow the Rhone back to Geneva. It'd be wonderful.

Samuel applauded my craftsmanship in assembling a memorable itinerary. Then he added, "But?"

"But what?"

"Look closely."

"Yes."

"See anything?"

"No."

"Of course, you don't."

"OK."

"Look again."

"Still nothing."

"I'm black."

"Uh-huh."

"You're not."

"Uh-huh."

"So?"

"So what?"

Obviously, we were a mixed-race couple. It was obvious, I just never thought of it. I had never thought of it with Abduli and I didn't think of it now.

Nevertheless, Samuel had opened the conversation. I guess things might have been different in Guinea. After all, as regards to sex, the French were pretty open about crossing color lines and Abduli was a government official—who was going to tell him to cease and desist?

Here in Geneva, things had been even keeled. At times people would stare at us—sometimes even point—but rarely. This was a very cosmopolitan city. Other parts of the country were indeed much more conservative. But, from my seat, who cared?

With just a whisper of uncertainty, Samuel agreed.

We had a great trip.

Invigorated by our travels and our time together, back at EHT we each plunged into our jobs—still spending several nights a week talking business and making pleasurable memories.

My move to CSTF meant that I felt I was about as far up the promotion ladder as I could go. It is important to cite that I had not achieved this on my own. Through my years with the organization, I had been graced by the mentoring of some of the most outstanding talent in the field. EHT attracted many of the top experts from around the world. I had had the unrivaled opportunity to work with the best of the best: Kim Lee, Sally Strasbourg, Jonas Brighton, Marc Le Blanc, Alejandro Rodriguez, George Abban, and others.

I was where I was thanks to the generosity of these exceptional people. They had openly and candidly shared their knowledge and guidance. They had pushed and pulled me to where I was.

And, where I was, was where I had hoped to be. I felt I was seeing the big picture. In spite of, or perhaps because of, Samuel's queries on our first date, I felt we were all doing a good job of identifying and mobilizing tools that could provide real impact in terms of benefiting people—helping them overcome the global problems of poverty, malnutrition, ignorance, environmental degradation, and political instability.

It was, I had to agree, a work in progress—but there was real progress. We were able to merge and integrate solutions to identify common denominators—transforming these into implementable measures that would lead to positive results.

We were making headway. We were doing our jobs.

With positive feelings about my professional and private lives, I thought it might be time to try another vacation with Samuel. This time, I'd decided we'd really put the system to a test. We'd fly to Rome and then rent a car to drive to Brindisi from where we'd take a ferry across Ionian Sea to Corfu, crossing to Athens and then another ferry to Izmir and continuing by train to Ankara from where we'd fly to New Delhi. We'd travel north through Nepal and Bhutan before turning south along the Brahmaputra River, ending in Dhaka and flying back to Geneva.

Samuel was shocked and titillated by the audacity of this suggestion. We—black and white—would be effectively on show across a great swath of the world's cultures. Who could resist such an opportunity?

We did it.

Back in Geneva, we digested our great adventure. We had seen fantastic sights. We had met extraordinary people. We had had a good time. Through all this, the mixed-race issue was no more of an issue than we had experienced during our tour of Switzerland.

Most people seemed to have the position—better you than me. If Samuel and I wanted to mix races that God may have never intended to mix, so be it. Apparently from the perspective of many of the intolerant, it's maybe difficult, but possible to endure such (unnatural) behavior as long as my family does not do it—look, don't touch.

In the end, it was pretty much what we had imagined.

Once again, a sort of stability seeped into my life—this accompanied by a level of contentedness to which I was unaccustomed. I had spent over five years at EHT. I was approaching my forties and I felt at the top of my game. I had a solid relationship and a solid job.

A Stumble Then a Fall

In everyone's life, at some time, our inner fire goes out. It is then burst into flame by an encounter with another human being. We should all be thankful for those people who rekindle the inner spirit.

—ALBERT SCHWEITZER

I THOUGHT I HAD reached my peak, but apparently not.

By my fortieth birthday I had moved on to become a special advisor to the DG. This was a tricky spot for me.

Our boss, Mateo González, had been vice president at the World Bank before coming to EHT. He was bright. He was hardworking. He was impatient. He was a misogynist.

I really want to be careful here. My boss was not a womanhater. If you'd ask him, he would say, to the contrary, he adored women. And he did. All types and all sizes. But this adoration was of the corporeal type and not the professional variety.

Professionally he, forced by the dictates of the institution, endured women. First, he really had no choice; forty percent of his staff was female. Second, if he focused solely on the message and not the messenger, he was able to appreciate the products of his female staff. This notwithstanding, he would have preferred to have had an all-male workforce—only dealing with women during his leisure time.

Unlike people Samuel and I had encountered, who publicly begrudgingly accepted mixed racial couples because, privately, they hoped they could distance themselves from such (they felt, aberrant) twosomes, the DG could not ignore or distance himself from women. He could not opt for a separate but (almost) equal arrangement. So, when he received a superior product from what he considered as an inferior individual, his thoughts were immediately to wonder how truly excellent the product would have been had it been done by a man.

This was a thorny environment for a senior female advisor—any female advisor.

Strangely, in an unexpected way, my relationship with Samuel helped with my relationship with the DG. As everyone, our boss knew we were an established couple. Although, I suppose he was not a proponent of interracial relations, he accepted my commitment and made no unsuitable overtures, as he did to many of my female coworkers.

When all was said and done, we had a dicey work relationship—but one that seemed to be somehow satisfactory to both of us—satisfactory but uncertain.

It was a delicate dance.

In retrospect, I entered my forties nearly as naive as I had been as a PCV in Fomi. I wanted to do good and assumed others wanted good to be done. This was not good in terms of good reports or good data; this was good in terms of good impacts—making people's lives better.

Samuel would frequently warn me that I was building up for a tumble—paraphrasing Jimmy Cliff—The higher you climb, the further you fall.

He would recall our discussion on that first date, spotlighting the fact that I was still full of hope. With a bit of regret, he emphasized I needed to modulate this with a big dose of reality. He would repeatedly cite his grandfather's words. Roughly translated from the Tswana language: Life ain't fair.

His injunction: don't expect to find fairness.

If you do find it, he would add, understand it is as rare as a bloom from the *bobbejaanghaap*—the hoodia cactus of the Kalahari that only flowers when the precise conditions intersect—at times dormant for years.

My forty-first anniversary brought about unexpected, and unwelcome, alterations. Samuel's father died. Samuel had been named as his father's successor. This was a life-changing event. Samuel was at the threshold. Intellectually, he resisted heeding the call from home. Instinctively and emotionally, he knew he could not refuse.

We spent hours talking about our tomorrows. We both knew all too well the poignant story of the first president of Botswana, Sir Seretse Goitsebeng Maphiri Khama, who, in 1948, married the very British and very white, South London-born Ruth Williams. Lady Khama had died just three years earlier—buried next to her husband as all good fairytales should end.

Like Samuel, Sir Seretse Khama was nobility, his father the paramount chief of the Bamangwato people. Like Samuel, Sir Seretse Khama's partner was an outsider. She was an outsider who was ultimately accepted and became part of the Sir Seretse Khama's community. She was an outsider who became the mother of Sir Seretse Khama's four children. Was this the pathway for me? Was this what Samuel wanted? Was this what I wanted?

Sometimes we would talk until sunrise.

My job, while still professionally rewarding, was becoming more and more politically uncomfortable. The DG was unpredictable. This likely meant my job security was unpredictable. Ironically, buried in the crews on the second and third floors, I was innocuous—unseen, unnoticed. My job there quite secure. Reaching the first floor and the DG's doorway, I suddenly was at risk.

Leaving with Samuel for new lives in Botswana would remove this risk.

Was I ready for Botswana?

It was not a question of skin color. This had long passed being an issue for us and was unlikely to be a major stumbling-stone should I accompany Samuel. It would be noticed, it would be the source of commentary, but soon it would be normal, and life would go on.

It was really a question of culture.

No one knew better than I the spectrums of human cultures. I had no doubt I could adjust to Botswana as I had to Guinea (for all her courage, Lady Khama had never been a PCV). I had no doubt I would find terrific people and amazing places. I might even manage to get a position at the University of Botswana or the Southern Africa Development Community whose offices were in Gaborone. We would have our home. We would have our family. We would have our lives.

Was this the course I should chart?

I was torn. I could not decide.

Finally, Samuel broke the logjam. After the tenderest of love-makings, he softly whispered in my ear, "You should stay."

It took me several seconds to get my bearings. He wasn't talking about staying in bed, he was talking about staying in Geneva. It just wasn't that simple. It wasn't just a quick flip of a switch. It was a highly consequential decision.

I could only reply, "What? Are you sure? I should be with you?"

"Perhaps. But I think you need to be where you feel you are making a difference—making a difference now-now, not waiting for the results to pop up."

"I guess . . ."

"No, you don't guess, you know. You've worked long and hard. Christ, you've been at it nonstop for years! It's your life. In spite of the challenges, you are now truly sitting at the right hand of the leader. Your inputs, your interpretations, your actions have direct influence—no waiting. This is what you need."

"Hmmmm . . .."

"We're good together, we're very good together. And, who knows tomorrow? But this is not the time for you to drop everything here and go to Botswana. It's hard enough for me, but I must do it. You shouldn't."

"Ahh . . ."

"Let's drop it. It's concluded. I'm going to start making my plans. You carry on. We're special. I'm sure our paths will cross. But for now, we have to go our own ways. Just let it go."

I did.

I should say I was shattered. By my standards, Samuel and I had been together for a long, long time—it felt like forever. He was terrific in all ways. He was beautiful.

He had been my most enduring partner. He had been the man with whom I had been the most connected—although we never had those discussions about marriage and family. In fact, these topics only surfaced when there was the question of both of us going to Botswana.

We had had so much.

Now it seemed to wash away, like years of detritus scoured from a stream during a thunderstorm—gone.

I should be devastated.

I was rattled and unhappy.

I don't know if I loved Samuel. We also never spoke of love.

I don't use the word "love" very often. People are always talking about how much they love.

"I love spaghetti!"

"I love daisies!"

"I love rabbits!"

"I love blue aprons!"

People are always loving things.

They are also always loving people.

"I love Tony Bennett!"

"I love Madonna!"

"I love Colonel Sanders!"

"I love Richard Nixon!"

Everyone is full of love.

Alas, perhaps sadly, I did not and do not feel that love is that omnipresent. Love is rare. Love is special. Love only happens on very extraordinary occasions—maybe it does require being star-crossed. Maybe it requires the *bobbejaanghaap* to bloom.

We like many things. We are attracted to many things. We are enamored by many things. But love is scarce.

If I didn't love Samuel—and I may well have—I sure as hell liked him a lot.

Now we had taken separate paths—not really by force but by choice. Let me say it was dictated by what we tried to see as an objective assessment of the situation. The same techniques we though we used so successfully at EHT.

Gone!

And, I did miss him so!

We continuously hoped for the best. We attempted to be optimistic—the glass was really half full. Samuel had said we were so good together that we certainly would find ourselves once again in each other's arms. I yearned for that. But I doubted it.

Among all whom I would call my lovers, my bonds were strongest with my beautiful Samuel. Nonetheless, if I look back, inevitably the winds of time blew out the flame of passion. Separation did not make the heart grow fonder, it washed away the memories and the emotions—it made relationships fade.

Samuel and I called, wrote letters, and made plans to meet up. Yet, with almost gut-wrenching anguish, I knew it was over.

Samuel had said, "Let it go."

He had meant for now.

The truth was forevermore.

During this same period, since Lady Luck seemed to often kick you when you were down, my father died. I went home for the funeral. Mother was crushed. Susan had everything in hand.

Six months later, Mother died. I made the long trip one last time. Susan had all meticulously organized down to polishing the shoes her kids would wear to the grave-side ceremony. She informed me that she was soon moving into the family home ("it was so much larger that her little place"). I put my few remnants in storage, gave my little sister a hug, and flew back to Geneva.

My crumbling private life was bolstered by a hyperactive professional work-load. My gender concerns about the DG aside, he did seem to be serious about the work of EHT and about international development in general. He was definitely interested in demonstrating the efficacy of his leadership. To a large extent, this involved demonstrating the efficacy of EHT's approach, results, and tools.

While I celebrated my eighth work anniversary in Switzerland, EHT had been up and running for practically half a century longer than I. When first established in 1946 by the founding Venetian merchant families, in a post-war period, a year after the UN and several of her specialized agencies were initiated, economic development was a high priority. Then, as colonialism waned and newly independent countries struggled to gain footings, the scope of development grew and deepened. However, as the Cold War faded, modern, shiny technologies competed with funds for needy segments of an everchanging global population. Groups like EHT found themselves in increasingly competitive environments. The world's economic development buffet was no longer large enough to offer everyone a seat. Only the most aggressive were able to keep their place at the table.

Today, under González's leadership, it was necessary to clearly show that EHT was at the cutting edge—impactful and efficient.

Understanding this imperative, I had prepared a proposal for the DG—a series of in-depth analyses of EHT's past, present, and future. My suggestion was to look at sustainability. Over the last twenty-five years, had EHT's inputs succeeded? Were people better off today thanks to interventions by EHT a generation ago?

If the answers were yes, the DG would be in a very strong position to flaunt the EHT program—seeking more support and greater influence.

EHT was technically founded upon the approach that there were more commonalities than differences among the crucial problems facing global development. Practically, this translated into devising strategies for problem solving from a carefully selected set of countries, dissecting the common factors, and melding these into realistic actions to mitigate the problems.

Accordingly, if this worked, taking a sample of actions recommended a generation ago and examining their impact today should either validate this methodology or highlight areas requiring adjustment.

Regardless of the outcomes, the initiative to undertake such a self-analysis should reflect well on the leadership—on the DG's office—on González himself.

The DG agreed.

There would be a thorough study.

A high-level team of outside experts was assembled. I was charged with being their liaison. They were charged with assessing the works of EHT over the past twenty-five years.

The study took nearly a year.

It fully occupied my time. It sucked up my energy. Slowly, and I guess thankfully, Samuel and my parents became vague shadows.

The study (my study) was commended across a wide spectrum of those engaged in international development as being ground-breaking, innovative, and even praiseworthy. It was given significant prominence—González basking in its glow.

When concluded, the study results were indeed illuminating—in both good and bad ways. Overall, the consensus of the expert panel validated the approach. Core and major problems were found to be crosscutting, with common but flexible solutions and good means of addressing shared issues among a much larger affected population. The panel even went further, concluding that actors who employed the converse approach, underscoring problematic differences rather than accentuating the similarities, were, in the panel's opinion, doing so not to address the essential problems in the best possible way, but to build their own portfolio as being a specialized group who addressed very precise and unique concerns. This counterstrategy, furthermore, was often practiced more to attempt to attract donor funds as opposed to using the best tools possible to assist the disadvantaged target populations.

Undoubtedly, the panel summarized, vulnerable people around the globe suffered from a mutual collection of socioeconomic ills. They compared these to health ills. Public health workers had, according to the panel, acknowledged for a long time that if they could address the top twenty diseases in the developing world, they could reduce early mortalities by over forty percent. The same principles, in their view, applied to socioeconomic afflictions.

These facts notwithstanding, the panel found that, while the approach was correct and the methodologies for problem solving derived from this approach also proper, the sustainability over the twenty-five-year timeframe was much less than anticipated. Implementation of identified actions over the short-term resulted in improvements in the quality of life for the intended beneficiaries. However, this was expected to be the beginning of a process where these improvements amplified and expanded through time to greater and greater numbers of beneficiaries. This so called "oil-drop" effect was found sorely insufficient.

The shortcomings, moreover, were not attributed to weaknesses in the identified actions nor in the processes set forth to carry on these actions—the failures were in this carrying-on principle. Things did carry on for a year, sometimes even five years. Nevertheless, things were rarely still progressing after twenty-five years. There was not enough momentum to carry these activities through to their hoped-for much larger endpoint. Some of this loss of steam was accounted for by the fact that often the initial catalysts were supported through projects—extra-budgetary resources. When, in due course, the responsibilities where to shift to regular budgets and staff, there simply were not the means to carry on.

This weakness in design was exacerbated by politics. Donor politics were fickle. The favorite color of the month changed with amazing rapidity—donors themselves were seldom ready to follow actions over a generation. Country politics evolved around election cycles (if these existed) which were much shorter than a generation. Young countries still had archaic government structures dating to the colonial period along with trained staff shortages that accompanied independence. These all combined into a perfect storm that made long-term sustainability the exception and not the rule.

The panel wrapped up its review stating that the phenomena that had adversely affected sustainability should be lessening in the new millennium. Economies were changing. Developmentalists as a group, and EHT in particular, should continue with their established and now tested methodology, but focusing on means to ensure the processes were integrated into local institutions, communities, and economies.

Overall, the DG was happy.

The dust began settling on the expert panel's report and work once again settled into a slower cadence. It appeared as though senior management was ready to say, "We did our pioneering study. We've honestly looked at ourselves in the mirror. It's time to move on."

And, to them, moving on meant a return to the same established ways of doing business—the status quo—no true desire to adjust according to the conclusions of the study.

I was not ready for such a myopic view.

I decided I needed to look more carefully at this issue of sustainability as it related to those areas where I had personally been engaged. After all, I was now a seasoned EHT operative. How many of those efforts I had initiated when I had arrived were still flourishing?

I dug through my box files. I contacted colleagues—past and present. I researched the current status of those actions I had wrapped up and carefully slipped into a box file as closed.

It took the better part of nine months before I began to see any results. What I found at first perplexed me, then it alarmed me. In at least three-quarters of the follow-ups I made, when the initial funding to implement the prescriptive measures expired and, as so well described by the expert panel, the beneficiaries were struggling to find ways and means to keep the forward motion going, second-phase funding came through the International Center for Democratic Ideals.

On the surface this appeared to be a welcome and even generous, but not totally unexpected, arrangement. ICDI's professed mandate was to promote democratization. Tools and policies addressing and mitigating social and economic disorders were ways of helping the common man. If, once road-tested, these gains were further promoted and wrapped in the flag of democracy, what harm could be done? A better-off citizenry was good for democracy.

Unlike most EHT activities, ICDI worked on a cost-sharing basis— their grants requiring matching funds from host governments. The hope was that the combination of external and internal support would allow the core actions to continue through time.

However, strangely, within three years of receiving ICDI support, eighty percent of the activities began to falter. Looking deeper, this backsliding was due most frequently to noticeable reductions in overall financial support. Although second-phase support for addressing the initial problems through partnerships with ICDI was indeed reduced, aggregate financing should have continued for multiple years, often increasing as beneficiary governments were generally contractually required to contribute proportionally more through time.

This apparently was not happening.

I followed this thread.

My contacts in the concerned countries verified the budgetary shortfalls, finding that ICDI support, cloaked in the original project framework, had often been redirected to the political leadership.

This was, at the very least, worrisome.

I tried to uncover more about ICDI. This was hard. They described themselves as nonpartisan and transparent. They had a variety of wishy-washy literature full of bromides. Yet, it was very difficult to learn more—to find details of substance.

Nevertheless, I was able to confirm that conservative—very conservative—political groups across Western Europe and North America were the major ICDI donors. While the spiel for public consumption was the promotion of Western-style democracy, as the surface was scraped away, it became clearer that the real intent was to support right-wing governments with whom the donors of ICDI would subsequently enter into very favorable trade relationships. Call yourself a democracy, let us (the donors) exploit your natural endowments, and everybody was happy.

Equally troubling was the discovery that much of EHT's operating capital came from ICDI, rerouted through other channels to make the connection more difficult to trace—but there, nonetheless.

It was all smoke and mirrors!

ICDI, with all its shady network of conservative political interests, was indeed likely the major supporter of EHT. I guess, and it was logical when I objectively thought about it (taking away all the romantic mystery about the progeny of Marco Polo helping the poor and destitute today), the resources of the original founding families could not realistically still serve as the sole groundwork for such an expensive operation as EHT.

Overlaying maps of countries where ICDI's pro-democracy interventions had resulted in very favorable trade agreements with ICDI donors, compared to priority countries where EHT claimed to be making a difference, the two maps were the same. EHT was a conduit for ICDI.

It was simple conservative rhetoric. If good business was good for everyone, better (that is, bigger) business was better for everyone. Obviously, very lucrative contracts with ICDI donors spurred host country economies—the influx of new capital certainly trickling down (or so they said) to the most vulnerable—the most needy who were the priority for EHT. It was symbiosis.

It was bullshit.

It was a sham.

I was unsure what to do with my revelation.

I decided I was an advisor to the DG; I should advise the DG.

He was apoplectic.

But his apoplexy was not about questionable financial and political linkages—it was aimed at me.

Without going into all the gory details, I had gone where no one was intended to go. I had disturbed scabs that were untouchable. I had done the unpardonable.

While it wasn't quick and it wasn't painless, the final conclusion was that I had to go. I had to go, but there was no cause. I couldn't be sacked for doing my job. Still, I couldn't stay. It was very messy.

I ended up getting a lawyer. My lawyer ended up getting a settlement that made each of us rather wealthy.

I was now unemployed, but financially comfortable.

I was, also, professionally unscathed since part of the settlement was to invent some pretext for my departure. I left with full honors and formally with the great regret from EHT's management at having lost an exemplary employee. To all, I was leaving to take a most lucrative and influential post somewhere with someone, no one really knew where or with whom—no one really cared.

I was gone.

Going had not involved too much. Over the years I had accumulated little in my small apartment in Satigny Commune. I just folded things up and left.

My quandary was not how to go, but where to go? What to do?

I thought of *Things Fall Apart*, by Chinua Achebe, (that I had read in Peace Corps) telling of the Igbo people's encounters with white men and related uncharted transitions. Apart from the rather inconsequential (in my view) loss of a job and the adjoining requirement to change my residence, the real mind-boggling issue was that my world had fallen apart.

As Samuel had warned me, I had set myself up for a fall.

I had climbed to the highest vantage point to see the big picture. I had been part of the global effort to paint that big picture in humanistic tones that faithfully helped all. The global effort, however, had been a theater—I'm unsure if a comedy or a tragedy—and, as Shakespeare had said, we were just actors.

It wasn't about people; it was about money. Should I be surprised?

My naivety had just shown through. How could real life be anything else?

Thinking of Peace Corps brought back thoughts of Guinea. I had nothing better to do, why not go back for a visit?

Years before, I had resisted the temptation of going back to Guinea. I should have listened to myself this time. But when my house of cards collapsed,

I felt like I needed to wander in the wilderness. I set my sights on Guinea where it had all begun—this time going in the back door.

After I got visaed-up in Geneva, I took a train to Paris and flew to Abidjan. I then took public transport across a politically shaky western Côte d'Ivoire to Man, the capital of the Tonkpi Region. After a brief rest, I continued on to Danane (wishing Samuel had been with me) and then crossed the border into Guinea, traversing Lola and arriving in Nzérékoré.

Of course, it was all the same and it was all different. There was still the same vegetative cloak of humidity, the same hustle and bustle of the run-down—but running hard—capital of the forest region. There were still refugee camps, but these were farther from the city center due to continued frictions with the town folk. Madame Philo, who had run the restaurant where I so often ate, had apparently died of AIDS. The Cocotier, one of the hottest spots at the time, was gone and forgotten. Satellite television was everywhere, but there still wasn't enough food in the market.

Life went on. I had not left so much as a footprint in the dust.

After a week of digging where there was no past, I took a taxi up the N2 to Gouécké—continuing to Kankan, Babila, and on to Fomi. Back in "my village" I was just as much a stranger as in Nzérékoré. The chief had died, his successor a son who had been in France at the time of my posting. Most of the older generation had passed on while the younger had moved on to the cities—Kankan or Conakry. The village was really only still going due to plans for the great dam. It apparently was still a work in progress, with few real concrete details—no one really knowing how it would affect the village—all dreaming it would bring riches and television.

There was no place to stay in the village. There was no one to take me in. I had left not a single footprint. I went back to Babila and then, the next day, at sunrise, got into a taxi for Conakry.

So much for going home.

I had arranged my itinerary to fly from Accra to New York. It was often easier to fly between anglophone countries than between anglophone and francophone. Therefore, I had planned to fly from Freetown to Accra. I now had to reach Freetown.

Sierra Leone was turbulent—just less so than Liberia. I managed to take the hydrofoil to Freetown, following the breathtakingly beautiful coastline that hid so much fear and despair.

After a few nights in a cheap Lebanese guesthouse, I took the helicopter to the island that was home to Lungi International Airport and, in the early evening, hopped on a 737 for the two-and-a-half-hour flight to Kotoka Airport in Accra.

This was, I felt, the end of my wandering. In Accra, I checked into the Labadi Beach Hotel. The sixteen-year-old luxury hotel, which had hosted many important personages from Queen Elizabeth to Jimmy Carter, was situated right on the beach of the same name. I spent two weeks baking in the Atlantic sun, much as I had over two decades previously when I was vegetating at the Novotel in Kaloum.

The only break I took from the chaise lounge on the beach was a day trip up the shoreline to Cape Coast and the old slaving fortress of Elmira. Like Gorée near Dakar (and so many others), this was a major portal that funneled Africans to far-off lands, to unbelievable abuse, to mistreatment that, in some cases, continued to the present.

Back in my chaise lounge I sipped Star beer and napped. Whether asleep or awake, my mind whipped up a mosaic of human events—like a family tree seen from on high—a fading tableau on a wall in the Alhambra. There were petrified people forced on rickety ships in Elmira mixed with villagers from Fomi waiting for tomorrow's riches, combined with Liberian diamond hunters fleeing a rebel patrol. It was all stirred together. Some had been ripped away. Some could not wait to get away. Others did not know how to try to get away. People, moving to and fro.

My dreams floating on the beach. Were they symptoms of fatigue and stress? Harbingers of things to come? Or, simply nonsense—visions provoked by too much sun and too many beers?

Then, through wandering, but still not knowing where I was going, I boarded the Boeing 757 for Kennedy.

It was an eleven-hour flight. There was plenty of time to ponder.

As the plane's tires tore themselves free of the tarmac, leaving Africa behind, I recalled the words of Sir Richard Francis Burton, who, in the 1850s and 60s, explored many remote corners of the world, including the Great Lakes of Africa—words that had so excited me when I first read them during Peace Corps training:

> Of the gladdest moments in human life, methinks, is the departure upon a distant journey into unknown lands. Shaking off with one mighty effort the fetters of Habit, the leaden weight of Routine, the cloak of many Cares and the slavery of Civilization, man feels once more happy.

I had first come to these shores as a budding volunteer. In the ensuing years, just as these lands, I had greatly changed—I did not know if it was for the better.

I was now returning from, not departing upon, a distant journey. If the reciprocal of Burton's observation was true, this could well be the saddest moment of my life. I didn't know.

I was going home. It was not my homes in Fomi or Nzérékoré, or even Geneva. I was going back to the source—to my roots—wilted may they be. I was going to the US of A.

I had left as a youth; I was returning as an aging adult.

Youthfulness made me think of youths in general. Today, young people were the major segment of developing countries' populations. Africa, Latin America, South Asia, Southeast Asia—all were overflowing with youth. AIDS (increasing adult mortality), reduction in childhood diseases, improving economies and communications—all had combined to make the younger generation both demographically and politically very important.

In my travels and in my work, I would frequently have opportunities to engage these youngsters. They would often react, "You're a woman."

"Yes."

"Where are you from?"

"America."

"Wow! Are all American ladies like you?"

"No."

"How come you're here?"

"I'm trying to help."

"Don't you like it there?"

"It's fine. I'd just rather be here."

"Did you have a television at your home?"

"Yes."

"Did you have a car?"

"Yes."

"Could you play basketball?"

"I suppose."

"Then why are you here?"

"Like I said, I want to help."

"Can I go to America?"

It was often like that. They wanted to come to El Dorado—the land of milk and honey—the home of Levi's and CNN. America was the end of the rainbow in the minds of so many.

Now I was going (back) to America and I felt I'd rather have been going anywhere else. I'd really have liked to have jumped into Sir Richard Burton's trunk and escaped into the wilderness with him.

As I stared out the window into the blackness, I felt dizzy—I felt I was standing on the rim of a deep, deep well, looking down, seeing nothing. The edge crumbled and I was spinning into the nothingness like Jimmy Stewart in Hitchcock's 1958 film *Vertigo*.

I was going to America.

New York spilled from the blackness like the backdrop in a theater. It just appeared.

Before I got my bearings, I was in a taxi headed to Novotel Times Square. It wasn't that I really liked Novotel. Truth be known, I felt it was overpriced for mediocre accommodation. Nonetheless, it was what I knew. It was about all I knew.

Under any conditions, I did not know New York City. Under my present conditions of seeing myself a stranger in a strange land, it was even more anonymous.

I spent a few days losing myself in the throngs of the city's byways. I even went to see *South Pacific* at the Beaumont, fondly remembering (vaguely) seeing the movie with Mitzi Gaynor and Rossano Brazzi with my parents and recalling (vividly) my mother playing insistently the soundtrack on her Victrola.

I visited the Metropolitan Museum's Art of Africa collection, but it made me feel even more out of place and I left after only an hour of viewing the collection of twelfth century Yorubaland lost-wax castings. These immediately brought images of my Benin bronze—Samuel.

I knew no one. I visited bars and restaurants thinking maybe I would meet someone—after all, it worked so well in Conakry.

I met no one.

Clearly, NYC was not my destiny. I pulled out my tattered and faded address book and tried to reach out to any of those folks in DC with whom I had, at least for some time, maintained contact.

I could not reach anybody. Naturally, it was over a decade since I had even tried to call any of these individuals. Addresses, telephone numbers, lives—they all changed remarkably over ten years.

Old chums or not, it seemed our nation's capital was a better match for me. If I still felt I wanted or needed to focus on international development, there was the World Bank and a large covey of consulting firms, not to mention USAID and a slew of international NGOs.

I took the train to DC.

With no pre-established entry point, I opted for a different tactic—I'd first find an apartment (as I had before) and set up some sort of a base before I began seeing what direction the Fates took me.

In my earlier life, I had found the library at George Mason University to be very helpful, so, once again, I chose the Virginia side of the capital, finding a nice apartment in Fairfax along Chain Bridge Road, right next to Bell's Bird Sanctuary Park.

As opposed to my first residency, this time my budget was not razor thin. On even a local scale, I was far from rich. But I was somewhere beyond comfortable. I had, in my own right, made considerable savings while at EHT. Then, the settlement required for my ignoble departure increased these monies several times over.

I even bought my very first new car: a Volvo XC90—hailed as a luxury crossover SUV. It was nice. It was so nice, I felt out of place driving it while halfheartedly looking for work.

I didn't really have to work. I just didn't know what else to do.

I was a well-educated, experienced, pre-menopausal woman. What should I do?

My health was good. EHT had in-house medical staff and we all received the best care. My increasingly irregular periods, growing difficulties sleeping, and mood swings were maybe more due to the (early?) onset of menopause than the continued effects of midlife-crisis stress.

This physiological probability notwithstanding, I felt the stress.

I felt the stress of being alone.

I felt the stress of waiting.

I needed something new and shiny to erase much of the pain, or at least frustration, flowing around my recent past.

I needed to move quickly into the next phase of my life. But I had previously leaned on others through such times of transition.

Who was there to help now?

I had no real family. Susan and I had no common ground. There might have been some first or second cousins around somewhere, but I had never met any. There were no living aunts or uncles. There weren't even any close old classmates.

Since separating with Samuel, I had had no meaningful relationships. There had been a few "ships passing in the night" episodes, but nothing worth mentioning.

There had only been my work from the high perch of EHT—a perch that had come crashing down.

I still thought of prices in my mind in Swiss Francs. I still thought in the metric system. I still blurted things out in French as often as in English. I still said, "good day" to all, shook hands with everybody, and unavoidably demonstrated time and again how outside the mold I had become.

Throughout my childhood, Mother was persistently harping (in my view) about having faith in God—so often reciting that tired aphorism, "When God closes a door, he opens a window." It definitely was not due to my faith, but somehow it did seem a window opened.

It first opened, literally, in the ladies' room of Oh George Taphouse, on the other side of Highway 620 from George Mason's campus.

I was using the facilities after a good dosing of good beer, sharing the rather tight quarters with another woman about my age, when the outside window blew open as a thunderstorm rolled through. The rusty hinges required both of us to get the damn thing back in its casement, after which I unconsciously grunted a, "*Mon Dieu!*"

My co-conspirator replied with, "*Quand même.*"

"*Quoi??*" I asked.

Thus, Josephine entered my life. As we got to know each other better, she became just plain José.

José, not surprisingly, was on the faculty of George Mason. She was part of the Film and Video Studies Program—teaching Documentary Filmmaking and Visual Storytelling. She had grown-up in Roanoke, her father a successful banker and her mother a lawyer. Before her divorce, she and her very-well-off, oil-company-executive husband had lived in Houston. When the childless couple split, she had gone back to school (happily paid for by her ex) at Georgetown before taking the position at George Mason.

José became more than a friend—she became a sounding board. She had no inkling of the world from which I came. But she had a whole truckload of common sense. She was a good listener—I guess dealing with me as though she were planning a documentary of my heretofore unknown life.

We'd have drinks together several times a week. Then, we'd go out for dinner at least once a week. Sometimes we'd double date with guys we'd found somewhere—laughing the next day, inevitably, about what jerks these "boys" (as we loved calling them) were.

We bonded.

José was special.

As she got to know me and my story, she slowly felt comfortable throwing some suggestions my way.

The first was to make sure I had closed the door on my love affair with international work. To do this, she proposed, given we were living in one of the most active epicenters, I should see how groups like The World Bank and some NGOs saw me as a credible employee or contractor.

This made sense and it was, importantly, a rude awakening that I needed to experience.

I was confident. I had unique professional skills. I had years of experience. I had (in my humble opinion) a fantastic CV.

I spent three months making phone calls, making unscheduled appearances in offices, and making appointments, as well, with people I did not know. I had used George Mason University's resources to compile a list of possible employers in the DC area. I went down the list one-by-one. When I reached the bottom, I went back through the list, telling my contacts I was simply following-up.

Nothing! That's exactly what I got for my efforts. Zero!

Most were coldly indifferent. Some were honest (from their seat), saying I was of another generation—development work today being of a different league. Sadly, according to many, my generation was to be held responsible for most of the transnational transgressions of the day. New blood was needed.

Amazing!

Whatever remnants of my former life might have been left standing, fell apart now.

My forecast tumble was complete.

I was, quite truly, on the verge of falling apart myself.

Was this the just reward for doing what was right? Was this the result of years of study and work?

Why had I ever left home?

It was so unfair!

Then I recalled, once again, Samuel's words, as he remembered the wisdom of his grandfather: "Life ain't fair."

What was I to expect?

José's reply was, "I could'a told ya so."

My new friend then added the necessary reassuring postscript, "*Du courage!*"

This seemed to work better to get me in an upbeat mindset rather than thinking of Mother's venerable admonitions to, "Have faith, have God."

It was time to retool.

I decided to audit a few classes at George Mason while I tried to see what the options were for a forty-something single female. The College of Humanities and Social Science had a graduate-level Cultural Studies Program with two very interesting upper-level classes: *Culture and Political Economy* along with *After Colonialism.*

As I had done years ago, before even leaving these shores, I was able to sit in on these classes as long as I agreed to contribute actively to the discussions—my background considered as an asset to the overall class (finally getting some appreciation for my bonafides, I snorted to myself).

These courses were fascinating for me. They basically reinforced my existing biases. While they did provide some additional perspectives, it was more like listening to a well-loved familiar song. I knew the basics. I had the firsthand experience. I was, nevertheless, still greatly attracted to the relevant processes, challenges, and possible outcomes.

José, with her clear-eyed assessment, chastised me for staying in my comfort zone. If, she impugned with a smile, I really wanted something new, then I had to look somewhere new.

The second semester, I tried to change my focus to lesser-known and less comfortable (for me) subjects. I departed from graduate studies and managed to be able to sit in some undergraduate-level classes in the Department of Social Work. The aim of this academic group was to "Facilitate the development of cultural skills that would foster positive impacts which would, in turn, be transformative for people and their communities."

This seemed like a little different, perhaps a good twist of the old core themes that had so far interwoven themselves into my life. Rather than sitting on the hilltop and looking down on all the ills (trying to mitigate these, of course), this was possibly an alternative route whereby one jumped into the muck at the bottom and tried to push up. Was this the retooling I needed?

I asked José

José always had an opinion and she was always happy to offer guidance.

José was the product of a mixed marriage. Her mother was a Southerner and her father a Northerner—she born in Alabama and he in Illinois. After marriage, they had settled south of the Mason-Dixon Line in the Blue Ridge Mountains in southwest Virginia.

As a hybrid, José was a manifestation of the two parent stocks; socially she was a Southerner and culturally she was a Northerner. She wholeheartedly endorsed the time-honored but waning principle of southern hospitality. People needed to get out of their shells and get into the stream of life.

However, José was adamantly opposed to the historical bigotry and prejudices—racism—seen across much of the South. She was for an all-inclusive and egalitarian openness.

Accordingly, José felt that if I was dallying with the issues of social transformation of people and communities, I should meet her Aunt Beatrice who lived in Marengo County, Alabama—part of the "Black Belt." José assured me that since March 1965, when Aunt Beatrice marched with Martin Luther King from Selma, her aunt had been deeply involved in trying to help those people and communities in the most need.

To drive her point home, José invited her aunt to join us for a home-style Thanksgiving dinner at her house. After the turkey and pumpkin pie, Aunt Beatrice settled into José's comfortable armchair with a glass of Port and regaled us with stories of the social shambles that was rural Alabama. After her second glass of Port, she fixed me with her somewhat cloudy obsidian eyes, saying, "Dear, you didn't have to go to another continent to find people worth saving, you could have just come to Alabama."

We all agreed—José and I matching Aunt Beatrice's Port ounce per ounce with our sour mash—we should meet at Aunt Beatrice's for Easter to examine the topic in more depth. Aunt Beatrice exclaiming, "Easter in Marengo County is ever so lovely."

José then served pralines and coffee.

Before I get too far astray, I should at least offer honorable mention to Irv—Irving Bernosky. Irv was three years my junior— divorced, balding, and malcontent. The Bernosky's were a very well-to-do family in northern New York State who had found their riches in scrap iron. At Cornell, Irv had met Azra Kakarn, the daughter of one of the richest men in southern Florida, Ejlaal Kakarn, a Pakistani immigrant who had found his fortune making component parts for the US automobile industry.

The two Cornell students found more than a magnetic attraction to steel; they found love. Sadly, a Jewish-Muslim union was welcomed by neither family. The more their families resisted, the more they clung to each other. They fled to San Francisco, married, and had two children. Irv, who was an extremely clever fellow, started a computer business in the late 1980s. He did very well.

Azra stayed at home until her children could enter kindergarten, then took a position with a major brokerage firm. They were the American Dream. Great jobs, beautiful home, super cars; they had it all. Then, Azra started wearing a hijab and she pulled their kids out of public school, placing them into the Madrasa at the Gharb Masjid. Overnight, Irv's family had become strict Muslim.

Azra could not be deterred. Irv could not accept the drastic changes—he was, after all, Jewish. He was not going to convert. He was happy to practice "live and let live," but this was far beyond tolerance—this was turning his family upside-down. Azra was adamant. Irv filed for divorce, asking to be given custody of the children. The divorce was granted, but the children stayed with their mother. Irv sold his company and his car—his part of the house going to Azra as part of the settlement. He returned to the East Coast. He started a small company to assist government offices abroad set up computer systems—he was again very successful. To keep himself grounded, he taught a course once a week at Georgia Mason on information technology.

Well before Aunt Beatrice's visit, Irv and I met by chance one evening when José and I were again at Oh George Taphouse. I had gone to the bar for refills of our highballs. As I turned to go back to the table, I ran smack-dab into a surprisingly sound stomach of someone behind me, sprinkling Bourbon on his pinstriped shirt. I said, "surprisingly sound" because the solid abdomen my drink sloshed into was in stark contrast to the haggard and aged (practically comic book) face into which I stared as I completed my pirouette. Only the eyes seemed to sparkle with a youthful energy.

I took a wad of paper napkins off the bar and indelicately dabbed his stomach. This solicited a kind of wrenching laugh from the recipient of these ministrations that many might think was best to be undertaken in a more private place than the front of a very populated bar.

Having broken the intimacy barrier, Irv joined José and me at our table and me, later that night, in my apartment.

I saw it as an amusing fling. A man of such seeming contradictions, but good muscle tone. Perhaps a memorable hook-up?

The one-off adventure turned into something else. We spent over six months intermittently tumbling (as well as fortyish lovers could) about his or my bed. It wasn't hot passion, it wasn't blow-steam-out-your-ears sex, it was simply comfortable.

It was comfortable at a time when I needed comfort and it was interesting. Irv and I were opposites in so many ways. While this didn't lead to a ground-shaking attraction, it led to engaging curiosity. Our stories were so different. And, we were each honestly interested in the other's tale. This led to a companionability that was equal parts physical and thoughtful.

Denial and Acceptance

The first step in the evolution of ethics is a sense of solidarity with other human beings.

—ALBERT SCHWEITZER

JOSÉ AND I WERE football fanatics. We were like Arsenal fans—passionate and loud. We had our team, our common causes, and we cheered vociferously, most often from the stands, as we drank beer and munched peanuts.

While we both did like football—albeit José continued to call it "soccer"—our most important teams were more in the social and political arenas than the athletic field. For these non-sporting squads, we tried not to simply sit on the sidelines. We contributed to and volunteered with action groups—trying to do what we could to promote social and economic equity.

We also tried to be realists. I hoped I had left my naiveté on the EHT stoop as I had left the building. Money and good-ol'-boy power grabs were the drivers. We tried to offer a counterbalance but were heavily outweighed. Yet, we were indefatigable.

Our unflagging fervor for our cause (bringing a bit of a wistful moment as I remembered back to "my farmers") was the glue that stuck us together. At another time, under other circumstances, we might have toyed at even becoming romantically involved, but this frankly was not something that our lives could accommodate.

José was wholly consumed by her work at George Mason—building themes from our cause into many of her films and stories. She also had an on-again-off-again relationship with Howard, a professor of developmental and social psychology at Georgia Mason. They would go months without seeing each other then leave for a long weekend in West Virginia, shacking up for seventy-two hours without seeing the sun.

Although José and I had a very open and candid friendship, I sensed Howard was a no-go zone and I really knew very little about their liaison. We concentrated our together-time on trying to nonchalantly save the world.

While José was an important part of my life, I too had a number of things in play. Irv and I were more regular than José and Howard, but we were not welded together at the waist. My class audits at George Mason continued to hold my attention. And, I had become active in a circle of Afrocentric RPCVs. When one added all this into the mix of other groups with which José and I were active together, it was a very full schedule.

As I was preparing for my visit to Aunt Beatrice's, Irv was preparing for a nine-month sojourn to a score of embassies and other official US installations around the world to oversee the upgrading of their information systems. We realized our time together had been a quirk. The gods controlled tomorrow. So, we separated as though we would see each other again soon—knowing this was far from certain. We'd have to wait and see.

Then José and I went to Aunt Beatrice's for Easter.

José's Aunt Beatrice lived in the Alabama Black Belt—a seventeen-county region of the state so called because of its rich, dark soils (pedologically speaking, this band of soils stretched from Maryland to Texas). This was, as well as an area with particular soils, a region of the state that had a relatively high percentage of black residents. Many considered the Alabama Black Belt as the birthplace of the American Civil Rights Movement.

Aunt Beatrice lived in Marengo County. The county was established in 1818 on land obtained from (many would say stolen from) the Choctaw Indians. The county was named after Napoleon's Battle of Marengo, the area having been settled Bonapartists in 1817. The county was home to many cotton plantations. In 1860, slaves accounted for seventy-eight percent of the population. Through the years since the Civil War, cotton was replaced by cattle, timber, and fishponds. Changing economies continued to leave roughly a quarter of the population below the poverty line.

Aunt Beatrice lived in Demopolis, the largest town in the county—a county that was still more than fifty percent black. On the Tombigbee River, the town, about 100 miles west of Montgomery (thirty-five miles east of the Mississippi border), off Highway 80, was home to over one-third of the county's population—the county seat of Linden, seventeen miles to the south, being about a third the size of Demopolis.

Easter, as Aunt Beatrice had promised, was a nice time in Demopolis. The afternoon temperatures were a full ten degrees warmer than DC, which was still shaking off the dampness of winter.

Like her niece, Aunt Beatrice had no specific religious affiliations—she was everything as much as she was nothing (spiritually speaking). Therefore, while we did not have an Easter egg hunt, neither did we attend services. To celebrate, Aunt Beatrice had made reservations for us at the Demopolis Bistro, starting with a seafood Cobb salad, followed by delicious West Alabama fried rice (also chucked full of seafood), and then topped off with chocolate mousse. It was an Easter feast to remember.

The next day we went to the Reynolds Activity Center where Aunt Beatrice volunteered three days a week. Aunt Beatrice did not want to make a big deal out of our visit to the Center. She did not want to disrupt things with a trio of old white women coming into a flock of black kids—the biggest portion teenage boys playing basketball. After all, her aim was not to introduce us to the objects of her attention. Her focus was on showing me that, if I was looking to get involved, there was plenty to do.

That evening, on her porch, Aunt Beatrice went into more detail. Alabama ranked number forty-seven in the country for residents living in poverty. Furthermore, the state ranked forty-eighth in terms of number of people living in hunger and food insecurity (Mississippi, next door, always beating out Alabama for the bottom of the list). Across the state, there were nearly 700,000 people living in poverty—fifteen percent of the population. Poverty was highest in the Black Belt counties. Things were tough and those most affected needed a voice.

However, that very year, the political leadership had been talking about a bill that would require voter ID—knowing full-well this would have disproportionly greater effects on the poor—keeping them from the polls—stilling their voices.

As intended, Aunt Beatrice's encapsulation of some of the dire straits to be found just across the street from her family home made an impression on José and me. We were pushing an agenda at the nation's capital, but there was unquestionably a great need in the hinterland.

The next day, we tried to concentrate on lighter subjects. We visited the Gainswood Antebellum House Museum and, crossing the river, drove around the Demopolis State Wildlife Management Area. On our last day, we drove up to Tuscaloosa to look over the campus and visit the Gorgas–Manly Historic District with the Gorgas House Museum—the building itself dating back to 1829. After a late lunch at Dreamland BBQ, we headed back to Aunt Beatrice's.

Enroute, Aunt Beatrice, chuckling to herself, remarked about the strange circumstances that, as she put, shined a light were a light was needed. With more than a hint of irony, she reminded us, "We ate at Dreamland, right?"

"Uh-huh." José and I grunted in unison.

"And," Aunt Beatrice continued, "for the past two days we've been staring at all sorts of artifacts from the Old South—that place in time so dear to so many."

Another, "Uh-huh."

"Well, ladies," she smiled, "haven't we just come from dreamland?"

"Of course."

"No," she admonished, "not the BBQ, the dream of rediscovering lost times gone by."

"Hmmm?"

"Yes," she intoned, "mark my words, folks here are living in dreamland. They dream of the second rising of THE South."

"OK."

"No, it's not!," she actually scolded. "I'm a Southerner. We have to move on. We have to look forward, not back."

"Indeed," the simultaneous reaction.

"Indeed, to you two," she cautioned, "but totally unacceptable to many hereabouts."

"One step at a time, Aunt Beatrice." José tried to calm her aging aunt's nerves as she warmed a little bit too much to her subject.

"Yes, yes, yes," the elderly freedom rider replied, "let's just hope it's a step forward and not back."

Back in the realm of George Mason, I reminded myself I was still in Dixie. While I returned to my groove—sitting-in on classes, hanging-out with José, engaging with various groups and factions—I thought back to Easter in Demopolis.

I had had Easters in Fomi and Nzérékoré and elsewhere around Africa. What were the differences?

I had always seen things as a bimodal assortment of events: here and there. From my angle, here and there were very different. If I was honest with myself, "here" was on top, "there" was not. "There" was trying to climb out of a hole to get to a similar level as "here." It was like a card for the old stereographs (I guess the predecessors of View-Masters) of the late 1800s, two images side by side—in my view, one of "here" and another one of "there." One shiny. The other tarnished.

My life had been divided, not equally, among "here" and "there." When I was "there," I was where I wanted to be. I was, I thought, having the greatest impact. I was helping those most in need. I was doing the most good. When I was "here," I was trying to get "there."

It was confusing.

Had I been in dreamland?

I thought of the stereotypes. I knew more of the realities, but I was still affected by the time-honored clichés. Underdeveloped countries were corrupt. Underdeveloped countries were ignorant (or awash with ignorance). Underdeveloped countries were where a few dominated the many. Undeveloped countries were basket-cases. So much of the world had pigeonholed countries trying so hard to, as we said, "develop" (they very likely would say they were simply trying to survive).

The corruption was so often flagged as the sign of collapse. Large portions of the funding for major infrastructure projects were diverted into private overseas investments. Public services were staffed with ghost workers whose salaries ended up in the bank accounts of politicians. Elections were theatrics with candidates determined before election day.

I recalled meeting a senior manager from an Italian road construction company while traveling in Zambia. He'd said, "If you really want to make money, build roads."

He had gone on to explain how, by merely shaving a few centimeters off the width of the road and millimeters off the thickness of the road's surface, millions could be pocketed—the windfall shared between civil servants ostensibly responsible for quality control and the company itself.

These were the ills of the third world.

These were the truisms that had added gravitas to my work—underscoring the misdeeds and the urgency of doing better.

These were the ailments of "there."

Yet now, as I opened my eyes and looked through a different lens, were these not the ailments of "here?"

Were not lobbyists just conduits for adding cash to politicians' pockets? Were not the ultra-rich twisting arms to have lower and lower taxes? Were not those with the means supporting reduced public assistance to health and education while their own families went to private schools and hospitals? Were not those in power trying to wrench the vote from the hands of those with a different political persuasion? Even if elections were fixed over "there," at least there was an effort to get everyone to vote. Here the tendency seemed just the opposite.

Yes, EHT was, to my chagrin, scared by malfeasance. But this was not, in hindsight, an isolated case of the greedy and unscrupulous mismanaging things for their personal benefit in the arena of development. This was simply another case of selfishness and exploitation that did not apply to here or there, but to everywhere.

It wasn't Yin and Yang. It wasn't a duality of worlds. It was just one messy ship sailing uncertain seas.

With this revelation, I decided to get a dog.

Maybe it would be more correct to say the dog got me.

I had just parked at Kroger and was heading in for my weekly stock-up when a lady approached me. She was probably younger than I, but her haggard features made her look years older. From out of nowhere, she was at my shoulder saying, in a husky voice, "You look like a nice person."

Not knowing how to react, I simply nodded.

She got closer, almost snuggling into my coat, pushing something into my hands, saying, "Do the right thing."

Then she was gone.

I looked down and found I was holding a fluffy wheat-colored puppy.

This was, or this was to become Suki.

I abandoned my grocery mission and went home. I put the pup on the kitchen floor, stretched out beside her, and examined her thoroughly. She seemed as jittery about me as I about she. I poked and prodded her. When I got to look at her teeth, I was aghast—her tongue was purple. Obviously, the lady had pawned off a sick dog—not knowing how to treat this dastardly disease.

I looked in the phonebook and found the nearest vet, rushing there with my afflicted puppy—afflicted by what, I had no idea. When I got her on the exam table and explained to the vet her problem, the white-coated lady nearly doubled over in laughter.

When she was finally in full control of her wits, she revealed, "Dear, you don't have any problem. This puppy appears to be very healthy."

"But the purple—"

"No worry," she smiled, "she's part Chow Chow, Chow Chows have purple tongues. It's normal. You're fine."

Hence, Suki and I began the process of getting to know one another.

Within a week we were best friends.

❖❖❖

My life, and I guess everybody's, was characterized by a series of ups and downs. The next event started as a downer. Aunt Beatrice died. It was sad that the world had lost such a unique individual. Yet, those who had known her celebrated having been touched by her extraordinary spirit.

José and I were, of course, going to the funeral in Demopolis. Unlike José, however, I was not on a tight schedule. I was, in fact, in a slump. The classes I had already audited had pretty much sapped whatever academic energy I had left. There were still no doors opening on the international front. Furthermore, there appeared to be few doors opening anywhere.

I decided it was time for a break.

After consultation with José, we decided we'd take the Volvo and drive down to Alabama with Suki. After the funeral, José would fly back from Montgomery and I'd be free (with Suki) to meander wherever I might.

Held at the Reynolds Activity Center, the funeral was more a celebration of a singular and unselfish life. Aunt Beatrice had enriched the lives of many.

Beatrice Brennon Crenshaw had been an icon in Demopolis. Born in 1910, she had had a long and full life. Her father had been a schoolteacher who had moved north from Mobile at the turn of the previous century. Her mother had given piano lessons and raised (or tried to raise) four kids— two boys and two girls. Beatrice was the youngest. The younger of her two brothers, only eighteen months her senior, had died at the age of four from complications from German measles. Tragically, her older brother had been killed by a cotton truck when riding his bicycle only three years later. She and her sister (José's mother) had survived to grow up in the New South.

Beatrice had attended the Alabama Central Female College in Tuscaloosa, intending to follow in her father's footsteps. Her sister, Amanda, nine years her elder, was always the more adventurous and went out of state to college—attending MacMurray College in Jacksonville, Illinois, where she had studied liberal arts. Jacksonville was just thirty-five miles west of Springfield where Amanda met her husband, José's father Alvin, (his middle name was Charles, so he went by A.C.) at The Cotton Patch, a popular chicken and biscuits restaurant.

Alvin spent his college vacations working at the Springfield Piggly Wiggly. Academically, he was going to the University of Illinois in Champaign where he was enrolled in the College of Business.

On this particular day in destiny, The Cotton Patch was full to the seams and customers had to share tables—the gods had smiled, and Alvin shared a table with Amanda. The chemistry had been immediate and intense.

The couple wed in June after each graduated for their respective colleges. They moved to Chicago where Amanda entered law school at the University of Chicago while her husband started an internship at the Continental Illinois National Bank.

While her big sister geared up for a career and a family, graduating from Alabama Central, Beatrice returned to Demopolis. She married Hank Crenshaw. She and Hank had known each other since grade school. He was a good guy. He worked at the post office and coached weekend sports. As Beatrice taught fifth grade, Hank moved up through several postal positions to become an assistant head of station.

While this was a time of harmony in their home, the South was far from harmonious. This was not only the Great Depression, this period represented the merging of the Jim Crow Era and, what was later to be called, the Lynching Era. Race was literally a burning issue.

In 1933 Reuben Micou was lynched in Winston County, Mississippi. Although one hundred miles from Demopolis, the effects had spilled over into western Alabama. The sixty-five-year-old black man had been in jail for the crime of arguing with a powerful white man. He was torn from his cell and murdered. Seventeen white men were subsequently indicted for the horrific act.

This spawned public displays of both condemnation and support across the region. The local Demopolis Klu Klux Klan members demonstrated in favor of dropping the charges against the seventeen who they claimed, "Did a service to society."

Local church groups marched the same day, demanding prompt justice against the murderers.

It was probably inevitable. The two groups clashed. They clashed violently—the Klan was armed. By the time the Klan members fled, there were two dead and four injured. One of the dead was Hank Crenshaw.

Hank had not even been marching for either group. He had simply been walking to the post office and was caught up in the melee.

Reuben Micou had unknowingly been the spark that had ignited the flame that had pushed Aunt Beatrice to stop teaching and become an activist (an obscure term in those days).

Hank and Beatrice had had no children. José's parents had passed away. In this setting, at the reading of Beatrice's will after the internment, José was surprised, but probably should not have been, to be the sole inheritor of the modest estate including the home in Demopolis, some antique furniture, a rather meager investment portfolio, and (unnoticed previously by anyone) 275 acres of land near Cuba, Alabama—snuggled right up to the Mississippi State Line.

José's initial reaction, once she absorbed the bequeathment, was to sell everything and get back to George Mason as quickly as possible. However, Mr. Weizel, Aunt Beatrice's lawyer, advised against any rapid decision-making. Mr. Weizel described the complexities of the various components of Aunt Beatrice's estate. Modest though it was, in these days of process and regulation, even the simplest affairs were complicated. The best tactic was slow and steady.

José hated waiting nearly as much as I. Nevertheless, Mr. Weizel's advice could not be dismissed. It was best to slow down—but how?

With almost a flirtatious quip, I so clearly remember saying, with no forethought, "Don't worry, I'll take care of everything."

It was meant as tomfoolery—just trying to break up the solemnity of the occasion.

Yet, somehow, it hit home with José, who replied almost naturally, "Of course."

From her viewpoint, we were good friends, I had nothing really serious that was occupying my time, so why not?

José saw my interjection in a completely different landscape.

If I had to try and interpret my silly babble of all those years ago, it was most probably intended in the context that I'd take José to a bar and supply her with enough booze that her future would become crystal clear.

She saw things differently.

José plainly saw this as the answer to my slump. It was destiny.

Once again, it may have been best that I kept my mouth shut. Or it may have been the hand of fate.

In any event, it was her home ground and her rules. She saw a role for me and I honestly could not say I was committed to anything else.

So, we did go to the bar, but it was José who paid and I who had pegs set on the road into my future. A plan was devised between gulps of Tennessee sour mash and handfuls of Georgia peanuts.

Only temporarily, mind you, I would move into Aunt Beatrice's house in Demopolis, liaising between Mr. Weizel and José as arrangements were made to settle the estate.

Everything in order, José caught her flight from Montgomery on schedule.

Moving into Aunt Beatrice's didn't involve much more than putting my car in the garage and getting a big bag of dog food for Suki. José was able to find someone from George Mason to sublease my apartment on Chain Bridge Road. She also sent me my few belongings remaining in Fairfax—all my stuff barely took up the space of four good-sized boxes.

I became a Demopolian.

There was a transition period to which I should have been very used. Things were different and so was I—I was an outsider in a close-knit community. Not so different from Fomi, of course. It was not so different, but actually demographically smaller and, in many ways, more sectarian. The town's population was about 7,500—less than a fifth that of the wider Fomi area that I had covered as an extensionist. Certainly, by comparison with the DC area, I was in the boonies.

It felt like a welcome change.

Much of the liaison work I was charted to carry out was really just discussing in depth face-to-face with Mr. Weizel the full context of the inheritance issues so that both he and I could brief José—she feeling the two perspectives beneficial in making basically irrevocable decisions.

The legal issues of probate were both intricate and straightforward (also, beyond my ken). The conclusions of how to deal with the assets were more involved. The investments were easily transferred into José's portfolio. The antiques were transported to Mobile for sale on consignment through a high-end dealer. I made the arrangements and ensured the items got to their destination in good shape. José decided to hold on to the house for the time being—maybe just so I'd have a place to stay.

The lands near the state line were the real mystery.

Both Mr. Weizel and I dug into this matter.

The lands in question were part of a larger plantation—Cuba Plantation—purchased in 1850 by Andrew Pickens Calhoun—son of our country's seventh Vice President. This was his second estate, adding significantly to the lands he owned at *Cedar Haven*, near Faunsdale, nearly fifty miles to the east. In 1863 the property had been sold to Mr. Tristram Benjamin Bethea, a Montgomery lawyer and politician. At his death in 1876, the acreage had passed to his son Henry. From that time on, the chain of custody as it were, was increasingly fuzzy. It seemed as though the plots had remained with this family until the Depression, at which time they had been sold to a distant cousin, Nathan, who lived in Demopolis.

Nathan had reportedly purchased all the lands at the old Cuba Plantation site—some 875 acres. At his death, Nathan, seemingly a life-long bachelor, bequeathed his lands near Cuba to Lilly Whitewater—who many local folks would call a "colored girl." She was of mixed race, but of a fair complexion of a paleness many good ol' boys would call "high yell'a."

Lilly's mother, Rose, had, in effect, been Nathan's common-law wife for decades. Racially mixed couples were not to be seen in Alabama. Although, the 1967 US Supreme Court decision of Love v. Virginia had abolished all bans on interracial marriage, Alabama did not remove anti-miscegenation provisions of the state's constitution until 2000. Incontrovertibly, Nathan and Rose's relationship had to be kept under wraps.

They had been very successful in masking their union. As far as anyone in Demopolis knew, Rose was a seamstress who did occasional work for Mr. Nathan.

Given the obvious mixed background of Rose's daughter, and the long history of covert interracial pairings across the South (some voluntary, others not), no one asked about the girl's father. The less known, the better.

When Rose died five years before her hidden lover, Nathan could have deserted Lilly. He did not. While still surreptitiously, he continued to support her and her studies. At the time of his passing, he proudly watched the daughter he could not acknowledge as she worked as a nurse's assistant at Tombigbee Healthcare Authority.

When the story came out and Lilly was openly cited as the heiress of Nathan's estate, the town's ruling class went up at arms—this was completely unacceptable.

It was also completely legal, and it was Aunt Beatrice who, although not a lawyer, came to Lilly's aid and fought against the embedded bigotry of Demoplois' landed gentry.

With no statutory grounds, and a crumbling social base thanks to Beatrice's energetic defense, Lilly inherited Nathan's lands—giving Beatrice 275 acres of the old Cuba Plantation as a generous thank you.

This was the final piece of Aunt Beatrice's puzzle.

The best future of this acreage was unclear. Both José and Mr. Weizel decided it was necessary to take a good long look at the next course of action.

In Sumter County, Cuba (or Cuba Station, as some called it) had seen better days. In the 1850s through the 1890s its economy had been driven by slave-powered agriculture and railroad building. More recently, it had been severely depressed; Sumter County became the poorest county in the state.

However, this ignominious position had ironically shone a light on the county's plight. The state government had begun initiating efforts to draw out-of-state investment to Sumter. If they were successful, managing to attract significant capital, property prices would rise. It was not a good time to sell large tracts at the below par land prices inherent in the present faltering economy.

Once again, I encountered a situation where waiting was the tactic of choice. My assignment was basically finished. The decisions were made. I wasn't really needed. I didn't want to wait.

I was thinking of leaving, but I had no idea of where to go.

Over the past weeks, in pursuing my charges relating to Aunt Beatrice's will, I had had frequent occasions to make the seventeen-mile-run to the county seat, Linden.

As one can imagine, this was not a bustling town. Being the center of government for a county with a little over 20,000 inhabitants (slightly more than half the number of residents than there had been at the beginning of the twentieth century) was an important, but not terribly taxing job.

In my meandering through several county offices, I picked up a handful of fun facts about the area that was my new (if temporary) home. These came from multiple sources and across many years, as data seemed to be no more easily available in Linden than it had been in Babila where I had scoured for details about Fomi upon my arrival.

Given the plantation history with which I was now quite familiar after my exploration into Cuba Plantation, it was not surprising that the old families with deep roots still held onto much of the land. According to reports, over ninety-eight percent of rural land was owned by individuals (as opposed to corporations, tribal groups, or similar). Of this group, eight percent were non-white—this latter group owning in total four percent of the individually owned rural lands of the state.

Within this state-wide setting, the county, with more than half its population recorded as black, had a poverty rate of roughly twenty-eight percent, with one-third of children less than eighteen years of age living in poverty. Youth concerns were aggravated by facts like low infant birth weights—low weights were noted for fourteen percent of births (the national average apparently eight percent). It seemed the similarities with rural Guinea were not only in regard to the difficulties in getting current and comprehensive statistics.

Hopefully on the positive side, with a noticeable portion of the population living in stressful conditions, the county (as others) had a Family Assistance Project. This public effort, itself stressed for resources, was assisted by a nonprofit, The Community Engagement Group of West Alabama. Eileen Jackson headed up the nonprofit. Eileen could trace her family back to the Glennville Plantation in Russell County, on the other side of the state. She had crossed the state to attend the University of Alabama in Tuscaloosa from which she had been awarded a BSW in social work. Before becoming a college student (or more likely, in order to be able to become one), she had worked in Atlanta for five years. Moving from The Big Peach to Tuscaloosa to Linden had been a strenuous process—mentally more than physically. She still missed the things she could not find in a small rural berg in the Black Belt, but she was consumed by the work. There was so, so much to do.

I met Eileen at the County Clerk's office—each of us searching for hard-to-find items.

Eileen and I got along.

In no time, we were having coffee together whenever I was at the County Seat. We enjoyed each other's company. As two outsiders, we had a common bond. As two professional women who were seen as, in many ways, challenging the status quo, we had an even stronger bond.

As Aunt Beatrice's affairs were wrapping up, I told Eileen I was thinking about moving on, just didn't know where.

"Why don't you come and work with me?" she asked, throwing me somewhat of a curveball.

"Hmmm," was about all I could offer. The work in which CEGWA was involved fit very nicely with my most recent dabbling at George Mason, but was this where I wanted to go?

"I've funds for a short-term consultant. You'd be just the ticket!"

"I don' know."

"Yes, you do!" she stated emphatically, "you know this interests you."

"I'm not really sure."

"Come on. You've told me time and again about how you saw your efforts come tumbling down, yet how you also see common ground between those far off places where you worked and the grave problems right here in front of you."

"Well . . ."

"No 'well' about it. Just say, 'yes'. I've only got a little money so you can give it a try. If you don't like it, you can go your merry way. If you do, we can see if I can get additional funds. What have you got to lose?"

What could I say? I acquiesced—not begrudgingly, mind you.

José was fine with me staying in the house. Suki seemed OK with the yard. I was set.

I will not rummage to any length through that memorable period in West Alabama, nor the impact it had on my view of my surroundings. It is inadequate, but at least a start to say I was greatly affected.

What I had perhaps surmised, but what became blatantly clear was that poverty in rural Alabama rivaled that in Guinea or elsewhere in Africa where I had worked. Yes, the context was different, but the severe and debilitating effects on vulnerable people were nearly the same. Rural folk were confronted with the same dilemmas of how to find an acceptable quality of life. How could poor people find acceptable schools for their children and acceptable healthcare for their families?

To a large extent, rural Alabama was a parallel universe. From all indications, if you had money—not even if you were rich, but just that you weren't too poor—you could send your kids to an academy (a private school) and get your ill kin to better hospitals.

If you were poor, it was a totally different picture. The poor had no access to private services. To the contrary, the poor were ofttimes seen by the non-poor as the sluggards: blacks and "white trash." The poor were regularly seen as lazy. The poor were seen time and again as those who could do better but chose not to. The poor were even not infrequently seen by others as unworthy: certainly not a group warranting any special considerations.

In general, or so it seemed, the poor were the unwanted and the neglected. And, the annoying poor were in trouble.

If someone made $5,000 annually, this person was poor. Few would disagree. But this person was also eligible to pay taxes, further cutting into money that simply wasn't there.

Rural economies faded; rural communities shrank. Rural folk suffered.

It was a global problem with some special local twists.

I did get engaged.

I went door to door. I held small and large meetings. I contacted politicians. I wrote letters. I went to church services. But mostly, I talked with Eileen.

With the growing rumbles of new ways to suppress poor voters, my major focus was trying to develop channels where the poor would and could vote.

It was almost like European life in the 1400s with a privileged nobility (aristocracy) and a disadvantaged peasant or plebeian class. Southern aristocracy had existed since colonial times—their seeds continued into the twenty-first century. These seedlings tenaciously held on to the levers of power—relentlessly trying to bend the pathway of the future. For them, change and modernity along with diversity and empathy were threats to their dominance—a dominance they saw as God-given.

I saw my role, with Eileen's blessing, as being one of trying to inform those who felt the bottom of the barrel was their natural milieu that they could hope for better. They could achieve better. But they could only do so if they were educated and organized.

I have no idea if I was successful.

Eileen initially had enough funds for a three-month contract. Once bitten by the assignment, I agreed to stay if she could find more resources. She did. I stayed.

At the same time, I wondered. Was this the end of the road? I had unquestionably embarked on a task that could occupy the rest of my life and very probably another lifetime as well. I was getting very close to fifty. Was this my destination?

I thought not.

It was time again to move on.

I had been more or less financially secure before coming to Alabama—comfortable by even skeptical norms. While here, I had had very few expenses and a reasonable, if not overly generous, contract with CEGWA. Once more, I had the luxury of being able to do almost anything, but unsure of how to start doing something.

My mother had not been a big reader. But, when we went on vacations in grade school and junior high, Mother would read out loud to the other three of us. Her favorite book was John Steinbeck's *Travels with Charley*. Nostalgically, I picked up a frayed copy at a Montgomery used book dealer. I was attracted to the words Steinbeck, then apparently fifty-eight, penned at the beginning of *Travels*:

> When the virus of restlessness begins to take possession of a wayward man [or woman], and the road away from Here seems broad and straight and sweet, the victim must first find himself a good and sufficient reason for going. This to the practical bum is not difficult. He has a built-in garden of reasons to choose from.

My garden was full and ready to be harvested.

I put my bags in the Volvo, made a nest for Suki on the back seat with some old blankets, and took off.

I had heard of people flipping a coin to see which direction to take. I was not any more organized, it was simply that I wanted to go to Meridian, Mississippi first. Meridian was only sixty miles west, so it was a pretty paltry first step. Yet, as I had laughed with Samuel, it was the beginning of even the longest journey.

Meridian had been the center of the 1964 calamity when three civil rights volunteers from New York City had been slaughtered. As an indication of the brutality of the acts (or maybe because the dead were outsiders), an all-white jury convicted seven Klansmen of "depriving victims of their civil rights."

Meridian today was highlighted as a model of the New South. The city had modernized and diversified—reportedly doing well economically, unlike many of its neighbors.

I spent a few days to amble about and get my sea legs under me. No more office hours. No more clock to watch. All I really had to do was make sure Suki got her chow.

Then, as if a bell had sounded, it was time to move forward. My inclination was to go toward the Gulf Coast—always having been a lover of the seashore. I could easily go south to Pascagoula and then have Interstate 10 at my doorstep to zip westward or eastward.

For reasons I cannot to this day explain, perhaps that mysterious hand of Fate, I decided to do the exact opposite of my gut feeling. I headed northwest into the innards of the country—into the bowels of the great river systems that irrigated the heartland. I moved into areas that honestly held no attraction and about which I knew absolutely nothing.

Being contrary seemed the right thing to do.

I zigged and zagged through northeast Mississippi, western Tennessee, northeast Arkansas, central Missouri, western Iowa, and eastern Kansas—right up to Nebraska. It was not the same as my expedition through Africa when I had left Namibia, but it was still one helluva trip. From my vantage point, many things were just as new and unfamiliar in the midlands of the United States as in far-off Africa. I somehow bizarrely felt I was traveling in the shadow of Sir Richard Burton.

I was exploring my own backyard for the first time.

I say "I" at times, but most often I'm thinking, "We." Suki and I were a team.

Suki and I were not accosted, robbed, nor driven off the road. But we had many memorable experiences and near misses. We were in no hurry—investigating every half-hidden alley and stopping at far too many roadside attractions.

Slowly migrating north from the Black Belt toward the Black Hills (purely by chance and not by design), my most impressive observation was the multiple personality disorder affecting the country—everything was the same and everything was different.

The fast-food vendors, the stores, the grocery stores, the pharmacies, the gas stations—they were nearly the same throughout the 1,000-mile adventure (as a bird flies). The jeans, the sneakers, the T-shirts—all the same. The food, the groceries, the cars—the same. But, the culture—quite different. Wearing my anthropologist's hat, I could easily recognize the shifts, as we moved along the byways, when one way of life bled into another. It was truly remarkable.

We continued on our northwest tack as though navigating by the stars. At this rate, I figured we'd hit the Canadian border somewhere east of the Rockies. What would happen then?

What happened well before we reached that point was that Suki badly cut her paw when we were walking in a vacant lot in Norfolk, Nebraska. I'm not sure what caused the gash, but it was a gusher. I took her to the closest vet who kindly got her in as an emergency. Four hours later, when she came limping out from the back of the clinic, she was well repaired, but sutured up. She would need her sutures out in two weeks.

We could have continued along our celestially guided course in the hopes of finding a vet en route to remove the stitches. But I decided we needed to stay where there were with folks who knew the problem from the onset.

I got a pet-friendly room with a kitchenette in a motel, appropriately called the Heart of Norfolk, that rented rooms by the week. We, Suki hobbling, took stock of our new locale. The town of over 20,000 was just over one-hundred miles northwest of Omaha. There was a nice park surrounding a lake where Suki and I liked to stroll.

Going to and from the park, I noticed an ordinary-enough house flagged as "Johnny Carson's Childhood Home." This further underscored to me the obvious: there's something different everywhere. The corollary, of course, also true: there are commonalities everywhere.

Suki couldn't go too far, so while she rested her foot, I walked about town and visited the public library. I had categorically no knowledge of the state of Nebraska nor the town of Norfolk. So, I decided to try and get at least the barest of background.

I did my homework.

The area had been settled in 1865 by German stock coming from Wisconsin—as always, people looking for good, cheap land. Nebraska achieved statehood in 1867. In 1879, the *Fremont, Elkhorn and Missouri Valley Railroad* came to town on its way north to the gold fields of the Black Hills. This spurred considerable growth. In 1885 the state built an Insane Asylum in the town. Over the years the economy had been maintained by a combination of light industry and agriculture.

I probed a little deeper. Madison County, surrounding Norfolk, had 700 farms with the major crops: grains, oil seeds, along with peas and beans. Cattle were the major livestock component of the agriculture portfolio, which was worth, annually, over $300 million.

I noted that effectively one hundred percent of the farmers were, according to the census, white. This brought me back to Marengo County and I did a quick comparison. The overall population of Norfolk was ninety-one percent white—this an immediate contrast to Demopolis.

Madison County had twenty-five percent more farms than Marengo. And these Nebraska farms were twenty-five percent larger. However, over one-fifth of the Southern farms were operated by blacks. Furthermore, the total value of the crops and livestock from Marengo County was less than $20 million (forty percent of the farmland in Marengo used for woodlots).

Marengo and Madison—different and similar. I scratched a bit more. In the former, eighty-four percent of students graduated from high school, ninety percent for the latter. This was pretty close. For the southern county, seventeen percent finished college—in the northern cohort, the number was thirty-eight percent. A big difference. In Marengo, the average income for working women was $19,000—in Madison it was $26,000. Another big difference.

I felt like I was moving along a spectrum—not a rainbow, for there was no pot of gold at the end, of that I was sure. The shared factors woven into the uniqueness of each place were the essence of this country. Yet, to be able to see and appreciate the similarities and differences, one had to take a careful look from above. As before in my mental ruminations, the big picture was coming into prominence—both in terms of its utility and in regard to how hard it was to really get to this vantage point—not to mention knowing what to do if and when you got there.

One day, after about a week of research, I was leaving the library and inadvertently glanced at the bulletin board. There was a sheet of paper with bold felt-pen printing: "Temporary Position Available." In smaller script below, the notice indicated interested parties should contact the *Norfolk News Register*—the local paper.

As I was inexplicably wont to do, I called the newspaper. I was informed that the lady who covered the city desk had just started maternity leave. They were looking for someone to fill in for her. This chiefly involved dealing with letters to the editor as well as providing two to three articles a week on local events.

I stopped by to talk with the paper's President/Publisher.

Not too long before, as Suki and I were passing through the outskirts of Des Moines, I had had my birthday: the BIG five-o. There was no one other than my pup with whom to celebrate, but I had had no thoughts of celebration. This was a milestone I had expressly ignored. It was the threshold for moving into becoming old. It was unwelcome. It was terrible. It was inevitable.

And now, crazy as it was, I was going to talk to a newspaper publisher about taking a temporary assignment doing something I had never done before. I had heard of early onset senility—perhaps this had grabbed me unbeknownst to anyone.

Yet any infirmity notwithstanding, I went to the *News Register* and had a really good discussion with the publisher. He, Mr. Reeder, was very progressive and unexpectedly enthusiastic about having someone completely outside the box to deal with local affairs (naturally, under his careful oversight). After I had sketched my background, he was intrigued about how I would contribute to local news stories. I was, in fact, startled at how he felt the filters through which I would view local matters would be very interesting to his readership—they being overly used to a, possibly, more narrow outlook.

He offered me a six-month contract (Lynsie Brock, the regular city desk holder, having twenty-six weeks of maternity leave).

I accepted.

Back in the motel room, as I fed Suki, I wondered how nutty I was.

This would turn out, in all likelihood, as a totally self-inflected wound.

I would completely embarrass myself (not that I hadn't done so many times before).

There was no good reason to do this. All logic aside, I was jumping into another ditch. But, what else did I have to do?

As it turned out, it was great.

The paper had a small and cohesive team—only five members (including Mr. Reeder). With the exception of myself (and including Lynsie), they had all spent years working together. They were in tune and laid-back.

While the world was, as usual, in turmoil, the level of urgency that seeped down to Norfolk was minimal. Commodity prices, snow removal, and flu shots seemed to be the order of the day.

I found the letters to the editor very illuminating, at times insightful, at times galling, and most generally unpredictable. They often focused on community specifics and historical souvenirs of which I had little, if any, knowledge. However, if I tried to look at the big picture (doing so with Mr. Reeder's blessing), it was amazing how the fundamental issues pushing local residents to write were so similar to the issues that weighed on folks from Fomi or Nzérékoré to Geneva or Demopolis.

Basically, people everywhere were looking for the good life. They wanted acceptable food and shelter as well as acceptable health and education. They wanted an acceptable quality of life within their context of what constituted "acceptable" in their culture and their community. They were not looking (or at least not the majority) to be overnight successes nor overnight millionaires. They were not looking for the lap of luxury nor a free pass. Simply put, without undue suffering, they wanted to be able to have what they perceived as a normal life.

From this optic, I was able to craft suitable replies to the writers; often I did not address the unique issues raised but provided what I hoped was insight to the bigger picture.

Mr. Reeder agreed with my approach. He even printed an editorial about my temporary position with the paper and how I would be replying to subscribers, and residents in general, as, as he skillfully called it, "An objective third party."

Adding to my contributions to letters, I did successfully prepare two to three short articles a week about local concerns. Identifying topics was no problem. Everyone—and anyone—was more than happy to tell someone from the paper about the burning questions in their life. I could merge these into a meaningful theme for a weekly feature. Again, as with letters, I could not go deeply into the local context, but I could offer a wider framing and perspective that I hoped would be helpful.

To my satisfaction, the feedback Mr. Reeder received was positive. People seemed to like seeing their own preeminent subjects put in a broader background. The outside aspects and possible solutions let them know others were confronted with the same worries. Additionally, the mechanisms others used to address these worries were often good guides to local residents looking for suggestions for what to do next.

Outside the paper, things were probably as should be expected. Suki was back to normal; she still loved to walk in the city's parks and then go for runs in the surrounding hills. I had good, but casual relationships with my coworkers, my neighbors (I was still in my motel room—now paying an even lower rate by the month), and with my everyday contacts. I had, all the same, no meaningful social life and was, by my own choosing I guess, again experiencing an extended period of celibacy.

Although, if I dwelt on it, my socializing (or lack thereof) was frustrating, on the whole I found a fresh perspective in Norfolk.

I honestly enjoyed the opportunity to try and meld my own bag of experiences with the crucial events affecting the lives of people on the North American Great Plains—far from where I had done most of my work. The commonalities reinforced my professional philosophy of a high degree of universality in humankind. The comparatively slow pace of life (for me) and low level of stress (professionally) were welcomed. But I was missing something.

Being a hermit did not work for me. My best friends—my touchstones—José and Eileen—were far away. My work at the paper served as a conduit to get to know a lot of people—I had a lot of acquaintances, but few friends. There were quick lunches or after work drinks with a variety of Norfolk's citizenry. Yet, a real local social life was evasive.

When wrapped up in Aunt Beatrice's affairs, I had let my assignment overflow and consume my social life. Indeed, José had forewarned me to be careful of Southern men.

This didn't really make sense to me. In my experiences, Californian, Guinean, French, or even Botswana men were just pretty much men. I didn't see how anyone from the southern US would be that different.

Nonetheless, I still felt as though I was Aunt Beatrice's guest in Demopolis, and I didn't want to ruffle any more feathers than I already had by just being there. I did whatever I could to keep a low profile.

Things changed a bit at CEGWA. Here, I still ruffled feathers—but, the feathers of those who were just inherently opposed to CEGWA's work. So, I didn't mind.

Marengo County was not a dry county, but alcohol sales were curtailed by law on Sundays (and Christmas). To bridge the "juiceless" Sabbath,

Saturday nights were, in a local context, hyperactive. I would occasionally go out on Saturday to cut loose, ending up in some stranger's bed or a motel room.

This was infrequent, discrete, and almost anonymous.

While Madison County Nebraska had many distinctions when contrasted with Marengo County, it shared dry Sundays with its southern cousin.

With this rationalization, I opted for a similar pattern of cut-loose Saturdays—most often with similar results.

The difference this time was me. I had not seen CEGWA as a long-term career possibility. It was serendipity. It was a learning experience. It was a chance to contribute. But it was not a vocation for a lifetime. I felt differently about my work at the paper.

To my own astonishment, this was showing signs of being something that I could do for the rest of my life. My hopscotching about seemed to fly in the face of job stability. It was too soon to judge. But perhaps there was something here to hang on to.

This possibility, nearly subconsciously, prompted me to take my social life (or lack of one) a little more seriously. Didn't I need a circle of closer friends and perhaps even a partner?

This, of course, was much easier concluded than accomplished.

Most singles my age were the products of one or more divorces. Some were shattered by their experiences. Others were ecstatic. Some had a yard full of children. Others were courageously looking for offspring. There were ex-military, ex-teachers, ex-scientists, and ex-politicians. There was a large field of play.

There was no one-size-fits-all. I tried several samples, never finding one that truly fit—even in the short-term.

The closest to a good fit I found was Hal. He was a local product who, like me, had gone east to college. He had landed a fine brokerage position at Morgan Stanley in New York City. His star was rising.

Then, his father (his mother had already passed) developed Alzheimer's. Hal was an only child. His father had, up until his illness really blew up, managed a builders' supply started by his grandfather. Hal felt he had to go home to look after his father and the business.

Hal and I had some good times.

Hal and I had potential—or so it seemed.

Still and all, it was like tasting a cup of coffee you know is too hot. We only sipped at a relationship, not wanting to get burnt. There seemed to be a lot of inertia to overcome.

For better or worse, José and Eileen remained my circle.

As we entered the midpoint of one of the most severe winters in recent years, it was time to look for an escape hatch from the northern tier. It was time to get far enough away from Hal to be able to objectively assess our relationship. It was time for a change in scenery—at least, temporarily.

I talked to José and Eileen at least twice a month, but now I really wanted something more tangible. With José to some extent more house-bound by winter than Eileen, I suggested we three meet in Alabama for Easter to spend a week simply vegging and telling tales.

This was met with full support.

Eileen proposed we meet at Clear Springs Park where there were hot springs where we could soak our aging bones and wounded souls. This was, she informed us, the site of an 1890s spa near Ozark, in Dale County—about 170 miles from Demopolis. I could fly from Omaha to Montgomery via Atlanta and José could meet me there—Eileen picking us both up for the drive to Ozark and the old spa.

Terrific plans categorically endorsed by all.

Everything went as expected. Our flights were on time. The mild Alabama climate was comforting. We thoroughly enjoyed our time together and our soaks in the mineral springs that we hoped would wash away the scars of the years.

We had a wonderful time, fulfilling all's expectations. We each rein-forced the other's trepidations as we all entered our sixth decade on this, as we saw it, indomitable but distressed planet.

I got back to Norfolk rejuvenated and energized.

Five days later I passed out in a coma.

On the River's Shore

Serious illness doesn't bother me for long because I am too inhospitable a host.

—ALBERT SCHWEITZER

I WAS REALLY SICK. But I was totally unaware. I was gone—my mind disconnected from my body. My mind disconnected from the world.

As I now revisit my past, this period is, of course, a blank. I can only recount what has been recounted to me—I believe it to be true.

I passed out at home. I just fell in a heap on the kitchenette floor. It was early evening, the time to feed Suki. Seeing me on the floor and not her bowl of chow, she began to bark. When her prodding yielded no results, she began to howl. This, a most unusual event, apparently caught the attention of a neighbor who called the manager.

In any event, the manager came in, saw me on the floor, and called an ambulance. She kindly followed the same to the hospital, providing admissions with the sketchy information she knew. Among my personal details was that José was my emergency contact.

While the ER doctors tried to find out what had happened to me, the admin folks contacted José. The precise details are still unclear to me, but it seems the doctors were stymied early on. Unable to get any meaningful status report, José requested—demanded—I be transferred to the Mayo Clinic (she agreeing to cover the costs if need-be—also insisting on babysitting, for she knew it would not be for a long time, Suki).

The three-hundred-fifty-mile flight by air ambulance I guess went well, as all my medical records as from twelve hours after my crumpling to the floor, came from Mayo. And, I assure you, there were many, many pages of records.

My condition digressed, according to these voluminous records, from a coma to a persistent vegetative state. I became a hunk of protoplasm kept alive by machines.

This was not to say the people at Mayo just put me in a room in a bed and forgot me. They were constantly seeking for the cause of my failing condition.

Ultimately, after much exploring and conjecture, they concluded I had primary amebic meningoencephalitis caused by the minuscule amoeba, the tiny single-celled organism *Naegleria fowleri*.

The doctors opted for an experimental treatment involving a cocktail including the relatively recent drugs chlorpromazine and voriconazole. It seemed it was a question of trying to find the best mix of meds and then lighting a candle—maybe many candles.

This disease has a very high mortality rate. At the time I contracted it, there were only four documented survivors in North America.

This very rare form of, usually fatal, parasitic meningitis occurs when the amoeba comes into the body when water containing the heinous creature gets into the nose.

As the doctors, with José's help, pieced together the probable scenario, the "brain-eating amoeba," as it was called, which liked warm water, had probably inhabited the spa pools where I had so happily splashed about with José and Eileen (neither of these ladies showing any symptoms, thankfully).

While the high doses of strong meds (and very possibly the candles, which I do believe José lit) did manage to destroy the parasite and my body somehow clung to life, my weakened and ill brain had to retreat. I was in a vegetative state for twenty-one months—a period sufficiently long such that more than half those so afflicted never regain consciousness.

I did wake up.

I had lost almost two years of my life. My body was atrophied and emaciated. But I was alive.

I awoke in a grim bed in a grim room.

A doctor, stethoscope grabbing his throat like the pincers of a crab, was at my side as my eye flittered open.

Everything was fuzzy.

Everything smelled sterile.

There was the hum of machines.

"Welcome back, dear," the doctor said in a smooth voice, "you were very lucky, we thought we'd lost you."

I couldn't speak.

The doctor explained what had happened to me.

My mind screamed.

My eyes exploded; my nostrils flared.

I was furious. I was more than a little happy to be alive. But I was furious.

I had been to places with Ebola, typhoid, malaria, viral hemorrhagic fever, and the plague and I'm nearly killed by some goddamn protozoa from some goddam swimming pool! It was mind boggling!

The doctor had the nurse inject something into my IV.

I was gone again.

I awoke again.

I awoke again, as I learned, at St. Ann's.

St. Ann's was referred to by many as "The Center." This was undoubtedly in reference to St. Ann's functions and structure, but in my case, it was the right term—simply referring to the fact that St. Ann's had become the center of my universe.

St. Ann's was located in Homer, Minnesota, seven miles downstream on the Mississippi from Winona—a little over fifty miles east of Rochester and the Mayo Clinic. I had been transferred here, again under José's loving supervision, when I was deemed to be disease-free but vegetative—this a more suitable place for long-term care (of a zombie).

St. Ann's was indeed a suitable place for a whole spectrum of care. My own case involved care of a senseless being kept alive by technology. There was also, for others, memory care, hospice care, and just old-age-care. Moreover, St. Ann's offered a whole portion of its surprisingly large campus to retirees in good health who needed a place to stay where others took care of the chores while they gallivanted in their *Winnebago* or took a cruise. It was a big and diverse place focusing on the needs of aging baby boomers.

It was my new home.

It was here I was impatiently waiting to get better.

I had truly been very, very lucky!

Not only had I survived a disease that literally makes mincemeat out of most of its victims, I had come out of a stupor that generally leaves its prey, if not dead, permanently handicapped—often mentally disfigured.

From all initial indications, I had come through this ordeal with all my mental faculties. But one could not go through what I had and come out unscratched.

My muscles had degenerated. My whole skeleton had become nearly immobile. Additionally, in an ironic twist, the injuries I had incurred when boarding the plane in Dakar had resurfaced in spades.

I had managed to survive the plethora of deadly diseases that romp across the African Continent to be laid waste to by a critter in warm Alabama waters. But, my years in Africa had left their mark. The ligaments and tendons I had torn and stretched falling on the tarmac that night in Senegal had come back to haunt me. In addition to my overall mobility problems resulting from my illness, my left leg, upon which I had fallen all those years ago, now refused to work properly.

I began a long course of physical therapy supplemented by acupuncture and deep massage. I did whatever I could—whatever anyone suggested. I had escaped death. Now, I needed to regain life. I was desperate. I needed to become normal again. I needed to get my legs under me and get on with it.

There was no time to waste.

Alas, reality is truly a bitch (as one of my professors often lamented).

My body had been ravaged by a terrible disease. For months my brain had shut down to heal. It now apparently felt ready to take control of things, but the things which should be controlled were ill-prepared for their job—I could not even walk to the toilet.

Another word about my surroundings before I get back to my tale that I can now recite from my own memory. As I've said, St. Ann's was big. In many ways, St. Ann's was all about crowd control. There were lots of residents with lots of issues. Individuality, especially for the relatively unhealthy, was not much of an option except for those vagabond retirees who kept some sort of townhouse on the campus but were more times than not absent.

For the enfeebled majority, like me, who lived in the commons—the various shared spaces were more like dormitories than homes—we were part of a flock being shepherded. Our herders tended to be bevies of young women and men overseen (at least in principle) by an aging supervisor who was hard to distinguish from the residents themselves.

While we all had private rooms, those who were able were encouraged (read nearly forced) to eat in the common dining area. They were also encouraged to spend at least several hours every day in the other public areas.

There were many spots where the residents could, and in the view of the overseers, should congregate.

There was a common TV/movie room. There was a common game/craft/hobby room. There was a common mediation room. There was a common solarium/reading room. There was a common exercise room cum gym. There were even spaces subdivided into cubicles where some could try and maintain some sort of part-time business or professional activity while still being part of the larger whole.

Weaving through this maize of chambers were the gaggles of youth: pushing wheelchairs, stabilizing walkers, picking up fallen crutches, bringing glasses of water or cups of tea, turning on TV, or picking up the debris the residents left in their wake. These youngsters, when new arrivals, were cheerful and moderately energetic. However, as they gained experience, these attributes waned in favor of aloofness and almost slothfulness—after all, why break a sweat for a bunch of infirm old people (not that I considered myself an "old person").

It suffices to say, while I was not thrilled about my surroundings, I was thrilled about being in an able enough state to complain about them.

Additionally, as I took deep breaths, sucking hungrily (the air tasting faintly of Pine-Sol), I greatly appreciated being alive (if not in the best of shape—as they would say in Guinea, not "*en forme*"). I had a clear head and a (relatively) serene atmosphere where I was able to reflect, hopefully objectively, about my life—where I'd been and where I was going.

I felt lucky.

In spite of, or more truthfully, probably because of my close encounter with death or a permanent vegetative state, I honestly felt extremely lucky.

Not only lucky to have survived a dreadful disease that snuffs out the life of most it encounters, but lucky to have led the life that led me to this awful disease.

Unlike so many I had met along the way; my life had never had any master plan. I had seriously considered the options offered by Mr. Corrigan and, after due consideration, thought I would be a teacher. I had not become a teacher, albeit I had often taught.

My university studies had led me in a different direction, and I was grateful. Yet, I was also not a practicing anthropologist, albeit I had frequently used these skills.

I had fallen into Peace Corps by accident—an accident for which I would be forever beholden. Doors and windows were opened that I otherwise would never had known even existed.

I had been fortunate. I had seen people, places, and things seen by few of my neighbors. I had had experiences (good and bad) that were difficult for the average American to imagine.

Yes, nothing is free. We all pay for our decisions and I had had to accept the consequences of my decisions. I was middle aged with no husband—no children. In fact, I was nearly without family.

Susan and I still exchanged Christmas cards. José had contacted her when I fell ill. José kept her up to date as I had vegetated in my bed at St. Ann's. Once I returned to this world, Susan had called about every three months. These were perfunctory. We were from different spheres—I guess we had always been.

She would briefly but enthusiastically expound about her children and her husband's job. She would ask a few polite questions. Then she would say, "Bye for now."

There was really nothing there.

My empty bed and my empty nest were the price I had paid for my, in my mind, exceptional life.

Had it been worth it?

I believed it had.

But, was I really sure?

My time in what was now called "rehab" allowed ample—more than ample—opportunity to ponder. Time to seek for answers to questions I myself asked.

At first, I was bed-bound—unable to even hobble to the loo, the bedpan and the meal tray were the only companions in my less-than-comfortable institutional bed. There was a TV on a shelf in one corner. José had sent me a transistor radio and kept me supplied with a variety of reading material.

I found the TV tiresome. I did listen to NPR on my radio. But mostly, I thought long and hard about how I ended up in this bed—no family to surround me—no husband—no children. Only the flock of unknown caregivers.

My thoughts were initially mostly about my thoughts.

I had been told (more than a few times) my brain had fully recovered from the potentially disastrous attack.

Had it really?

I began scouring my brain—reassuring myself that things were as they had been.

I began a slow walk through my life.

At first, this was solely looking at the outside: where I'd lived.

Starting from my dorm room at St. Mary's (the irony was not lost on me that my journey had somehow started in the arms of one female saint and was again in the care of yet another), I revisited my life—trying to make sure all the circuitry was functioning and the memories were as they should have been.

I entered each room. I swung through each apartment. I toured each home. I roamed each neighborhood. I wandered through each town. I went back to Cambridge, Goldsboro, Bull Run, Fomi, Nzérékoré, Lambanji, Windhoek, Beltsville, Satigny, Fairfax, Demopolis, and Norfolk. They all seemed to be there. They seemed to be as they should have been.

I then checked on every bedroom I had occupied, at least for an extended period of time. Where was the bed in relation to the door? Where was the head of the bed? What kind of mattress was there? What kind of curtains or other window dressings? Was there a closet? What was in it?

I re-examined each office I had occupied. How was the desk positioned? Of what was it made? Was there a computer? What kind? What about windows? What about the desk chair? What about other furniture?

I re-lived big slices of my life—sometimes looking more deeply inside.

But there were places I didn't go. I didn't revisit the men in my life. That was for another day. This was, after all, not a self-examination of the way my life had turned out. This was a self-inspection of my brain—of my memories—of my thought processes.

This was a desperate effort to convince myself I was once again normal—or as normal as I had ever been.

This was a frantic means to achieve some level of acceptance that, even if my limbs were not cooperating, my mind was back with me and operating on all cylinders.

Slowly, as I walked the corridors of my mind, or possibly because I walked these pathways, my mobility began to make tiny improvements. I was able to make it to the bathroom, precariously balanced on the strong shoulder of one of my caregivers. Then I was able to shuffle to the toilet myself, bending heavily over a walker.

Next, I was able to slide in and out of a wheelchair and have those same muscular caregivers push me to one of the common spaces for a change in scenery—for the sound of human voices—for the sight of new faces—for the introduction to new smells (not all good).

I was far from running about, but I was gradually and haltingly moving about more.

Every other day I had two hours of physical therapy. My limbs and my core (as they so loved to call it) were massaged, twisted, pulled, pressed, and contorted. Ice packs, heat packs, whirlpools, and traction were applied. At times, when being agonizingly bent and unbent, I felt like I was Geneva's beloved François Bonivard who had been imprisoned and tortured in the dungeon of Chillon Castle (on an island in Lake Geneva) by the Duke of Savoy from 1530 to 1536 (the object of Lord Byron's poem in 1816, *The Prisoner of Chillon*). He had survived and so would I.

Feeling better about my mental state—my memories—I decided I needed to see what parts of my previous life were still there to hook onto today. Propped up on pillows, with a lap desk, a handful of Bic pens, two yellow legal pads, and a stack of #10 envelopes, I began to write letters.

I was, of course, already in close contact with José. Eileen and I exchanged letters and cards on a regular basis. I was sporadically in touch with Susan. But that was the extent of my mailing list.

I now wrote to Hal. I wrote to Irv. I even wrote to Samuel.

I had all the stuff to write dozens of letters. But, to whom to write? Other than these three guys, I hadn't a clue.

And then, several weeks after my first valiant attempt at reconnecting, I got the letter I'd sent to Hal back, marked, "Return to sender, addressee unknown."

A while later I got a polite but very phlegmatic letter from Samuel. He was married, they were doing well, he wished me a speedy recovery.

I never heard from Irv.

I wrote one more letter to the *News Register*, thanking Mr. Reeder and all the staff for their collegiality, highlighting how much I had enjoyed my work in Norfolk.

I then gave all my stationary to one of my caregivers.

As my strength improved, I was able to do more with less—the less being without the nearly full-time support of my caregiver of the moment. I was able to get into and out of my wheelchair basically unaided (from a chair—not yet from my bed). When my hands and arms built-up, I was also able to propel my chair myself.

Soon I was able to put the latest book or magazine sent by José on my lap and, after a spin through the commons to greet my fellow inmates, wheel myself into the solarium. Persistently, my aim was to sit in the sunny surroundings and read and relax. Inevitably, after a few paragraphs, the book or magazine ended up face down in my lap and I was immersed far into the innards of my mind.

This time, my introspection was not retracing my steps—it was questioning these very steps.

Some directions had probably, or perhaps better put, possibly, been out of my control. But not everything. Likely, not most. Throughout, before being thrown into St. Ann's arms, I had (willingly or unwillingly) been at the helm. How often had I misread the signs? How often had I reacted from my gut and not my brain? How often had I slipped?

Had I, in fact, been lost and didn't even know it?

I needed to (again) be comfortable with myself.

I honestly didn't know if I would reclaim my equilibrium.

I could have become depressed.

I was very close to getting depressed.

I easily could have depressed myself.

Sitting and thinking and sitting and thinking can be risky—especially when one engages in days (not hours) of self-analysis.

This was not the circuitry check I had so meticulously undertaken while still confined to my bed. I now felt most of the synapses were working about the same after as they had been before. The wiring might be frayed and a bit the worse for wear, but it still did OK.

This was not walking where I had walked before. This was dissecting the paths, trying to dig into the groundwork. This was questioning. This was more onerous.

Still and all, I managed somehow to fly to the stratosphere of my mind and look down at me, myself, and my life. This was, I guess, that big picture I had so sought for so long.

It was like looking the wrong way through a telescope. Everything was surreal and a little fuzzy—smaller than I had thought.

It seemed to always circle back to that topic: a plan—a life plan. A self-determined trajectory that would guide the user to a meaningful and happy life.

Was it really so?

Was it really about a plan?

Some people have plans.

Susan had a plan.

Indeed, nearly everyone I knew appeared to have a plan—everyone but me.

From my seat on the sidelines, Caroline, Shiela, Bill, Anthony, Joel, Abduli, André, Martha, François, Samuel, José, Irv, Eileen, and even Aunt Beatrice all seemed to have had plans—truth be known, probably more than one each. I suppose when they thought of me (if they did), they may have thought I, too, had a plan. But as I thought of me, I could recognize no true discipline nor adherence to anything resembling a real plan.

Evidently, as I now saw things from my seat in my wheelchair, I had, in spite of the seriousness with which I had addressed the assignment, failed Mr. Corrigan's homework. I plainly had not had the wherewithal, what my dear departed father would have called, "moxie," to take life seriously. I had manifestly failed to demonstrate the necessary tenacity to chart a course, to stick to it, and to reap the rewards.

I was flotsam. I was, and had been, so it seemed, drifting aimlessly. I had been tossed about by forces whirling about my realm—moved, at times, violently, from one shoreline to another. Though perhaps weathered by these forces, I had also gone where I otherwise would not have gone—done what I otherwise would not have done.

It had not been a carefully orchestrated strategy.

In my meanderings, I had encountered many people (frequently obstinate, driven, ambitious individuals) with clear and regularly lofty goals—specific distinguished targets in life. I had seen them climb ladders in DC, in Conakry, and in Geneva. I was not of their ilk.

My own case, I guessed, was much closer to random motion—Brownian Movement.

And, it wasn't an avenue resplendent with rainbows and rose gardens.

Now, with St. Ann's help, I needed to take this snapshot from the telescope and see how it could be improved as I prepared to enter, what so many erroneously called, the autumn of my life.

Confession is said to be good for the soul, and to whom better to confess than my present hostess, St. Ann. But, not only was I not very religious, I truly had no idea of what to confess.

I inherently felt I should confess—I should identify and take responsibility for the errors of my ways. I should willfully and openly accept and rectify my mistakes. I should promise to do better.

I felt all this.

I frankly didn't know how to go about it.

Had I actually erred? Had I miscalculated, misjudged, or misbehaved?

I felt the answer was yes. But, what then?

I made, I hoped, no pretext of being anywhere near perfect. I was, I knew, as flawed as they come.

But, was I more flawed than others? Was I more flawed than Samuel or José? Was I more flawed than mother or Susan?

If I wasn't, why was I worried?

Objectively, I must be. I must now, under the guardianship of St. Ann, be paying for the carelessness of my earlier life.

But was it so?

My mind bounced and rattled about.

I felt like I was one of the Japanese battling Beigoma spinning wooden tops, thrown, gyrating madly, on the field to topple or be toppled.

I felt I should fight.

I felt I should repent.

I felt confused.

It wasn't necessarily that I was having second thoughts about the cost-benefit analysis of my life—I felt that it had been worth it.

It was more that I was peeling off the next layer. If I felt it had been worth it, what did this say about my value system? Was my acceptance of my current situation just an acquiescence of the here and now—a rolling over for reality? Or, was my assent founded upon a clear and objective look (from on-high) of the pros and cons?

My mind swirled.

It was like watching a toilet flush: in the northern hemisphere clockwise, in the southern counterclockwise, at the equator straight down. But this time, somehow in my mind, straight up. It made no sense. My eyes closed to avoid water splashing in my face.

The nurse said it was a relapse. The doctor came by and said I was doing too much too quickly. My caregiver simply said I was knackered.

I knew not.

Whatever happened with my churning brain, it had wiped me out.

I was given some new meds that basically put me back in bed and sent me to Never-Never Land.

I don't know how long it lasted. St. Ann was not very good at keeping time. Days, weeks, months—they all melted into the same slurry.

Then I felt like Sleeping Beauty. They told me they had changed my meds again. I awoke for a second time. This time, not from a coma but from a drug-induced haze.

The takeaway from it all: don't overheat your brain. It is still frail.

Mother had always said, "Many hands make light work." I needed to modify this a bit for my present situation: better putting hands than brain cells to work for the moment.

I talked to my caregivers. I had seen the cubicles in one of the common spaces. My young helpers indicated these offices (as they called them) were available to residents who were well enough and strong enough (mentally) to take on some sort of part-time work. This could be consulting or other tasks that could be done by long distance and via remote control. However, most often, through arrangements St. Ann's had with online vendors, the tasks involved working a few hours a day as a customer service representative for any of the several partnering retail companies.

First, I had to mend some more before I could see how to train my body and keep my mind at bay. Then, I needed tasks for my mellowed mind.

As always, in spite of my strong inclinations to the contrary, it was slow—a step at a time.

Gradually, I was feeling stronger. Belatedly, I was feeling more in sync with my world as I now saw it. Warily, I forced myself to do things that would have in other circumstances been my nemesis. Guardedly, I pushed my boundaries.

I wheeled my chair into the Formica-encrusted booth (by any other name, the "offices" to which my caregivers referred), not being the first to leave black smudges on the wall as my tires bounced off the toe rail. I took my pad and pencil from my lap and placed then on the counter. I took a deep breath. I picked up the handset of the black push-button telephone with a gizmo that hooked onto my left shoulder.

I smiled—to myself or the gods, I did not know which—maybe both.

I wetted my lips, scooted back in my chair, blinked twice, and sought my most charming voice, chiming into the handset:

"Good morning. I am sorry you had to wait. This is customer service. How can I help you?"

Autumn's Leaves

Happiness is nothing more than good health and a bad memory.

—ALBERT SCHWEITZER

Naegleria fowleri had consumed five years of my life. But it had not made hamburger of my brain. I had been blessed.

At one point, before my backsliding, I had attempted to dismember these blessings as I had attempted to disjoint and exscind all parts of my life, past and present.

This had led to nothing more than engulfing my weakened body with mental energies trying to interpret processes and actions for which there were no easy interpretations.

Although I could try to assess my past and judge my present, this was, in fact, an effort in futility—diverting my nearly spent spirit in directions that could only gnaw away at my slow but steady progress toward good health.

Even with St. Ann's help, initially I could not duplicate in my brain the circumstances of years gone by.

At first, I could only recall snippets of causes and effects—of actions and reactions.

These slowly multiplied.

Then, they all seemed to be there (How could I know?).

The pieces were there.

They slowly settled into comfortable slots in by brain.

They were there, but they were different.

The lens through which I looked back had changed. Near death had colored everything.

What is now obvious to me was that, to figure out good or bad decisions, one really had to be there at that place and at that time. Anything else was simply frittering away whatever meager vigor I managed to amass along my road to recovery.

What was, was.

I did recover. Possibly I did not reach one hundred percent, but I certainly achieved ninety—and that was pretty damn good considering where I had been.

I had been so fortunate, not only medically, for ultimately overcoming this challenge, but also financially.

EHT had been what kids in my high school would have called a "cherry job." Not only did it pay well, it had a great benefits package (raising, of course, the wisdom of my decision to go head-to-head with senior management—but we won't go there). After five years, an employee became vested. After reaching that threshold, unless fired for cause, the employee had a monthly pension and, even after leaving the organization, could retain the health and life insurance packages as long as the ex-employee paid the premiums him or herself.

The final official EHT departing story, to save face on both sides, was that I had returned to the States to take a senior position with some sort of highbrow think-tank—or some similar invention. Pure rubbish of course, but I did return to the States and I returned with my insurance coverage intact. This proved to be an inestimable boon. This had paid for nearly all my expenses from the ambulance in Norfolk to my last night at St. Ann's.

While José had done so, so very much behind the scenes, she had not visited me at St. Ann's. She took (exquisite) care of Suki, provided reading material, called, sent get-well cards, and even looked out for any expenses I still had coming in. But she stayed in Virginia.

She told me later she couldn't bear seeing me die. She knew the facts. She knew *Naegleria* would kill me. She honestly said she wasn't strong enough be around for the inevitable. She would make the arrangements at the beginning and the end, but she could not watch me eaten away.

I understood completely.

Now that the unthinkable had happened and I was being released in surprisingly good shape, she immediately arranged for us to meet—all three of us including Suki.

José shied away from St. Ann's completely—it was like if you didn't see it, it wasn't there. She had a cousin in Des Moines who lived in a big family home going back to the turn of the last century—a cousin and a house where we could meet and relax.

I took a bus to Minneapolis and flew to Des Moines.

I had nothing in terms of baggage—barely able to fill a carry-on.

Fearing the worst, José had sold my car and donated my few possessions to charities in Norfolk. I had even less than when I had first flown across the Atlantic as a new Peace Corps volunteer.

It felt good.

In every way, it was a new beginning.

I may have been closing in on the autumn of my life, but for me it was spring.

José and Suki were sitting outside the arrivals' gate area when I got to Des Moines. Our reunion was emotional, tearful, and joyous—Suki even piddled on the airport's red and blue carpet out of pure happiness.

José had already rented a car and, jubilant, we drove in a comfortable silence the fifteen minutes to her cousin Hugh's home—savoring the moment.

Hugh's house was a well-kept vintage residence in a neighborhood that was quickly approaching the century mark. The property had a big backyard that backed onto a green space laced with oak trees.

The doorbell had not even finished its first kneel when the door was opened by a smiling, balding, slightly overweight man about our age with a nose that truly resembled José's.

Hugh was actually, once the story was told, José's second cousin. Hugh's tale tried to connect dots that had been covered with dust for years. As all family trees, theirs was twisted with age—but, unlike some, still standing.

Hugh was the youngest son of José's mother's aunt. José's grandaunt had moved to this Des Moines neighborhood in the 1920s. Her husband, José's granduncle, and his bride, came to the city from their birthplace in tiny berg of Chapin, in Franklin County, one hundred miles due north of the state capital. While her grandaunt raised five children, her granduncle built a common labor job into a sash and door company—Ford Millwork.

Through the years, the Ford's once deep Iowa roots were diluted as family members moved about the country in search of work, education, or love. Hugh was to all intents and purposes the last of his immediate family's direct lineage to keep his hands in woodworking.

Hugh, his wife Angie, and their teenage daughters Millie and Alexa, led what, to an outsider like me, seemed to be the typical American life. While I knew all too well that little was as it first appeared, the latest iteration of the Ford Family seemed textbook middle America.

Hugh was now the owner and manager of Ford Millwork—Angie was the bookkeeper. The girls attended Roosevelt High School, one-and-a-half miles from their front door, and the same high school their parents had attended. By all accounts, the company was doing good business and the girls were doing well in school.

Hugh and Angie graciously opened their home to us and, having no pets of their own, opened the backyard to Suki (begrudgingly, also turning a blind eye when she slept at the foot of my bed in the upstairs guest room José and I shared). This sincere hospitality was all the more appreciated since this was the first time Hugh and José had met face-to-face (over the years they had exchanged Christmas cards and talked on the phone).

Hugh and Angie's bedroom was on the main floor. The girls had separate bedrooms at the front of the second floor. José and my room was on this floor, but at the back, and the window opened to the green space over the back fence. While we all shared the same bathroom upstairs, it wasn't really crowded. There was a small attached cubicle (not to be confused with those of St. Ann's); Angie called it a sewing room (she didn't sew). It had evolved into a de facto diminutive sitting room outfitted with old and frazzled furniture that otherwise would have found its way to the Salvation Army (surprisingly similar to the décor Dr. Clark had chosen for the Center all those years ago). For José and me, with Angie's blessing, the sewing room became our sanctum to reconnect.

After a suitable period of introductions and chitchat, José and I, with Suki at our heels, and with steaming mugs of Angie's quite excellent coffee, fled to this small harbor fitted with throwaway artifacts simply to talk. Suki curled up at my feet.

As was inevitable, my Suki girl had aged as we all had. Her muzzle was now mostly white, she'd gained a bit of weight, but it was plain to see that José had taken wonderful care of her. It was also clear that she had established a deep bond with her second *patronne*.

She licked my toes as José and I practiced random speech. We talked about anything and everything. The common thread, the once-only whispered truth was the total amazement at my being there in the flesh. José was principally focused on seeking absolution for a sin I would not accept she had committed. She definitely had not abandoned me. Yet, by not coming to St. Ann's, she felt she had. In spite of all she had done, and continued to do, she believed she needed forgiveness for something she had not done.

As I explained what I remembered and what I had been told, about my ups and downs, about my meds, my thoughts, my burdens, my challenges, José realized she had done well. She could have done nothing on the shores of the Mississippi. She had been, however, of tremendous and unforgettable help doing exactly what she had done in Virginia.

When we only had dregs in our mugs and it was time to feed Suki, José and I went downstairs, finding the Ford family circled around the TV in the den directly below our sanctum. I invited all to dinner out, asking Millie to choose the best place in town.

With no second thoughts, Millie immediately identified the 801 Chophouse as the place to go. I had to push to the back of my mind chophouses I had visited in Nigeria and Ghana, enthusiastically endorsing the young girl's choice.

Fortunately, Hugh and Angie had a Toyota Sienna, because the Chevy Cobalt José had rented would never have carried us all downtown to the restaurant.

Millie had made an excellent choice—the fair was superb. This was a meat place—no comparison to its African counterparts. There was a delicious appetizer of carpaccio that took me back to Geneva. I encouraged Hugh to have a twenty-four-ounce Delmonico steak (billed at nearly twice the price of bus fare to Chicago), but he opted for the less extravagant ribeye while the rest of us, except José, chose prime rib—José having sea bass. In spite of the delectable main courses and the delightful accompanying potatoes and fresh vegetables, we all managed to find room for homemade ice cream to top it all off—although, I felt I needed my wheelchair back to make it to the car.

The next day, Hugh and Angie were at work, the girls at school, and we had the house to ourselves. We sat with a full pot of coffee at the kitchen table and José went over the unpleasant but necessary task of my personal affairs—she having had power of attorney during my stint at St. Ann's.

I had absolutely been very, very fortunate to have had the extended health coverage after my departure from EHT. Moreover, gratefully, the settlement received (what was now years ago) at the time of this departure had been well-invested—favorable markets quickly adding significantly to my total assets. Nonetheless, as José painstakingly explained, my EHT health insurance did not cover one hundred percent of my expenses. Furthermore, during my "Sleeping Beauty Period," as José began calling it, there had been a number of financial crises that had taken away the gains. Overall, my portfolio had lost over one-third of its value.

These negative facts notwithstanding, I was still more than solvent. When the financial dust had settled and all the bills were paid, I had more than enough to live comfortably. More dumb good luck—another potentially devastating storm weathered.

I was sitting in a kitchen, whose owner I really didn't know, with all my earthly belongings in a carry-on in the guest room. More than that, I was seated across from my best, my dearest friend (who had past the toughest tests of true friendship a thousand times over), my dog was curled up at my feet. I was (more or less) of able body and mind. What more was there?

When we had attended to business, we took some time to wander about the city. José had a week off and there was ample time to see some new sites. We walked about the campus of Drake University. We visited the Fort Des Moines Museum which honored black and female military. We went to the Wells Fargo History Museum. We happened upon the Norman E. Borlaug Hall of Laureates—attracted by the impressive building, not knowing the essence of its cause.

Entering, we read about our departed host, Norman E. Borlaug—a native Hawkeye and winner of the 1970 Nobel Peace Prize. Borlaug, a plant pathologist, was considered as the "Father of the Green Revolution." Through the Rockefeller Foundation, he had undertaken groundbreaking work in Mexico to develop better-producing crops. These improvements had then been applied on a larger scale through a partnership between Rockefeller and the UN's Food and Agriculture Organization that led to significant increases in harvests in India and Pakistan and the birth of the Green Revolution.

This was of personal interest to me as the initial catalyst for the work I had done with Peace Corps in Guinea had been the Green Revolution—*la Révolution Verte*. This had been the flag flying over so many agriculture programs across the African Continent—*Vivre la Révolution Verte!* Sadly, like many revolutions, it had not sustainably achieved its aims. Nevertheless, it had shown a light on the importance of agriculture (heretofore, often a largely ignored sector of national economies) in the broadest sense—an emphasis that continued to today.

One afternoon, Hugh took off from work and accompanied us to the Iowa State Historical Museum. He proudly ushered us into a small chamber filled with glass cases of ornate glass hemispheres encircled in metal rings, about the size of a silver dollar—hundreds of glass hemispheres. Under their thick glass domes there were wonderful images—flowers, horses, trees—nearly anything imaginable.

These were, Hugh informed us, horse-bridle rosettes. They were decorative. "Kind of like a lady's earrings," Hugh told us.

Opening his arms expansively, Hugh then proclaimed, "This is all my grandfather's!"

As it turned out, Hugh's grandfather had had a very large rosette collection that he had donated to the museum—an unusual legacy, but a footprint, nonetheless.

José had wanted to accompany me shopping so I could increase my meagre wardrobe. But I really wasn't ready for the ordeal (as I saw it) of a buying spree. My limbs were still healing. It was good to walk—it was good to walk as much as I could. However, I did get tired and needed to rest more than I would have liked.

This should have been all about doing and not waiting—but sadly sometimes I simply had to wait a while for my strength to come back (in truth, I also liked the feeling of "less is more" in regard to my personal baggage).

The days flowed all too quickly by and soon we were seated at the kitchen table, the family out, preparing our goodbyes. I still was (by design) nearly as possession-less as when I had arrived. I was now reunited with Suki (and this was terrific!), but I had assiduously avoided any and all discussions of, or plans for, my future.

José and I had carefully weighed into the past and enjoyed the present. She frequently tried to open the door to the future, but I always pushed back. As this was our last day, she decided to push harder.

"You've got to think about what you're going to do. It's not enough to simply marvel that you are here."

"Hummm."

"No 'hummm,'" José, almost sharply, declared, "You've got to get your shit together."

"OK."

"What's OK? What are you going to do? You can't stay here? Are you coming with me back to Virginia? What in the hell are you going to do?"

"Not sure yet."

"Of course," she, almost angrily, continued, "you're just gonna breath the air, stick your fingers in the dirt, and thank God you're alive."

"Anything wrong with that?"

"No! But there's more!"

"More what?"

"More to living."

"But, as I recall, I'm the one who nearly died."

"But, you didn't."

"Nearly."

"Get over it and get on with it! Damn it, you've got to do something."

"Why?"

"You just do."

"I've enough money. I've Suki. I've got you. Maybe I'll just buy a *Winnebago* and drive about?"

"OK, do it!"

"Maybe I will."

"Listen, my dear, dear friend—you need to do something. Even if you have enough money and don't need to work, you need to do something. You told me how your mind pulled you into a pit of self-analysis. If you don't get your act together, you'll find yourself back in the pit. Next time you're in an institution, it won't be because you've been bitten by an amoeba, it'll be because you've driven yourself mad!"

That was it—that was the trigger. She'd pulled it.

"Fine," I practically pined, "I'll think about it."

"What'll ya do?"

"I'll think about it."

"May I offer something?"

"Sure."

"Here goes." To her credit, she didn't look smug. "A colleague of mine from George Mason has recently taken a position at Adams State University in Colorado. He and his family moved there last semester. He is now heading up the Business Administration program. Not long ago, he wrote me, enquiring about possible candidates for a position at the school. They are looking for someone to handle the undergraduate Introduction to Anthropology course as well as input into the Prison College Program. This is not tenure track—it is not even full-time. With these limitations, they are having a tough time finding the right person. I think you'd be the right fit."

My immediate reaction was "hell no!"—who'd want to do that? Nonetheless, I didn't say this to José. I was noncommittal and polite, "Thanks, I'll think about it."

"Do!" she all but implored. "Here are his contacts," she added, pushing a slip of paper across the table to me.

Reluctantly, with that, she let the subject drop and we talked about mundane things before we went out to the backyard to play with Suki.

José flew back to Virginia the next day. I rented a car, grabbed my little bag and Suki, bid the Fords goodbye, and drove west, unsure of my destination.

We zigzagged down rural roads, avoiding the Interstate, basically following the sun. After almost four hours, we found ourselves in Peru, Nebraska—population less than 900, almost 200 miles from Des Moines and less than two miles from the Missouri River separating the states of Nebraska and Missouri.

The surprise for me was that, although the small berg of Peru was home to Peru State College, a public four-year institution with a student body of nearly 1,500, there was apparently no close-by accommodation. We got something to eat at Zach's Bar and Grill and were directed to The Hill House as a good place to stay—the House was in Brownville, about ten miles downriver. The House was, moreover, located next to a park which had been one of Lewis and Clark's campsites, and which was bisected by the Steamboat Trace Trail that followed the river.

It was a good place to spend the night and a good place to have long walks with Suki in relative seclusion.

We spent three nights and two days at The Hill House.

I had been happy to return to the mainstream—to think of myself once again as part of humanity. Now somehow, I felt I needed to be in my own backwater for a while.

It was like at St. Ann's.

I had been so happy to venture out from my room—a room where I had spent so many days—so many years. Initially I viewed leaving my room as venturing out—venturing out to the unknown. My room had become my refuge—a safe place.

I needed to go beyond the four walls that had contained me for so long. I needed to see other people. I needed to communicate. I needed to live.

But, at first, I could only take the outside in small doses.

With a sigh of relief, I would return to my room after a visit to the commons. My room was my touchstone. It was, for a me, a place of survival where I was protected from the ever-present dangers that threatened us all.

Dangers that threatened us all? And then I began to think of the refugees of Nzérékoré, or the Herero and Namaqua of Namibia, or of so many others. So many people who were really living in the shadow of omnipresent danger—it seemed totally unfounded that I counted myself in their ranks.

I was not.

I knew I was not.

I was in nowhere near the life and death conditions that endangered so many around our globe.

Nonetheless, I was now hypersensitive to being—to being alive—to have this living being threatened by anything whatsoever (real or imagined).

Whatever was, was. I did not want to, should not go down this path—I should not dwell on these thoughts. José was (as always, I guess) right; I had to close the door, lock it, and look ahead.

On our third morning on the shores of Missouri (a much, much shorter period than that spent on the shores of her big sister, the Mississippi), I was settling the bill.

The lady at the reception desk asked, "Where ya go'n?"

"Not really sure," I replied honestly.

"Well, we hope you enjoyed your stay."

"I did."

"You with the College?"

"Nope, why do you ask?"

"Oh, do'n know—you just kinda look like a college-type of person."

"Thanks." I guessed this was the right reply, I wasn't sure.

"Sure, have a safe trip."

We continued west. Maybe, I thought, I was like a homing pigeon heading back to my own birthplace. Maybe, but I doubted it. This was simply more random motion.

After nearly five hours on the road, we pulled into Sehnert Dutch Oven Bakery in McCook, Nebraska. The historical plaque at the entry to town confirmed the town had its origins with the arrival of the Burlington and Missouri Railroad. Like so many towns across the Great Plains, McCook was a "railroad baby."

At the bakery, I got a chicken sandwich for Suki and then a cup of coffee and a bran muffin for me. I sat on a stool at the front of the bakery, watching mid-day traffic move down George Norris Avenue, wondering what it would be like to live in McCook.

This brought back to mind, not sure exactly why, the words of the receptionist this morning, "You from the College?"

I reached in my jacket pocket and brought out the piece of folded paper given to me by José. It read:

Dr. Eric Hale, Business Administration Program

Adams State University,

Alamosa, Colorado

What the hell—why not?

There was a payphone in the back, near the restrooms, and I called the operator to get Eric's number. As the gods would have it, he was in, he was happy to get my call, and he would be glad to see me whenever I got into town—no appointment necessary.

It was done.

Back in the car—we were still driving west, but now with a slight southerly change in tack. Alamosa was too far for us to make it that very night. Instead, we made it another 300 miles (a long drive, overall more than the eight-hour flight from JFK to Dakar) to Rocky Ford, Colorado—birthplace, as the sign at the entry to town told us, to the state's thirty-seventh governor and apparently home to lots of melon growers. Unlike Peru, Rocky Ford had plenty of accommodation including the Elks Lodge, the Arkansas B & B, and the High Chaparral Inn.

The next morning, after an uninspiring breakfast, we were back on course—150 miles southwest. Most of Alamosa is on the West bank of the Rio Grande (I seemed to have developed a penchant for rivers these days—possibly a sign of my having avoided narrowly the River Styx). Coming from the northeast, we came first to the town's East Alamosa neighborhood. Here we found the Riverside Inn of Alamosa, only two blocks from the shoreline. Better still, we could walk across the Broadway Avenue Bridge and go to Cole Park where Suki could have a good run for her stiffer, aging legs (she now a septuagenarian by some's calculations)—now even more cramped after long hours in the car.

We took a gamble and took the room at the Inn for a week.

Right before the close of the business day, after a good walk with Suki, I called Eric. We agreed to meet the next day in his office at ten o'clock.

Eric's office was housed in a modern brick and glass building rather overly typical of educational institutions around the country. The office itself was neatly arranged and its occupant proved to be equally neat. He was in his mid-fifties, clean-cut, wearing a plum-colored golf shirt under a lightweight, light brown sports coat. He looked very professorial.

He was, equally, very down-to-earth, friendly, and open. He heaped praise on José. He recounted his fortune at having had the good luck to have found this excellent position at Adams State. He modestly extolled the virtues of the university, the town, and the state (a little overboard on the salesmanship to my taste). He described succinctly the position they had and the type of person for whom they were looking. Then he asked me about me.

I didn't even have a CV, let alone a proper suit for a university job interview. But I was undaunted. I really was, moreover, ambivalent about the opportunity, so I was relaxed enough to be me.

I gave Eric the ten-cent version of my background, thinking the whole kit-and-kaboodle would be an overload. I quickly highlighted my academics, skating over most of my overseas and health histories.

This was apparently enough—at least for Eric (I guess they were desperate). He indicated he only sat on the search committee. But, so far, the searches had truthfully turned up nothing. Not many folks with any qualifications were interested in part-time non-tenure positions. If I was really interested, he'd be happy to bring my name to the committee. If the committee agreed, I would need to get him a CV. And then later, if selected for a final review, I would need to provide copies of my transcripts and diplomas.

It wasn't like I had anywhere else to go or anything else to do. I had taken the room for a week, after all.

I wasn't, if I was honest with myself, thrilled about the university, the town, or the state—in spite of Eric's best efforts at salesmanship. But, it sure as hell wasn't any more difficult than Fomi or Nzérékoré.

Things happened quickly.

Within twenty-four hours Eric called me at the inn. The committee had given their conditional go-ahead. Final decision, though, was pending arrival of my CV, academic credentials, and three letters of recommendation. I needed to focus on these tasks if I wanted the job—sweet and simple.

This was the time to turn back.

I did not.

I told Eric I'd get right on it and I'd call him once I had an update.

Eric was considerate and pleased I was moving forward. He did ask if he could make one small suggestion before hanging up.

With my consent, he concluded with, "While you're waiting for the documents to arrive, I would recommend, if you don't have them, you get a cellphone and laptop. Grande Computer Systems on Second Street offers a really good discount for Adams' faculty and staff. Given your promising status, I'll drop off a letter at the hotel reception and you can go there with this and pick up the needed tools of our trade. Just an idea for your consideration."

I thanked him, hopefully not too profusely, and went for a walk with Suki. I did not want to unlock locked doors, but I was still unsure if I was choosing the right path. Well, never too late to drop out.

I got on the phone and made arrangements for all my academic documentation. I could get letters from José and Eileen, but who else? I smiled to myself as I thought, facetiously, I could ask Mateo González. I settled on Mr. Reeder as my third reference—he was a little off target but would provide a good perspective on my writing skills.

I went to Grande Computer Systems and got kitted-up with moderately priced items that connected me to the latest technologies and the outside world—the outside world being the world outside my room at the inn.

I called José and Eileen to ask them for referrals and give them my cell number and new email address. José was thrilled. Eileen was more lowkeyed.

I tried the *News Register*. Mr. Reeder was out. I left my cell number.

I went for a walk with Suki.

We passed by the hotel office on the way to check for any mail. I noticed for the first time that the front desk had an assortment of brochures for local sites of interest. One caught my eye: the Luther Bean Museum at Adams State. This, tweaking my memories of the Museum of London, was reputed to have a good collection of southwest and European art. There were samples of Native American pottery and weaving next to cowboy paintings and bronzes (recalling how I had first seen Samuel).

Reading on in the brochure, the museum was housed in a building that had been Adams State's library from 1930–1954. The university itself, named after three-term Colorado Governor William H. "Billy" Adams, was founded in 1921. The museum, established in 1975, was named after Dr. Luther Bean, Adams State faculty from 1925 to 1952 and Director of the Education Department as well as Director of the San Luis Artist and Crafts School (Alamosa being in the San Luis Valley, a six-county, 8,000 square-mile, area embracing the headwaters of the Rio Grande with an average elevation of 7,600 feet).

It would be interesting to see the place—at least from the outside, as I undoubtedly could not go in with Suki. Furthermore, it was a nice walk. We only had to drop down to Main Street after crossing the Broadway

Bridge—the museum was twelve blocks going west, adjacent to the main Adams' campus.

It was a good walk for my legs (and my core). We sat in front of the building for a while watching the passersby. The structure itself reminded me much more of red brick factories I had seen years ago in Chicago (during my pre-Peace Corps attraction) than of a museum—I guess this was naturally a sign of the times—an indication of the year when the old edifice had come forth.

As we walked back the way we'd come, I noticed for the first time the Valley Campus of Trinidad State Junior College.

When we got back to our room, I used my new laptop and the inn's Wi-Fi to find out more about Trinidad State. Ever since being surprised by Peru State College, I realized that tertiary institutions could be found practically anywhere, and in any of many permutations.

Trinidad State was established four years after Adams State. The main campus for the two-year college was in the town of Trinidad, a little more than one-hundred miles to the southeast near the New Mexico border. The school, approaching 2,000 students on the two campuses, reportedly offered some fifty programs ranging from gunsmithing and nursing to cosmetology and aquaculture.

Trinidad State was only a little over a half mile from Adams State.

The next day, I left Suki in the room, crossed the bridge, and went to the Milgros Coffee House with my shiny new laptop to work on my CV and cover letter. After what seemed like a whole pot of coffee, I was satisfied with my products—saving them to a flash drive.

I then continued on down Main Street to Main Copy Source to print my documents. There were lots of folks wanting stuff printed and I had an hour wait. Wondering what to do, I looked out the front window of the store and realized I was right across the street from Trinidad State.

I wandered across to their campus—more of a business park atmosphere than a typical college campus. I ambled through some corridors and then sat on a bench in an airy atrium to, as appeared to be the practice of the day, play with my new cellphone.

I felt a presence and looked up. There was a slender, gray-haired woman a few years older than I who was smiling down at me. Her lips, embellished with a thick layer of crimson lipstick, parted as she asked, "Can I help you?"

"Oh, hi," I said, a bit startled (actually, I might have jumped in shock as she addressed me), "I'm just killing time."

"Well, I'm not sure if you're in the right place. Here we say time waits for no one."

"Oh boy, do I know that. But today, I'm waiting, and I hate to wait."

"For someone from the school?"

"Oh, no," I replied, realizing I was saying 'Oh' far too much, "I'm having some things printed across the street and simply randomly wandered in here."

"We're pretty experienced with wanderers."

"Are you on the faculty?"

"Yes." She smiled even more broadly. "I teach psychology for students in the Health Science Program. You teach?"

"Oh." There it was again. I kind of stumbled, "not really. Not yet."

"Yet?"

"Oh, yes," I said, trying to catch up with my brain, "I'm applying for a position next door at Adams State."

"Really. What's your field?"

"I've wandered through many fields, but my formal studies were in cultural anthropology—but that was a long time ago."

"Amazing!"

"Why's that?"

"Well, we've an open position in our Agricultural, Food, and Natural Resources along with our Law, Public Safety, Corrections, and Security Programs for someone to teach the Cultural Geography class. Mr. Snyder, who was here for years and years, recently retired."

"Oh, that is interesting."

"By the way, my name's Donna Winters."

I introduced myself and gave her the two-cent rundown: staying at the inn, just got here, have a dog.

Donna was either extremely welcoming or inquisitive (or both). In any event, she invited me for coffee the next day at the nearby Nestle Toll House Café.

Leaving Trinidad, I crossed the street and got my copies, now waiting impatiently for me. I was close to Eric's office so (even though I'd said I'd call first, I didn't want to wait) I got an envelope from the nice folks at Main Copy, wrote a quick note to him on photocopy paper, updating my situation, and then popped by and, finding him out, pushed my package under his door.

Although I was now the proud owner of two pieces of cutting-edge technology, I was (for better or worse) old-fashioned. I preferred the written word—written by a flesh-and-blood hand with a pen or pencil—and face-to-face exchanges. Bizarrely (or maybe understandably), it looked to me like the more we (the societal "we") got high tech, the less well we did low tech. At the risk of being highfalutin, the better we perfected our information technology, the less well, the less precisely, the less tersely, the less effectively we used information (communicated). Anyway, just a thought.

Donna and I had a most pleasant cup of coffee—actually, about four cups each—at the café. We shared short newsreels of our lives. As I had been weighing-out my life story when out and about in Alamosa, Donna probably got about a quarter's worth. I imagine I got about two-bits from her too.

She had been born and raised in New England—Vermont. She was the second child of the Winters of Wells River—Wells River a small village of 325 inhabitants on the New Hampshire border. After college (getting a bachelors in psychology at Champlain College in Burlington, eighty miles nearly due west of home), she had married Elliot Richards from Woodsville, New Hampshire, right across the Connecticut River from Wells River (and, Donna added tangentially, yet nearly matter-of-factly, as though I should have known, Woodsville was also the home of the Bath-Haverhill Covered Bridge built in 1829). Elliot's family owned the Richards Funeral Parlor—he destined to replace his father as the area's chief mortician.

Elliot, whom she had known since her teens, had seemed to be a gentle and quiet man, on an even keel. Just the sort of partner someone would choose to start a family—just the sort of end-of-life chaperone one would choose for solace at a time of grief. Behind closed doors, however, Elliot had proven himself to be a savage misogynist. He had brutally abused and humiliated Donna.

They were hometown kids. Their parents knew each other. This wasn't the way it was supposed to happen. Donna tried to tough it out. Donna prayed. Donna cried. Donna was embarrassed. Donna was physically and psychology scared. Donna got a lawyer and a divorce. Donna also got a good settlement that paid her tuition at Connecticut College in New London where she obtained a Master of Arts in Psychology—all the more poignant after her recent experiences.

Thereafter, she had moved about, coast to coast, sampling different colleges and different educational philosophies. It was the philosophy and not the salary that had drawn her to Trinidad. The idea to (hopefully) prepare students in two years for a possible life-long career was very much in line with her views as to the role of tertiary education. The extensive menu offered at Trinidad was the determining factor that led her to Alamosa. Here students had a choice and here students got a job.

By this point, we were on our third cups of coffee.

Donna left the past for the present, "Any thoughts about applying for the position at Trinidad?"

"Honestly, been so drawn-and-quartered that I haven't thought too much about it. Do you think it's a real opportunity?"

"I do."

"Guess I'd better think some more. The slot I'm aiming for at Adams is not full time. If I could piggy-back the two positions, it'd be wonderful."

"Probably could—they both need qualified people who'll work part-time for quite a bit less than the highest wages in the business."

"Worth looking into then."

With that, one more cup of coffee, and some closing trite talk about things to do in Alamosa, we wrapped up our extended confabulation.

Nearly sloshing in coffee, I walked back to the inn as Donna went back to Trinidad.

I liked Donna. She reminded me in some ways of José. They were both smart, strong-willed, independent, and innovative. Their major divergence, as far as I could tell from this cursory examination, was in their presence. José styled herself in an understated, casual way—little makeup, staid jewelry (if any), and folksy, mostly plain, clothing.

Donna was just the opposite. She used makeup—she knew how to apply it and she applied it liberally without it seeming garish. She wore jewelry—big colorful chunks of jewelry. And, she dressed to the nines. She was very stylish. She was chic to a point that could have seemed out of place in a bucolic setting like Alamosa, but somehow did not.

I liked Donna.

Donna and I met from time to time for coffee.

I had told her of my homeroom trauma in career planning all those years ago. Looking back, it was almost as though it had been a reading of tarot cards (hopefully The Hierophant for much-needed wisdom) foretelling a place for teaching in my life.

Donna was pensive. Her normally buoyant demeanor was swept up in a seriousness I had not seen before. She eyed me intently, saying in a soft voice, that belied her stern gaze, "I don't have to tell you how important teaching is."

"Of course not . . ."

"Just never forget. You have the trust of others—a trust you yourself have not really earned. A trust that can too easily be broken."

"Of course . . ."

"It's a big responsibility."

"Of course . . ."

"Yes, I know you know. I just feel so strongly."

Donna then told me about her fifth-grade teacher, Mr. Leonard.

From any vantage point, Mr. Leonard had been an example of what not to be.

He had been a self-professed disciplinarian. He had a hack paddle at his desk. If anyone, boy or girl, did anything that upset Mr. Leonard, he called the offending party to the front of the class, told them to grab their ankles, and gave them several vigorous whacks with his paddle.

Word slowly filtered out that Mr. Leonard's wife was a teacher at another grade school. The two would have competition to see who could give the most hacks in a given day. It was not about discipline. It was about power.

Then, this part probably unknown to his wife, Mr. Leonard used to invent all sorts of pretexts to lift girls up over his head—he looking up their dresses as he claimed to be demonstrating some obtuse scientific fact or helping the child get to something out of reach. It was sick.

The irony was that Mr. Leonard, when not hitting students with his paddle or ogling the girls' undergarments, used to enjoy dangling his finger in a bowl of mercury on his desk. He had died of mercury poisoning four years after Donna left his class.

Lesson learned—maybe not by Mr. Leonard, but definitely by me: teaching is serious stuff.

I was ready to get to it.

Much as I had painfully learned when dealing with my first job at Three Mile Island, things take time. There's a lot of waiting involved. College positions in Alamosa were no exception.

Our one week at the inn turned into five. My distain for waiting painted these days in stringent shades. Suki was, however, most happy as she had developed a real attraction to Cole Park. She had her special places and thoroughly enjoyed going to the furthest corners of the park to get the best workout possible (for both of us).

Then in rapid succession, the cogs fell into place.

Both Adams and Trinidad were state schools. Both ultimately (with Eric and Donna's pushing) offered me part-time positions. Both had HR offices and, to my surprise, different recruitment processes. Nonetheless, within twenty-four hours of each other, they each had contracts ready for me to sign on the eve of the anniversary of my fifth week in town.

I had finally followed my plan with Mr. Corrigan. I was a teacher.

I was a teacher and I was queasy about it.

I had honestly convinced myself through the years that I would be a terrible teacher—at least, classroom teacher. I felt I had already done a lot of teaching in the broadest sense. Starting as an extensionist and really continuing through my work at the newspaper, nearly everything I had done had dealt with trying to educate people—educating generally adults.

Now I found myself in a classroom—at the head of a classroom.

Fortunately (I think), my pupils were principally young adults—some verging on middle age. There was no throwing of erasers or pulling of pigtails. Quite a number were married. Several had their own families. Most knew they had to be at least pretty serious students if they were to get their diploma or certificate and get a better job or a promotion as they hoped.

It was OK.

In fact, outside the teacher-student dimensions (which were my major worries), it was frankly very rewarding to try and stitch together my own education and life experiences into a curriculum that met the school's requirements and the student's expectations while being, I hoped, interesting and challenging.

One of the biggest surprises was how much I enjoyed the Prison College Program—the part of the job mix that had initially raised the strongest level of trepidation in me.

The school had a well-developed program for the incarcerated—years ago called correspondence, now referred to as distance learning—for those behind bars seeking an associate or bachelor's degree, or just wanting to do something different. The classes were all based on selected printed texts provided to the student-inmate, who in turn provided his or her contact person at Adams with written homework and exams.

There were nearly a score of course options—each course having a lead instructor with one or two assisting colleagues. I was lead on the courses covering anthropology and sociology and assisting with political science and psychology. For my lead courses, I was in frequent correspondence with my inmate pupils. I encouraged them to call if they had questions and if they had access to a phone—several did.

I was astonished at how smart, I'd really say erudite, many of the prisoners were. I recalled the words of my sophomore chemistry lab tech (a very clever senior, or so he thought), "If you think you're really, really smart, try to steal something—something big—and get away with it."

Obviously, these guys (they were all guys) weren't really, really smart by these standards (they did get caught), but they sure possessed nimble minds from my perspective. Comparatively, they made faster progress than my non-jailed students—but I guess they had a lot more time to study.

While on the topic of progress, in retrospect I think we all made progress. It was good. My students, in and out of prison, seemed to enjoy their classwork and I found I enjoyed being seated at the head of the classroom.

This latest page of my life seemed promising.

Since leaving Des Moines, I had anticipated little—one step at a time.

I suppose I was so surprised to still be able to roam the countryside and taste the air, that simply being was enough. I was still amazed I was indeed awake in the moment.

Cherish that moment.

Don't let the slivers of time seep away.

Nonetheless, as the days since my illness melded into months, more was needed. Each day seemed to require that special challenge, that unique task, to convince me that my exceptional reawakened being was translating its inexplicable presence into suitably exceptional action.

It was practically an addiction—each day I needed more stimuli to keep me going.

Then I found teaching—my *raison d'être*. Yet, each day I had to take it up a notch.

I managed.

Who would have thought?

I liked to think Mr. Corrigan would have been proud (frankly accepting that, if he were still alive, he would surely be completely indifferent).

And, outside school, my life began to fill up.

Eric proved to be a valuable colleague. He invited me home to meet his wife, Renée, and son, Thomas (not Tom). That first invite turned into many others. There were potlucks at their church, dinners at the Rotary, and after soccer game cookouts. I was a welcomed addition to their trio—in many ways treated as the sister Eric and Renée had never had.

I got to know the Hales pretty well (as I'm sure they got to know me). They were, in my eyes, the stereotypic American family. I did like them, and it was with no disrespect that I found them to be like Susan's family or Hugh's family in Des Moines—something that should be painted by Norman Rockwell.

We (the "we" being these cliché families and me) were not opposites. We were indeed not Yin and Yang. We matter-of-factly lived in different spheres—different spheres that hopefully happily accepted each other, even if they did not understand each other.

Donna was my other bastion. Her sphere was closer to mine, but we definitely did not completely overlap. We did, however, get along very well together. Moreover, as a single female, Donna offered openings to distractions beyond fraternal dinners and barbecues. She and I would go out and, as they used to say in Nigeria, "Play life."

Donna had an off-again-on-again partner, Stan Handcock—Donna's ups and downs reflective of her desires to have male companionship without any long-term (or medium-term, for that matter) commitment. One evening, Donna, Stan, and I went out for dinner and (unbeknownst to me), by prearrangement, we were joined by David Cosby. David was my unannounced blind data.

David and Stan worked together at First Southwest Bank—Stan dealing with mortgages and David with commercial accounts. They were both out-of-towners—David originally from Seattle and Stan from LA—West Coast Boys.

Whether due to scrupulous preselection or simply dumb luck, David and I seemed to hit it off. At least once a week we went out as a foursome or a twosome.

After a couple months, a snail's pace by my standards, David and I became romantically involved (as prudish plains people liked to say). We enjoyed each other and it seemed like a natural evolution.

David had married his high school sweetheart after getting his MBA. He and his wife and two children had lived in their hometown of Seattle—he had worked for Boeing as mid-level management. After twenty-two years of marriage, his wife, a very specialized medical technician, had what he could only describe as a mid-life crisis. With no word to anyone, including her own family, she left with a guy from her lab, fifteen years her junior, to sail across the Pacific. No one had heard from her since.

David had been devastated. He'd been depressed. He'd been exasperated. Then, he'd been angry. Finally, he formally submitted a missing person's report to the sheriff, saw his lawyer, filed for divorce, (as required by law) announced the divorce in several local newspapers, and, when the divorce was finalized, moved to Colorado—his now grown children staying on the West Coast.

As David's and my relationship developed, Suki and I moved from our very extended stay in the inn to an apartment on Tinkham Lane, still in

East Alamosa, and close to Sunrise Park where Suki could find new special places and make new friends.

There was a new normal.

I balanced two schools and basically two households as I spent more than a few nights at David's house on Weber Drive, on the western shore, in the northern part of town—also close to Carrol Park to Suki's approval as she too spent the night when I did.

On weekends and holidays, we would get out of town—sometimes roaming afar, but often going to the Great Sand Dunes National Park, only thirty-five miles to the northeast. The thirty square-mile park (a monument since 1932, but only a national park since 2004) boasted the tallest dunes in North America: 750 feet tall. It was another-worldly place we enjoyed visiting—making us feel we had been far, far away from the daily routines of Alamosa.

Yet, daily routines there definitely were. Classes, students, inmates, friends, lovers, all merged into a broth (on bad days, I'd call it a "slop") that seemed to nourish my body and my soul.

Donna and I maintained a close friendship.

One day, back at the Nestle Toll House Café, for absolutely no reason at all, I blurted out, "We should go to Disney World!"

"What?" She obviously felt she had misunderstood.

"Yep." Thinking a little before I spoke again, only a little, I said, "we should go to Disney World—would that be a blast?"

"What?" she repeated.

"Think about it, a couple of no longer spry chicks in Disney World—what could be better?"

We were still not in sync, but my mind had run ahead, "And, ya know what?"

"What?" she said, now the reflexive reply.

"I'll call José and Eileen (I'd already told Donna about my good chums), we'll make it a quartet."

Finally, it seemed like the ice had melted, Donna was at least a little clearer about my outburst. She was minimally able to interject a, "Why the hell not?"

So, we did it.

We all made arrangements to meet in Orlando. Donna and I would fly out of the San Luis Regional Airport just outside of town. José would leave from Dulles and Eileen, bless her heart, would drive so we'd all have a car in Florida.

It was a hoot.

We, in the eyes of most, a gaggle of old ladies, targeted the activities aimed at younger children—others being far too strenuous (physically and/ or mentally) for us. We took the Mad Tea Cup, Dumbo Flying Elephant, and Magic Carpet rides. We visited Cinderella Castle and House of the Whispering Willows after taking the It's-a-Small-World boat ride.

We saw endless marvels and bumped (literally) into countless people.

We discovered, scattered throughout all the activities, a series of nice eateries that served cute little glasses of wine. We made these nosheries our centerpieces so that we were always well lubricated with the fruit of the vine when we entered into one of the perilous places planned to bring great delight to children (and nausea to adults).

It was, what my father would have called, "A swell time."

We had a wonderful week, capped off with a gourmet dinner where either the deep friendship or the extra bottle of wine brought the glimmer of tears to the eyes of all.

Then it was back to the grind for us all . . .now with a new common bond of Micky Mouse and friends.

Back in Alamosa, life went on.

David welcomed me back with great passion—one would have thought I'd been gone a year and not a week. But this was good.

In fact, as we grew closer together, we decided that keeping separate households was silly. Certainly, for an underpaid college professor (more of an instructor really), an unnecessary expense.

I moved to Weber Drive.

When it had become clear that my time in Alamosa would be more than a stopover—around the second week at the inn—I had traded my now long-term rental for a low-mileage 2007 Edge from Town and Country Ford, right down Highway 285 from Adams State. Suki and I agreed, she'd take the back seat and I the front. It worked out well.

My apartment at Tinkham Lane had been furnished, so the only baggage I really had to move to David's was the professorial clothing I felt I had had to purchase to perform my pedagogic duties. Most of this was thanks to JCPenney—the store located along my daily walk between the inn and the schools.

I was no longer possession-less, but I had managed to keep everything to a minimum.

This was good because David was the opposite. He had every gadget and device to do everything and anything. Computers (yes, more than one), big-screen TV, electric can opener, and even an ultrasonic grill (that cost, believe it or not, $4,300!). I was basically able to slip into the household unnoticed.

I began to wonder if this was it.

Most of my life, I had felt like I was doing something that would lead to something else—like Peace Corps leading to my work with GRA which led to IJB which led to EHT—quite an alphabet soup. While doing something today, I was always waiting for something new tomorrow.

What was my tomorrow now?

This might be it—my apogee, opening the gate to old age.

Had my autumn started?

Cogent Ruminations

There are two means of refuge from the miseries of life: music and cats.

—ALBERT SCHWEITZER

THREE'S.

Growing up, we always said things happened in three's—good or bad. It seemed the highs and the lows all came as trios.

Probably not, but that's what we said.

I certainly had a triplet of rapid and unexpected events enter into my life back-to-back: one bad, one good, and one still not categorized. I lost a dear, dear friend, was separated from another, and had a new door open.

I had celebrated my sixth anniversary in Alamosa when Suki died. It was fast. It was so fast I had to convince myself afterwards I actually had had a wonder dog named Suki.

She had been fine. She had been stiffer, grayer, and less active. But she'd been fine. She was eating, enjoying her walks, and still always there at my side. And then one morning she wasn't.

I looked for her, finding her curled in a corner behind the couch. She didn't look well. But she smiled and weakly wagged her tail when I sat down beside her. Over the next forty-eight hours she ate less and less and needed more and more help to get outside. On the fourth morning she never woke up.

I was destroyed!

She had been a constant in my life—a life I saw as being unsteady at best, and chaotic at worst.

She had been with me when I had fallen deathly ill and she had greeted me when I regained my health.

She had seen me cry. She had seen my laugh. She had seen me drunk. She had seen me sober (and somber). She had seen me angry. She had seen me sad. But she had never judged. She had only loved.

I was shattered.

Three months after Suki's passing, David was offered an excellent position at Wells Fargo in Denver. It was his dream come true. The shift to banking from Boeing had not been easy, even with an MBA. Alamosa had provided a very successful training ground and stepping-stone, but he needed to move on if he was going to get to where he felt he needed to be before he retired.

He asked me to marry him.

I could not.

I still saw myself too much as a will-o'-the-wisp.

I could not.

OK. Then he said we didn't have to get married—we would just keep living together—we would simply move together. Everybody did it. I'd certainly find something in Denver and his significantly increased salary would allow us to do all kinds of things we couldn't do today.

These things weren't important to me.

I still could not.

He cried silently—but, he did not beg.

It wasn't a crashing end. It was more like fruit slowly withering on the vine. Under the right conditions, it could plump up. Or, it could end up on the compost heap (back to the farming metaphors as though still a Peace Corps extensionist and not someone dealing with a separation with someone who could have been her life partner).

It seemed unavoidable, if not inevitable, that we each go our own separate ways.

But, this unanticipated fork in the path did get me to thinking—not always a good thing for me, mind you.

I had had thoughts that this life in Alamosa was the apex—something that would be the vehicle that carried my partner and myself into old age.

This was definitely no longer the case.

But, what of this life of mine?

Probably (nearly certainly), I had not achieved the long-term (sustainable) success I would have liked. In my journey, I had very probably merely passed by and hadn't even left my mark. I was only one of millions moving about spiderwebs that randomly crossed but left little in their wake.

As I had moved about, I had found out (the hard way) a lot about the problems with our system—the unfairness, the biases, the myopia. I had seen more than my share of the weaknesses and the inequities, but I had not found the solutions. In the end, like everyone else, I had merely passed by.

Yet, even if I had gone by without a trace, I did have, and do have indelible memories etched into my brain that the amoeba could not eat away—wonderful and unique images and memories.

These were sensory as much as cerebral.

I remembered the smells. I recalled vividly the essences of manioc drying by the road, communal garbage heaps fermenting in the sun, the aroma of street gutters scumming-over with foul green algae, beignets being fried in palm oil, coffee plants in bloom, racks of lakeside drying fish, jet-fuel on the tarmac, and the scent on the air the first day of rainy season.

I remembered the sounds. The drumming rain on a tin roof, kids reciting in an open-air school, singing lofting up from the thatched roof of a church, women in the market, men in a palm wine house, vendors in the taxi park, wind through the palms, roosters crowing in the morning, goats and pigs screaming as they were tied on top of buses, the sounds of the *quartier*—nothing like those of a US neighborhood.

If this reminiscence was living in the past, then so be it.

Some people seem to be able to turn off their history. I can't. For those who shut out the past, a day is seemingly spent and then wrapped and put in the dust bin—these obdurate deniers foregoing memoirs, finding today's relationships far more important than yesterday's alliances.

This may work splendidly for others. It does not work for me. I need to remember and appreciate. I need to know I have been.

I realized I had no history with David, just as I had had none with Hal. We enjoyed the present and shared our contemplations for the future, but we had no past. We had no once-in-a-lifetime shared experiences. It wasn't a paring, as it would have been with Samuel, François, or my other old lovers, with whom I had shared so much growing and maturing. I came to realize these deep-rooted aspects were critical to really curing the glue that stuck people together.

David was leaving, but I would stay.

Then there was number three.

To my complete shock, I was contacted by someone from the White House. Not a high-up somebody, simply an everyday anybody—but this was still amazing.

As it turned out, Samuel was not only a chief and active in Botswana politics, but also active in the goings-on of the African Union. At a cocktail gathering after a recent African-Union-sponsored seminar discussing ways of using Botswana as an economic model for Africa (hmmm, that sounded familiar), attended by several people from the State Department, Samuel had been approached by these folks from the States, asking if he had any good references—people with a good grasp of African issues. He had given them my name.

Apparently, this reference had trickled down through the corridors, ultimately stimulating today's phone call.

It was the end of 2015. As my caller explained, the Obama administration was laying the groundwork for a high-level Presidential Commission on Poverty. The key participants (of whom I was apparently one—or at least a candidate) would be identified and the major themes outlined in 2016. The work would then be picked up by the Clinton administration in 2017.

I had initially assumed this was about third-world or global poverty—my invitation based on my involvement circling back to Peace Corps and my background with EHT combined with my work with GRA in Nzérékoré and IJB in Namibia. However, I was informed by my caller that the Presidential Commission was focusing primarily on poverty in the US—an underlying assumption being that strategies to address poverty in the US applied worldwide (otherwise put, poverty was becoming such a burning issue that planners were taking the extreme measure of assessing if strategies long-used in the third world could be applied to the first world).

My caller assured me the ever-present "they" had reviewed my dossier and found that my mix of international and domestic work could provide very pertinent insight into issues affecting poverty and its mitigation (I noting he had not said, "eradication").

This was altogether unexpected.

This was fully unforeseen—but possibly far-reaching for my career—far-reaching for me personally.

Still, I always had questions.

Was it right for me?

Before getting lost in the inner workings of my mind as it analyzed this question, I promptly reassured my caller that I was indeed interested and could be available. I was most appreciative, moreover, of the opportunity and looked forward to following the Commission's evolution.

It was done.

I was, by training, an anthropologist. Classically, this meant studying past and present human societies.

I considered myself a cultural anthropologist. This meant studying and trying to understand the variations between and within these human societies. In my case, this had focused on the cultural differences—the differences in attitudes, behavior, habits, and morals. This had been the crux of my approach to most of my work from my thesis at St. Mary's to my efforts with CEGWA in Linden. This had continued to be the core of my current teaching.

This fact notwithstanding, I realized, with considerable introspection, much of my entire life had been skirting the subject of poverty—probing inequities. Coming from overseas back to the US and spiraling all the way back to my first real job at DEP in Pennsylvania, there definitely had been dimensions of poverty in my work on the Three Mile Island problem. Quite simply, if you were rich it was less of a problem. Obviously, if it had blown, the rich and the poor would have been incinerated side by side. But my work had been the aftermath and the trauma that engulfed otherwise healthy people. If someone was wealthy enough, the trauma could be addressed by leaving—pulling up roots and going somewhere else (even if at a financial loss). If you could not afford to walk away, you had to stay in the shadow of the cooling towers and try to manage the fear that would never leave you.

In Alabama, poverty had been a reality. Poor folks had to fight to get access to public health and education—even if of relatively substandard quality. The rich had access to the best private schools and hospitals.

Poor folks had to fight to have a voice—sadly frequently finding nothing more than a whisper.

The majority of the inmates with whom I worked had come from poor families. They were often minorities imprisoned for relatively minor (nonviolent) offenses for which richer folk would have completely escaped incarceration by paying a heavy fine or otherwise assuaging the demands of a biased system that was labeled justice.

And, of course, it wasn't just Pennsylvania, Alabama, or Colorado. There were poor people everywhere—in many instances more today than there had been fifty years ago.

Still, it seemed to me, it was more about addressing the underpinnings of poverty (easily and repeatedly said—much, much harder to do in any durable way). Some talked about empowerment—empowering the poor. But in my mind, power was a phenomenon that was atypical of the majority. While we do indeed all have our own internal power (or powers), socially (as in society) speaking, power was not invested in all. It was not a question of raising a marginalized person to a place of power, it was quite simply a question of ensuring this person had the same inalienable rights as every other citizen. It was a question of, as was so often touted, giving everyone an equal shot at a good life.

As I thought of poor people, as I thought of a Presidential Commission, as I thought of power, as I thought of me—I realized I had basically been apolitical my whole life. I had been all about people and not parties. I had, as current events from any country around the globe would attest, been shamefully naive (again), thinking anyone of any political persuasion would naturally want to help the most vulnerable, the needy—the poor.

Politicians disagreed on policy. There were, of course, many ways to achieve the same ends. But, in my unseeing way, I had assumed (so, so dangerous!) that, while the ways and means differed, all were in favor of the ends—ending poverty (honestly, not probable, but a good aim nonetheless).

Clearly, as the fog lifted, it was evident to me that poverty was a tool. The aim was power. One of the many tools to keep those in power was poverty.

When your life was wretched, when you didn't have enough to eat, didn't have cloths to cover your children from the rain, when you were suffering terribly, politics was a faraway thought.

I thought decades back to my father and the Carlyle family. We had not been wretched, but we, or at least he, had been subservient. It had been all about power. With this family's power, they had been able to provide my family with a comfortable, an anesthetizing, lifestyle whereby by Dad worked and overworked to keep the Carlyle's in power (ultimately to the sacrifice of his health and finally his life).

I completed my trek down memory lane, recalling Samuel's family aphorism: "Life ain't fair!"

Fair or not, remedies were needed.

I continued my enigmatic contemplations.

As I dug deeper into my personal data banks, uneaten by *Naegleria*, buried deep in the medial temporal lobe of my brain, trying to see previously unnoticed patterns, I saw even more sharply how poverty was inextricably linked to a lack of an audible voice—a tangible and assertive presence. Poverty was due to muzzling certain segments of society. It was so often due to discriminatory and selective processes such as voter suppression.

Suppression of black voters had been a reality since the end of the Civil War. But this was much wider than simply a Southern issue. While I had been with the *News Register*, the paper had run a series of articles about voter issues in neighboring states—I guess it's easier to criticize your neighbors than you own household. Kansas and the Dakotas had of late enacted a series of processes making it increasingly complicated for Native Americans and other disenfranchised groups to vote.

All these thoughts were stimulated by the totally unexpected possibility of participating in a very high-level analysis of American poverty—the possibility of putting my studies and my experience to the test.

This seemed not only fortuitous given what was going on in my personal life, but also a stunning chance to be involved in very significant work as I neared the probable end of my career. It seemed an opportunity to leave a legacy (a subject I was only now beginning to consider).

To add to the appeal, it was a slow-coming prospect. This contact was only an outreach to determine my (readily and enthusiastically given, I hoped) interest in, and possible availability for the Commission. The organizers would be moving ahead with the arrangements while I would be able to keep teaching for nearly another year (plenty of time to give notice). The real work would only begin when the Commission was first convened after the election.

Most of the work would start in earnest in 2017.

After a flurry of activity (mostly inside my head, but some on the phone as I called José and Eileen for any advice, knowing I'd talk at length later with Donna), I went back to my teaching. It was kind of like when I had first contacted Peace Corps—my contact at the White House had promised to provide me with regular updates, noting my keen interest. Yet, regular from the government's perspective was hard to judge.

With David's departure, I had rented another furnished apartment near to my first place on Tinkham Lane. Who says you can never go home?

It was now 2016—a presidential election year.

The presidential caucus in Colorado was on the first of March. Donna was going to come by and we were going to moan over the returns as we sipped wine. She arrived, as planned, at eight o'clock, handing me a bottle of merlot when I met her at the threshold.

She was also carrying a rather big wicker basket with a red checked cloth covering the top. I thought she had brought some tasty treats to accompany the wine. However, saying nothing, she went straight to the couch and placed the basket on the center cushion. Then with great theatrics, but without a word, she motioned me to come close and then whipped aside the checkered cloth like a magician exposing a bouquet of red roses from under her hat. I peeked inside. There, curled up, was a fluffy puppy—a mottled black, tan, and white fleecy ball snoozing in the basket with not a worry in the world.

"Her name's Tally," Donna finally piped up through a beaming smile.

"Tally." Was about all I could add.

"Yeah. She just ate, so she's knocked out."

"Uh-huh, I can see."

"She a real go-getter. I promise. Wait til she wakes up."

"Uh-huh."

"The family of one of my students has the country store in Monte Vista. Their dog just had a litter—she's part Collie and part Australian Sheep Dog."

"OK."

"I've seen her mom—she's great."

"OK."

"I guess this is a surprise?"

"Ya think?"

"Yeah. I just thought you needed someone to take care of you."

"OK."

"No. Really. You're going through a lot and you need a pup by your side to take your mind off other stuff."

"OK."

"You'll see I'm right. You'll love her."

I finally got my bearings.

It was lovely for Donna to do. I honestly wasn't sure I was up to having a puppy in the house, but I'd give it a try.

"Thanks, dear," I belatedly inserted into my stream of monosyllabic utterances. "It was splendid of you to think of me and to do all you did to get little Tally here."

With that, I took my new pup (still sleeping) out of the basket and sat down in front of the TV with her on my lap as Donna opened the wine.

It was now Tally and me.

A little while later, back at the Nestle Toll House Café sharing coffee with Donna, she explained why her student from Monte Vista had named the puppy Tally. He had zoomed in on her Australian heritage and found Tally in the Aboriginal Kiroi language meant "near water."

Donna saw this as especially appropriate for me as I had recounted to her how I recently seemed to end up on the river's shore—even now on the West Bank of the Rio Grande.

I agreed. This was serendipity.

What I didn't tell Donna was that I too had explored the name Tally— curious as to the moniker of my new best friend. In some Middle Eastern languages, Tally was short for Taylia which meant lamb (my Tally truly soft and downy like a lamb). Tally was also short for Thalia, one of the nine daughters of Zeus and Mnemosyne—Thalia called the Muse of Comedy (my Tally certainly fitting into the category of comedy, as she was one funny girl).

However you cut it, the name seemed to be a perfect fit.

Shifting from my new four-legged friend (for whom I was very grateful), Donna pierced the bubble, "So, what about the White House?"

I'd, of course, told her all about my call. Yet, what was there to say? "No news, but I'm not expecting any. They said this was only the initial contact."

"Sure. Got it. But, when it's the second, third of sixth contact, what're you gonna do?"

"Been thinking quite a bit about it. Pretty sure, if they ask me to really commit, I'll do it."

"Big step."

"Indeed. It'd mean moving back to DC and that's not honestly a step I'd relish. But this is truthfully a once-in-a-lifetime chance (How many times had I said that?). I really have no idea how Samuel's recommendation filtered through the system to reach this point, but I don't want to squander the stunning chance—possibly my last opportunity to have an impact at a higher level." I did not add, but thought and, to leave some breadcrumbs of my passing.

"Pretty high and mighty thoughts, huh?"

"That's what worries me. Remember that old Jimmy Cliff song (ironically, I felt, I referred to Samuel's lighthearted warning, referencing this song years ago—Samuel who had opened the door before which I now stood), "The Harder They Come," when he sang about attaining such lofty status that a crashing collapse becomes an ever-increasing option—maybe an inevitability?"

"Yep."

"Am I very meticulously preparing for a fall?" (I was careful not to say, "Another fall.")

"Humm," the cryptic reply.

It was not I that fell. But there was a fall.

To my total dismay, on November ninth I discovered we were not having a President Clinton the next year, but a President Trump! I (along with many, many others) was flabbergasted!

Denial set in. It took me until Christmas to accept the impossible.

Just after Boxing Day, out of the blue (at least, to my mind), I received a call from my guy at the White House. Obviously, the whole commission thing was now a moot point. However, to my amazement, apparently the team that had been working on this throughout the year was not ready to abruptly chuck the entire effort into the garbage—they wanted to be able to see some sort of follow through—and it certainly was not (in their view) going to come from the new administration. So, they had fortuitously stuck a contingency in their hip pocket.

In the (what was thought of as the highly unlikely) event there was a major change in leadership, the White House team had made arrangements with CESP—the Center for Equitable Social Policies. CESP would, with some end-of-years funding, pick-up the work foreseen for the Presidential Commission.

I was familiar with CESP from my time with CEGWA in Alabama. The motto of the fifty-year-old center was, "Promoting equity and poverty reduction." It seemed to be a good fit for the work initially ascribed for the Commission.

In early February, as the new administration was trying out its wings, I got a call from Tod Hanson at CESP. Tod, after introducing himself, informed me that, at the beginning of the year, Cecelia Bakker, from the previous administration's Council of Economic Advisers, had joined CESP. The two had been working together to juxtapose the now defunct White House American Poverty Project within the CESP poverty reduction program.

He further elaborated that, as they worked up from the groundwork already well outlined, they were now in the process of identifying the team of experts to work on the newly forged CESP "Square Deal Project." As he knew I was already aware that I had been among the potential candidates when these activities were planned for the public sector, he wanted to reiterate that I was still on the list—was I interested?

I was.

Tod then confirmed my position with the new project, expressing his pleasure that I would be joining the team. He additionally highlighted that, as was certainly obvious, the Square Deal Project could not rely on long-term federal funding. There was a relatively generous allocation that had hopefully been secured from the most recent budget cycle that would be adequate to get things moving. However, it was widely accepted (he was sure I was among those who would accept) that this project would take at least five years—and more likely, a decade.

Accordingly, additional, non-federal support was essential. He and Cecelia had already contacted a number of foundations and were confident that the needed additional support would be found. Nonetheless, when bringing new staff onboard, it was important they realize that this position could be for a decade—and, it also could be for a year. Right now, there were no guarantees.

This was nothing new to me. Not my best-case scenario—but definitely not unexpected under the circumstances.

I doubled down. I was in.

From my side, I advised Tod (as I was sure he was aware) that I was currently employed—my employers requiring a minimum of three-months' notice. Given the recent political volatility, I had hesitated at informing colleagues I was leaving—no efforts had yet been initiated to look for a replacement. In light of my current responsibilities and the academic calendar, I would like to set a date after the Fourth of July as my start date with CESP. This way, I would finish the school year and help in assuring someone would be in my seat for the start of next fall.

This was agreeable.

I was going back to DC.

Still, in the here and now, I was in Alamosa.

With my course now charted, I advised colleagues and supervisors at both Adams State and Trinidad (as well as my landlord) that I would be departing over the summer.

As I balanced all my teaching activities, I began to appreciate more each day—the interactions with the students, the satisfaction at (hopefully) teaching principles that were important to me, the challenges of a really challenging job (or jobs, in my case). I also felt I was making measurable progress with the prisoners with whom I was working, and this was truly rewarding (hopefully for all involved).

That year, as I viewed my environs, it appeared as though Alamosa had had an exceptionally lovely and vibrant spring. Yet, it was highly likely (and corroborated by most with whom I spoke) that this spring was, in fact, very similar (if not identical) to so many others. Yet, to me it seemed stunning—a soothing cape covering the landscape.

My milieu seemed perfect; my milieu felt special.

I was savoring remorse (or the closest thing).

I had (once again) become implanted in comfortable surroundings with comfortable duties and comfortable friends and colleagues. A major move (at my age) was a major event. My subconscious seemed to be tugging at me— "don't go."

But I was going.

I needed a change (now-now).

Spring break was coming, and I enrolled in an educators' roundtable on cultural hegemony and climate change at University of New Mexico in Albuquerque, about three and a half hours nearly due south. This would literally rip me away from my static thoughts of being static. This would overcome inertia.

The seminar was about as opaque as the title had implied. Nonetheless, there were some thought-provoking working groups and a number of interesting people (speakers and participants).

On my last afternoon, after the wrap-up of the roundtable, I was driving about a bit as this was my first visit to this city of over a half a million people (nearly sixty times larger than Alamosa)—showing Tally the city (she'd been cooped up in the hotel room for far too long and was ready for a change in scenery). We were on a large thoroughfare, crossing an intersection on a green light at very slow speed given the heavy afternoon traffic when I heard a "wham" that seemed to come from my car. Having seen nothing, I thought I had just had a major breakdown and, creeping forward, pulled to the curb that was only twenty feet away.

When I got out to see the problem more closely, I was shocked.

About thirty feet in my wake, there was a cyclist lying on the road, his (I could see it was a he) bicycle lying by his side. Although there were no immediately visible terrible wounds to the person nor noticeable damage to the bike, there was already a huge crowd. Most of the cars behind me seemed to have stopped and for some crazy reason it looked for all the world to me like an old Western on TV when they circled the wagons—cars and people rapidly surrounding the supposed victim.

I stood like, as my mother would have said (there she was again, appearing out of nowhere), a "ninny." I am sure my mouth was agape, and I was just staring in disbelief.

Then there was the sound of sirens—lots and lots of sirens.

People from the circling crowd began to look directly at me and point their fingers—some admonishingly.

And, I stood there like a ninny.

The police came. The sheriff deputies came (I learned later I was very close to the Bernalillo County Offices—a quick jaunt for the officers). A great big fire engine came (screaming). An ambulance came.

And, I stood there like a ninny.

Everything became a blur. The cyclist was trussed (like a Thanksgiving turkey ready for the oven, I thought) on some sort of stretcher by the guys (they were all guys) from the fire engine. This pallet was put on a gurney and pushed to the door of the ambulance, where the guard changed and the fire guys (apparently reaching the end of their mandated turf) handed over to the ambulance crew. The EMTs then pushed the stretcher into the waiting white van (lit like a Christmas tree) and sped off.

And, I stood there like a ninny.

Finally, awaking as from a dream, I realized there was a police officer in front of me asking for my driver's license and the registration with insurance for my car. As he very politely perused my documents, he informed me I was last on his list. He had noted that I seemed to be in a daze, so he had spoken with all the other parties before coming to me. He was, therefore, happy to be able to tell me that I had not committed any infraction. All the witnesses (the cyclist still to make a statement) indicted I was crossing the intersection normally, under a green light. Moreover, the initial opinions (pending the hospital's word, of course) of the fire engine and ambulance crews were that the bike rider had only suffered minor cuts and scrapes—after all, he kindly added, my car was nearly not moving, so all the impact came from the force of his bike.

The officer somewhat curiously concluded that, while there were no citations to be issued, he was noting that there was shared responsibility. Drivers of all vehicles (bikes and cars) should be aware of their surroundings and do all they can to avoid accidents. Given the circumstances, it seemed as though both parties were distracted and, given the very slow speeds involved, could have possibly avoided contact if they had been concentrating on the job of sharing the road.

I smiled (probably a ninny smile).

As an educated educator, there was an assumption on the part of others that I understood what was going on. I guess all the more so since as an anthropologist (although no one at this place in time likely knew I was one of these), I was supposed to know about differences in habits and behavior. But such assumptions were completely wrong. This was all totally inexplicable to me—completely beyond my ken. Although life in Guinea or Namibia was different, there were common denominators—I had points of reference. An accident in Albuquerque exceeded any understanding I could offer—the actions I had dumbfoundedly witnessed were mystifying.

I surely was a ninny.

I smiled.

The officer left.

I was confused and lightheaded. But I was elated to get away with only a word to the wise—or so I thought.

Back in Alamosa, I was ready to jump back into classes, students, and paperwork. I was not so much refreshed by an excursion to Albuquerque as I was happy to be back—happy to have escaped with negligible damage from my altercation with the Albuquerque cyclist (I had belatedly inspected my own car, finding it had only suffered a two-inch scratch that was easily treated with touch-up paint).

I operated on parallel tracks. I tried (and think I succeeded) to continue my teaching duties, supporting my students, and having usual relationships with my colleagues. At the same time, I was in intermittent contact with Tod, getting updates on the preparations at CESP.

While the tracks did not cross professionally, personally, they were twisted into a Gordian knot. In spite of my commitment to go, in spite of my tangible preparation to leave my present posts, I was still having waves of doubt.

Years ago, I handled life-changing decisions with aplomb. Today, I was gripped by angst.

Then reality gave me a quick kick in the gut to get me back on track.

I was spending a quiet afternoon at home with Tally over Memorial Day weekend when there was a knock at the door. Responding, I found a rather frog-like man dressed all in black (for effect or not, I did not know) on my stoop. He was wearing some sort of device on his shirt (I was later told it was a video camera). He handed me an envelope, saying, "You've been served." Then he vanished.

Returning to the sanctity of my living room, I opened the envelope, reading the contents. The Albuquerque cyclist was suing me for negligence. Unbelievable!

I called Donna. Donna called Stan. We three met at the Nestle Toll House Café.

Not to get into all the blood and guts, but Stan had a good lawyer who was a tremendous help. My insurance company, informed from the get-go, was also superb. What had started out as a quarter of a million-dollar case accusing me of negligent driving and willful disregard for an injured party, transformed into a five-hundred-dollar case to repair a sleazy guy's bike.

While I was practically unscathed in terms of penalties and had no negative repercussions as regarded my driving record or insurance premiums, the entire event had left a scar. It had quite simply, in my view, been an attempt to extort money.

It had been shameful.

It was so shameful; it never should have got any traction at all.

It was a scam.

But, I guess, it was the way of the world these days.

My rancor was as much about the prevailing environment as the perpetrator himself.

It appeared as though, with the change of government, there had come a change in the national discourse. "Us" became "me." What had once been touted as, "kinder and gentler" had become the uncompassionate. It was us versus them. There were reports of the leadership referring to "shithole countries," by comparison to the greatness they ascribed to their nationalistic tirades.

In the new vernacular, apparently those areas of the world where I had spent so much of my career were now perceived by the uncultured masses as shitholes—this was not only a personal issue, but also an intellectually challenging topic for a cultural anthropologist.

It was amazing!

When possible, when my mind would get into overdrive, I would take refuge in the Nestle Toll House Café. As I stared at the steam rising from my coffee cup, I felt more than saw someone.

"Dr. Patterson?"

I looked up, brought back from the far-off places my mind was taking me. There, standing by my table was a young man in jeans and a T-shirt with a backpack—looking for all the world like one of my students—yet, I couldn't place the face (and I'm generally pretty good with faces).

"Nope. Not a doctor—just Ms. Patterson—or Paula if it's easier."

"Oh, OK, ma'am. Sorry. My name is Evans. Ms. Winters said I should talk with you—she said I might find you here."

"Fine. No problem. What's on your mind?"

"Well," Evans said. Getting the opening he sought, he gathered his thoughts. "I'm interested in Peace Corps and Ms. Winters said you had been a volunteer."

"Yes, indeed—but a long time ago."

"Well, can you tell me anything—offer any advice?"

I then spent about twenty minutes summarizing my Peace Corps experience, concluding that I would encourage anyone with a good imagination, a desire to see new things, and a good dose of tolerance to apply to Peace Corps—it certainly had changed my life.

While I had been speaking, Evans had taken the seat across from me and ordered two cups of coffee. I could see I had timed it about right as his cup was nearly drained as I wrapped up my accolades for Peace Corps.

Evans made a move as if to get up, then seemed to think better of it. He kind of slumped back in his chair, asking, "One other thing, Ms. Patterson, if you don't mind?"

"OK."

"Are you a baby boomer?"

I was taken aback. What did this have to do with Peace Corps? This was such a bizarre change of tack—such a non sequitur—that I was almost curious. I figured at this point I had to answer somehow. "I guess I am, never really thought much about it," I replied noncommittally.

"Sorry," Evans intoned, seeing the quizzical expression on my face. "It's only that I just overheard a group of students talking about how the baby boomers have got us all in trouble and are likely to destroy things for us younger folk?"

"Go on."

"Well, and I know this has nothing to do with what I initially wanted to ask you—it just flashed into my mind—that's all—these guys were saying that it's all the wars' fault—not really clear to me where they're coming from?"

"Not clear to me either."

"Well, they said—and it's sticking with me—that's why I even bring it up now—sorry—that your generation wasn't raised right—basically your folks all fought in the Second World War and somehow kinda got bent and didn't know how to raise kids right, what with all the impact of the war and all. Then your generation got raked over by the Vietnam war—kinda multiplying the aftermath of the World War—and this really messed everything up. Now you boomers are, according to these guys, old and frustrated and full of regret—even bitterness—and really don't care about the future. That's why things are so messed up today. That's what they said. Don't know. Just thought I'd ask what ya thought. It seemed kinda important. And, ya know, I didn't know if it fit in with that stuff you teach."

I was uncertain of what to say or do next. Evans' abrupt screed had somehow grabbed a bit of my curiosity—just a wee bit. I figured it was worth at least one poke at the bear.

"Interesting, Evans," I inserted nearly sleepily, "so it's the boomers?"

"Well, ma'am." He appeared a bit sheepish now, "I'm not blaming you or your folks. I was only commenting on what I'd heard. It wasn't really, ya know, my discussion. Not honestly sure why I even brought it up."

"No. No it's fine. It's always good to try and discover reasons where reasoning seems often so absent. And, I tell you, I agree, things are messed up."

My new pupil only nodded.

"I had never considered the roles of the wars—I'm sure they do figure into the bigger picture somehow. And, I agree my generation has a large part in the current drama—not necessarily a positive role, either."

This got another nod.

"I, however, obviously view things through another lens."

No reaction.

"My generation, regardless of the connection to our parents' history, was, in its youth, seen as revolutionary: antiwar, anti-segregation, pro-environment, pro-peace, pro-civil rights. People were burning their bras and their draft cards. It is difficult for me—and I imagine for you too—to understand how so many free thinkers, so many who thought of themselves as avant-garde, so many liberated souls today, forty-some years later, are now avidly pushing for something that has all the trappings of despotism."

No reaction.

"All the symbols—the principles—of the sixties and seventies seem to have vaporized from these people's minds. It very possibly is, as you say, a reflection of frustration and bitterness. But, why?"

No reaction.

"It could be the wars. I don't know. They certainly were terrible and left indelible marks on all they touched. I just don't know. But I do know—trying to be objective now—that the fifties and the sixties offered most people real opportunity—even happiness. In retrospect, this time of unsurpassed economic and social growth seems to have been a rare and gratifying period. Maybe folks are just pissed off it's over?"

My choice of words seemed to have awakened my (now unwitting) pupil.

He sat upright, made a show of looking at his watch, and, standing up, apologetically said, "Ma'am, I'm sorry to have bothered you. Thanks for the insight into Peace Corps and the other good chat, but I really gotta run."

He was gone.

Thereafter, somehow the Albuquerque cyclist and the boomer bash discussion merged in a weird way into a pulse that countered the gnawing of my better angels (or whatever the hell they were?)—those small voices resisting the verdict to go to DC. I took these (as I saw them) rebuffs as signs—validation of the foregone conclusion that it was time to move on.

In Guinea and Nigeria, I had witnessed new (to me) levels of corruption. At EHT, and even indirectly at DEP, I had seen unfortunate levels of mismanagement and poor decision-making. I had now, by this stage of my life, seen a lot—a lot, I guess, by today's standards, coming from shithole countries. I had seen beggars and thieves, chiefs and presidents. I had observed different cultures, different customs, different beliefs, meld into societies that were tolerant and capable of constructing a whole that was truly greater than the sum of the parts.

Throughout, my touchstone, my reference point had been the US of A. While I knew full well malfeasance and bigotry were present here just as all around the globe—I had naively felt these worries were more modulated here in my homeland. I felt our society was evolving into being more all-inclusive, more understanding—more honest (both socially and financially).

Boy, did I (once again) get it wrong.

With a prick, the balloon had popped. It had evaporated leaving only the time-honored visage of prejudice, selfishness, and demoralization. It had popped, revealing those images that we had thought we had relegated to the darkest shadows.

While, sadly, a move on my part would surely in no way affect these potentially ruinous factors, it would make me feel as though I had done something—as though I was doing something.

Idleness was not an option.

Unfortunately, much of the reaction to the deleterious actions would likely prove impotent. Evans had been right. We, the boomers, had seemingly done the worst of it.

Now, could it be fixed?

Finale

One truth stands firm. All that happens in world history rests on something spiritual. If the spiritual is strong, it creates world history. If it is weak, it suffers world history.

—ALBERT SCHWEITZER

EVERYTHING BLURRED, LIKE WATCHING a fast-moving train go by. Before I knew it, I was back in the ninety-degree heat, ninety-percent humidity, of our nation's capital in July. Between Tod and José, however, the transition was practically seamless.

I had already taken care of all the formalities (with José's help) for moving straight into an (excessively overpriced) apartment on Burning Tree Drive (an omen?) in Tyson, Virginia, where Tally and I were welcomed with open arms—the arms readily accepting the required six-month deposit.

CESP offices were located on Haycock Road, just off the I-66, in Falls Church. It was a short metro ride to work, getting on at Spring Hill Station and then off after only four stops at the East Falls Church Station if I wanted to walk a little—or, if it wasn't walking weather, changing to the Orange Line, getting off at the West Falls Church Station which was very close to CESP.

It was a testament to how well the organizers and promoters of the high-level Presidential Commission on Poverty had prepared, and how strongly they had believed in the need for functional continuity (in the face of a changing administration), that CESP was effectively able to pick up the leadership of this effort in a matter of weeks. By the time I arrived (a full four months into CESP operations), to a newcomer like me, it looked like a well-oiled machine.

CESP was in some ways reminiscent of EHT. They had five floors of a twelve-story building—they were a big deal. Two of these floors had been leased specifically for the poverty work (after all, they had a big budget they needed to spend before it was either cancelled or reallocated). There were nine clusters of three-specialists each—these supported by a team of five to ten assistants. Each cluster had private offices for each specialist as well as a bullpen where there were mandated daily specialists' discussions (ranging from fifteen minutes to six hours). The whole show operated on flex time. All staff working on what had become the Poverty Partnership (PP for short, of course) were assumed to be at work ("on seat," as they called it) from eleven in the morning until two in the afternoon—there were a lot of lunch meetings. Beyond this, people were free to come early and leave early, come late and leave late, or come and go. It all worked.

My team was formally known as the Culture of Poverty Cluster. In addition to myself, Fritz Seizemore, originally from Michigan, was a cultural economist who had worked at the IMF for eighteen years and Jayla Brown, hailing from the Peach State, had had a career with UNESCO from where she had recently retired as a departmental director. High level was what was sought and (with the possible exception of myself) high level appeared to be what was on the table.

The expectations were to not regurgitate all the same ragged platitudes about the poor and poverty. The expectations were to be innovative and realistic—assessing the current backsliding in many places in regard to social equity and economic opportunity.

The expectations were not to re-wage the now fifty-year-old war on poverty and its nearly one hundred linked programs, nor to review the Equal Employment Opportunity Act, nor revisit affirmative action. The fundamental assumption was that things had not worked as well as we (the societal "we") had thought they had. Anti-poverty, pro-poor sentiments were not as tenacious nor deep-seated as once thought. Views on gender, race, and ethnicity had changed significantly (not all in positive ways, as initially hoped some score of years ago), not to mention views on the rich and the poor. Accordingly, the expectations were to imagine new paradigms in respect to an honest appraisal of the country's current place in time.

I hoped we were up to the task.

We seemed to have, in spite of the clear lack of the hoped-for central government support, important financial and human resources.

If I could make a meaningful contribution to this effort that I saw as so timely and consequential, I would feel as though I had done something—I had left a footprint, albeit a rather unimpressive eight and a half D.

Inside and outside CESP, things were very different from Alamosa. I had, of course, theoretically known this would be the case. I had lived in DC before. I had worked for big, complex organizations before. I guess the combination of age and the slow pace of life in Alamosa County had lulled me into a leisurely, practically slumberous, lifestyle that was now being (rather aggressively) overturned by the tumult of the politics of the nation's capital.

Alamosa had been somewhat staid, with, at times, an almost stand-offish citizenry. While it had been nonchalant and informal, it had been accommodating—it had been low-keyed (though certainly not serene).

Now I was back in the race.

Every day was a rush—a new challenge.

However, as now a sixty-year-old, my energies were not fully what they used to be.

In addition to vacillations in vitality, there was (ironically) a strong cultural dimension to my necessary DC adjustments. The CESP PP team was far-reaching. I didn't honestly know the complete composition. It did, by design, reflect the country's wider population structure. This meant that, while there were some old farts like me, most of the staff was younger—a lot, lot younger. There were, naturally, many millennials. And, as I learned on a nearly daily basis, millennials and boomers were quite different (couldn't seem to shake the boomer question, I guess).

In Alamosa, I had taught millennials and post-millennials (even some from Generation X). Yet, this had always been framed in student-teacher relationships which were very, very different from collegial relationships between peers.

For our work, this temporal variation in viewpoint was good—strengthening the analyses. In the workplace environment, this variability in outlooks was simply considered as a given—built-into the interpersonal connections. This generational asymmetry was kind of a pet sub-subject of mine—a hobby, I guess (hopefully, not an obsession). It was an interesting twist, I felt, that I personally had gone to far-off places to look at cultural assimilation (although, I had started as a young student right here in DC) and now I was directly in the midst of it as my generation was replaced (I reassured myself, in the natural order of things) by younger, more enterprising (possibly?) individuals.

It never ceased to amaze me (to put it modestly) how one of my younger colleagues and I could look at exactly the same thing and see totally different things. To add to the perplexity, not only did we visualize differently, but we foresaw actions and solutions completely asymmetrically—it frequently astounded me.

Nonetheless, this was not a drawback—not an obstacle. This was (the new) reality. Intellectually, I enjoyed it—contrasting and comparing to my wit's end. Professionally, howbeit, it was a test. So often I knew what the needed tactics and strategies were. I had, after all, been to some of the most poverty-stricken areas and worked intimately with some of the poorest people (at least, as I saw it).

Alas, my own views of myself and the world notwithstanding, I had to learn that I was just one voice among many. The PP assembly functioned on consensus—majority rule. I was one piece—and, one piece only.

It was hard for me to rein-in my enthusiasm and my decisiveness. I knew I knew what to do. I knew I knew how to do it. I knew I knew that if the needful was accomplished, things would be better (no magic bullet— just marginal improvement). I knew we could quickly do things that would be meaningful. I knew I knew so much. I knew I had so much to offer.

All the same, I was but one piece (and, not even a very big one at that) on the chessboard.

Outside Falls Church, outside CESP, I tried to foster a modified approach vis-à-vis my heretofore typical way of living my life. I felt I had always been someone who, when necessary, would work twenty-four-seven. Taking work home had never been a question, it had been the way things were done. I had (in retrospect, probably mistakenly) always had (probably) an inflated view of the importance of my efforts and was at the ready all the time, any time.

Now, after decades of workaholism and passion, I could look back. Where had the seventy-five-hour workweeks and the professional celibacy got me? From my current vantage point, maybe not all that far.

I had established a certain set of professional credentials—otherwise, I wouldn't be where I was. If not wealthy (by any measure), I was financially comfortable (but most of this due to the settlement with EHT and not, so to speak, from the sweat of my brow). I had had wonderful experiences and accumulated a few very good and true friends. How did all this appear on a balance sheet?

We can only see through our own eyes, and I concluded that my view of my life was OK. Although there were mistakes a-many, I would not go back and make any great changes. I had lived my life. I was happy with the life I had lived. I had been lucky. I had been very lucky. And, if not financially wealthy, I was very wealthy in experiences.

There was no remorse.

There was no unfulfilled frustration.

There certainly was no bitterness.

But there was truth.

The truth was that, in spite of how I saw myself, I was no longer young (no longer even middle-aged). I felt I was in good shape (especially in light of my battle with *Naegleria*). But there was no point in denying it—I was old. Unquestionably, I was old in the eyes of others, even if not in my own.

It was time to turn down the dial. It was time to slow down.

I took no work home.

I let it be known that I did not welcome work-related calls after hours.

As, long ago, Martha had told me so many times when we were absently lounging on Azure Beach, I had to get a life. Better late than never.

Getting a life was, of course, easier said than done. As always, and in spite of my efforts to put a damper on overzealousness, my work continued to swallow up most of the hours of my day. It continued to fascinate me. It all too often totally absorbed me. Turning down the dial wasn't straightforward. There's always the unforeseen—what my friends in Guinea all those years ago called "*les imprévus.*"

As an example (that, to this day, I'm still attempting to categorize and file in my mind), one afternoon as I was trying hard to quickly wrap up the day's efforts in order to meet José for a drink at one of our favorite spots (part of my tamping-down), my phone rang. It was the receptionist. I had an unscheduled visitor. It was near the end of the workday, and the receptionist wanted to know if I would be able to see this person, or should he be asked to come back later.

One final task. Why not?

A few minutes later I looked up from my desk to find an above average height, lanky, but somehow sinewy man of indeterminate age standing in my doorway. With a long step, an extended hand, and a big smile he swept toward me saying, "Sorry to come so late and unannounced, I'm Rodney Mills."

Unsure what to do, and having no idea who Rodney Mills was, I offered him a captain's chair in front of my desk, moving around to situate myself in its twin before asking, "Well, Mr. Mills, how can I help you?"

Rodney saw the green light, going into a short biographical sketch, indicating that he worked for the Security and Exchange Commission's

Division of Enforcement. While much of his work was confidential, and he was not at liberty, sadly, to divulge the full context of his visit, he, again apologizing, wanted just a few minutes of my time to ask a few questions.

This seemed simple enough—and brief enough so as not to keep José waiting at the bar.

"OK, shoot," I agreed.

"Thanks so much. Let me just set the stage with those few details I am free to share," he replied in a soft but firm voice, eyes on his notepad, trying to look, I thought, contrite. "Our division is looking into international fraud and corruption—bad actors and bad acts on a very big scale. You are not involved, I know. But you could conceivably have some important information—in this job of mine, we have to follow all clues, however fanciful. We never know when we're going to stumble onto a real breakthrough. Things develop a drop at a time.

"Please know, I don't want to frighten you and I don't want you to think I'm snooping—really it's my job—and this stuff is pretty much public record—but, on the off chance you might, unbeknownst to you, have some leads to new sources, I would like to ask you some questions about your past work overseas, if that's alright?"

"OK." I replied, thinking he was well rehearsed and wondering if I was fanciful.

"I've seen from multiple sources that you worked for EHT, based at their headquarters in Geneva?"

"Yes."

"That seems like a great job and a great city. What brought you back to our shores?"

"Well." Now reluctantly having to shift from monosyllabic answers and risking being late for José, I felt obliged to be slightly more verbose. "It was fine while it lasted. But, as I believe is also in those public records you consult, EHT is not exactly all it claims to be.

"I had, as you may probably already know, the dubious charge of uncovering, accidentally I might add, the very strong links—a dependency I guess I'd call it—between EHT and ICDI—the International Center for Democratic Ideals—as you surely know."

"Yes," Rodney confirmed, "I know of ICDI."

"So, I found them to be antithetical to EHT's publicly professed mission and my boss found my concerns antithetical to working at EHT."

"You were fired?"

"Yes. Although publicly, a more benign face was painted on my departure."

"Did you actually ever get in touch with ICDI when you were still working at EHT?"

"No. My work never involved ICDI. My conclusions—later validated by multiple sources—were based on data gathered when assessing EHT's efforts—ICDI surfacing only as a fluke."

"Any subsequent contacts with EHT or dealings with ICDI?"

"Not really. I'm still formally an EHT pensioner as I was vested in their program."

"Did you ever come across a multinational company called Delpro?"

"No—who are they?"

"I can't truly go into detail, but they're a group that has many tentacles—at times camouflaging their actions in the robes of international humanitarian aid. Their spoor is found around the world—often smelly as one might think a spoor might be." Rodney giggled at his little joke.

I nodded my head— José was waiting.

"I know it's getting late, but one last question."

"OK."

"At EHT or elsewhere in your travels and work, did you ever run across a man named Robin McCandless—he's remarkable for his full head of snowy white hair that sets off a glowing pink complexion. Also, he lives in this general vicinity, at Candy Point, on the Virginia-Maryland border."

"Nope to all accounts—but I'll keep my eyes peeled."

"Fine. I apologize again for the interruption. And, I thank you for sharing what you could with me."

"No problem."

Rodney stood, put his card on my desk, adding, "Call me if you think of anything."

As Rodney retraced his steps through the doorway, I wondered about what I saw as a strange and cryptic conversation with someone who many would probably call a "spook." It was puzzling. It was eerie. How much of what we thought we saw was actually there? How much were we spectators of, rather than actors in life's theater?

I had a quick recollection of Ruth and Peace Corps training at the Center. During Dr. Clark's most rigorous trials and tribulations, when we felt dazed and lost, Ruth would make us smile with a time-honored joke.

"They must all think we're all mushrooms," she'd say with exasperation and a twinkle in her eyes, "because all they do is keep us in the dark and feed us shit."

Well, Rodney had made the darkness a little more obscure.

But then Rodney was gone, and I was back to the here and now. Arranging my papers, I turned off the lights, and was hot on my inscrutable visitor's heels to get a much-needed after-work drink with José—still not fully sure what had just happened with Mr. Rodney Mills and his questions.

I saw José at least three times a month. We'd have dinner—or we'd have drinks and forget dinner. We'd go to a concert or visit (again) one of the many splendid heirloom sites that garnished the Mid-Atlantic countryside.

At a minimum, I talked with Donna and Eileen once a month. We'd share all the latest scandals and just enjoy each other's company over long distance. We agreed we four (with José, of course) would meet, the gods willing, for Easter in Key Largo in 2019, after the midterm elections, when we'd all rant and rave or celebrate gleefully and raucously.

I also now made it a habit to go for long walks with Tally every evening—regardless of the weather or how many G&T's I'd had before the walk. After coming back with Tally, I'd set aside a few hours to try to organize and chronicle my notes—prepare the groundwork for this very telling of my story.

I frequently asked myself, "Why worry? Why waste my time on telling a story no one other than my mother would want to read—and my mother was long dead?"

Indeed, I had never been a prolific writer—I'm not sure I truly liked writing. I had written more than my fair share of progress reports, proposals, reviews, and other routine administrative and professional documents. I'd even worked for a newspaper, for God's sake. Still, unlike many of my associates, I had never written a book—never even thought about writing a book.

Why write a book?

Who'd care?

Why invest the effort in futility?

These were not easy questions for me to answer. In some ways, I attempted to rationalize my deeds by telling myself this was just a way for an aging spinster to spend her lonely nights. I would remind myself that this was better than doing crochet and I didn't have the inherent talent to paint.

Then, on other occasions, I would verge on arrogance, thinking my story was worth telling—thinking my experiences were truly unique and should not be lost to posterity. Then, I would be nearly embarrassed by my pompousness and self-aggrandizement, wondering if I should be doing crosswords.

My views on my need to transcribe my narrative crystalized slowly as I began opening my eyes more when walking Tally.

Through most of my life, I think I had lived in cultures where people greeted each other—be it perfunctorily, at least verbally, with a curt and un-smiling hello. In Fomi, it had been a beaming *"bonjour,"* while in Geneva the *"bonjour"* was cool but correct. In Alabama, it had been a gurgly "hey"—in Alamosa more of a nasal "howdy." However, and wherever, there had been some sort of acknowledgement when encountering another of one's species.

This time, though, my perambulations went unnoticed—unacknowl-edged by the mildest "huh" (whether an affliction of the here or the now or both, I knew not). It was as though everyone had put on blinders—no one even dared make eye contact. Individuals immersed themselves deeply in inner worlds—this greatly facilitated by the complex and omnipresent cell phones that carried the users to fantastical places.

Tally and I would go out for a thirty or forty-minute walk, crossing paths with scores of people, greeting or being greeted by nary a one. I quick-ly became acculturated. Soon, my fellow humans were as decorative as the trees imbedded in the sidewalk's border—and nearly as animated.

To compensate, I began trying to see what I had not seen before. No longer focusing on the citizens with whom I shared the pathways, I began to look through windows and doors at the citizens who lined these pathways (hopefully, not being seen as a Peeping Paula—if, indeed any of those being watched, watched the watcher)—individuals who had always been there, but whom I had scarcely recognized as my focus had heretofore been else-where (on the shared road, to use a phraseology that brought back painful memories).

I watched people in the kitchens and living rooms or tiny verandas of their apartments. I watched people in gardens and parks. I watched people in restaurants and cafés. I watched people in gas stations and convenience stores. I watched people in shops and studios, labs and libraries. I became a spectator to the humanity that populated my neighborhood—my neighbors with whom I did not speak, but upon whom I did spy.

In so doing, unable to know, I imagined their lives. I imagined many still stuck only miles away from their birthplace (and their death place). We all got up, did something, and went to bed. But what we did was so, so different. As I guess had been the case through time, and as I now imagined, the people who formed the foundations of society, whose doings during the day made our lives doable, spiraled through life in increasingly tight circles, like water twisting down a drain.

Hopefully these essential residents found happiness. I viewed them in parks and bars, in fast-food joints and sports fields. I imagined them as enjoying themselves. Yet, I also imagined that, to some, possibly the center of DC at 17th and Constitution Avenue, scarcely fifteen miles away, was a little-known world (a strange place to visit on the screen of a smartphone, but not in person). My imagination reminded me of a book I had recently read—*Elizabeth Street* by Laurie Fabiano. The story was about an Italian family in Little Italy, New York City. Many who worked so hard to get here, who worked so hard when here, seldom saw beyond the borders of their neighborhood.

I digress. Yet, it was the realization that I had been so fortunate to have been able to do what I had done that reinforced my decision to tell my tale. I had not been born with a silver spoon in my mouth. I had had the privileges of white Middle America (which were definitely significant—but that's another story)—but so had my high school classmates. I was no smarter. I was no more driven. I had quite simply benefited from the quirks of fate.

It was a story to tell, not because of what I had done, but because it was a story that could be open to many who are willing to take a chance on crossing the threshold.

As Tally tugged me about the alleys and lanes of our community within a community, it was fortunate I had a demanding job to counterbalance the recondite (and, at times, off-the-wall—especially in the dark and unwelcoming evenings of winter) contemplations that filled my head as I was towed through the arteries of suburban Virginia by my four-legged best friend.

Work was indeed hard.

As my loving father might have said, "Dear, it's a tough nut to crack."

After all, we were trying to save the world, or at least a big chunk of it.

In the spring, the PP venture reached its first anniversary. To celebrate, Tod made a brief speech, highlighting that all was well in the (our little) kingdom. The original funding was still holding and had been significantly complemented by generous grants from the Evers and Food for Thinkers Foundations. In short, our future was bright.

Tod then announced a rearrangement—more of a new layer as opposed to a restructuring of the current hierarchy. Two clusters were being melded into a working party. The cluster would still be the principal unit, however working parties would meet at least twice a month to coordinate. My culture of poverty cluster would be linked to the socioeconomic models' cluster. The trio of experts in this group were working on corollary abatement practices, triggers for escape, and ecological susceptibility factors.

I was sure we'd have a lot to work on together.

I am uncertain if our clusters and working parties made major substantive progress, but we certainly spent hours in introspection, in deliberation, and in discussion. We were coldly analytical. We were maudlinly emotional. And, we were always profoundly serious. We had thoughts. We had ideas. We had suppositions. We had hypotheses. We had theories. We even had dreams.

We sought solutions.

We sought impact.

We sought sureness—albeit we often found doubt.

Throughout (although, in my eyes slothfully), we moved forward.

While we had a truly high-level team, we still depended heavily on outside resources. We relied critically on official data to both formulate our recommendations and to monitor hoped-for improvements. However, even in a best-case scenario, routinely collected and collated government figures were not fully adequate—not casting a wide enough net for our needs.

And, we found ourselves in a far from a best-case scenario. With the new administration, although it had been at the helm for almost eighteen months, many key civil service positions were not filled (some vacant due to protest resignations, others through normal attrition, and still others apparently forgotten or abolished). Data streams were now being interrupted; basic public datasets no longer complete.

Had we had all the open-source data we could imagine; this would still have been incomplete for our needs. Therefore, we did a lot of contracting with universities, NGOs, and other local groups or specialists to collect needed data. To the extent possible, we tried to encourage local work be done such that it integrated colleges and universities in the hopes that practical real-life assignments might be beneficial to students.

In this way, I worked indirectly with a score of students—interfacing mostly with their professors. These students at times only crunched numbers, but frequently they were in the truest case our eyes and ears. In these incidences, they were on-the-ground—they were the face of PP.

One of the pieces upon which I was working involved transgenerational coping strategies. We had identified some of the poorest parts of the country—urban and rural. One of the sites was the River Glen neighborhood of Chicago. Here, the economic indications (not to even mention the social aspects) were rock bottom: nearly a quarter of the residents unemployed, median annual income less than $16,000, and median home value less than $25,000.

We were interacting with volunteer groups representing random samples of the neighborhood's denizens. This work, in situ, was undertaken by faculty and students from the University of Chicago's Departments of Economics and Sociology.

One of the interviewers in River Glen was Shadrack George, a PhD student in the Social Thought Program. Shadrack, through the university focal points, provided us with very thorough information. He also provided, at the express request of the interviewee, a message from a Ms. Lucinda Davis, an eighteen-year-old single mother and River Glen urbanite. Lucinda had asked the following be sent to PP:

> To those in Washington DC—my brother Shadrack has told me ya'll are trying to help us poor folks from the ghetto—we called it the "Nabe," but Shadrack said we could call it a "Ghetto." Shadrack said you're trying to get folks outta poverty. So, ya wanna find a way for us to get outta the ghetto and get outta being poor— and ya'll gonna do all that by remote control from Washington. Well, for us all, I hope it works. But, I ain't holding my breath. I was born here, and, like my mother, I'll probably die here. But, I ain't writing to complain—more than enough folks hereabouts to complain with. I'm only writing to let ya know that being poor don't mean ya's lazy or stupid. Government people down at La Salle Street always saying we're just a bunch'a drugged-up free-loaders—we got it easy watching TV and eating nachos all day—getting a check in the mail from all ya hard-working folks that pays for our beer and sneakers. Well, I just wanna make sure ya hear from me personal that all this just ain't so. We ain't just squirting out kids and gobbling up welfare. Most folks here wanna do good. Most folks here wanna work. Most folks here wanna have their kids go to school. Most folks here are damned tired of drugs, and guns, and violence. We sure as hell ain't living the dream! But, when you stick your head up, someone's always there to try 'n kick it off. We ain't asking to be special. We're only asking to be like ya'll—working, voting, paying taxes, and play-ing softball. We hear all the time that some folks somewhere 's trying to help us reach this dream—ya'll just the latest in a long line. So, I ain't got no idea if ya'll can do something, but, like I said, I ain't holding my breath. But I guess I should at least say "thank you" for trying. Sincerely, Lucinda.

Lucinda's communiqué was unusual, but not exceptional. People would try to reach out to those far away in whom they had little confi-dence—people they felt could not understand their issues nor solve their problems. But, people with whom (for better or worse) they were willing to give it a go with that chronic fatalism, "what have I got to lose?"

I, and I think all of us, welcomed these inputs. They not only helped put things in perspective, but they underscored the fact that a lot of people, in spite of (critically, not because of) their experiences and best judgement, were counting on us.

This was really no different than Guinea, Namibia, Nigeria, or about anywhere else. It was hard, very hard, for outsiders to understand the true happenings and forces affecting so intimately and profoundly the insiders. It was, honestly, more than hard. It was nearly impossible. With diligence, perception, persistence, and sensitivity we, the interlopers, might, maybe just might, get enough of an inkling of realty to get a grip on mitigating strategies. Maybe, but it was tough.

The probabilities were not in our favor.

Yet, this truth did not stop us—to the contrary, it pushed us to re-double our efforts.

We could not change American (nor human) history. We could not, in the short term, change American (nor human) culture, ethics, nor social norms. Nevertheless, possibly—just possibly—we could put in place some tactics that would ultimately lead to these changes, to improvements, to equity. It was a lot to hope for, but there could ("could" truly the operative word) be more of a level playing field in the future, if there was the will and if we were clever enough to figure out how to plant the needed seeds.

After we'd boiled it all down and come to a course of action that re-flected all our best thoughts, after we'd done what we could, it would be a waiting game. We could only watch and wait.

Were we almost there?

I'm not sure—we'd have to wait and see.

We were, of course, not alone.

Others were watching—interpreting—judging.

Leading up to the celebration of the Fourth, under the headline, "Is Local Think Tank Prescient?" the *Washington News Register* published a story about CESP's PP project:

> Liberal local DC center seeks to eradicate poverty. The Wash-ington-based Center for Equitable Social Policies, through its Square Deal Project, has assembled, what it calls, "a unique world-class team of experienced experts" to examine causes

of, and solutions for poverty. As the country sees increasingly growing gaps between the rich and the poor, this can only be considered as a task of the utmost importance—raising our fellow citizens out of poverty. One in ten DC households finds itself below the poverty line, with nearly one-third of female-headed households and one-quarter of black or Hispanic households living in poverty. Solving human destitution is a towering task with potentially tremendous impact—or, a boondoggle at tremendous cost for meager results. CESP spokesperson Tod Hanson told the News Journal the Square Deal Project was making remarkable progress, while cautioning the job was not only of monumental relevance, but also of monumental dimensions. Mr. Hanson confirmed the Project was transitioning from public to private support such that taxpayers should have no concern as to the use of their hard-earned dollars. Nonetheless, Mr. Hanson reassured the paper's readership that an initial draft of the Center's first provisional report should be expected before the 2020 elections. Mr. Hanson concluded with his hopes that the on-going project would provide essential policy inputs into the platforms of this election—inputs that would ultimately make people's lives better. Can CESP really hope to succeed? We can only wish them well.

This was but one example of those seemingly peeking over the wall into our garden. It was also an example of the largesse with which many viewed our (not very public) work.

While many of the PP crew probably considered themselves as "liberal," few if any had any expectations of eradicating poverty. This was simply too far-fetched—too grandiose—for even the most adamant supporter of our cause (my mind going back to my initial thoughts on this nomenclature when first contacted by the White House). Mitigating the negative impacts of poverty was a long way from eradication.

Yet, at the end of the day, any more or less measured publicity for our efforts was probably welcome. We were trying very hard. We had a big job ahead of us.

As I thought of our big job (in my eyes, our big responsibilities), I at times wondered if there were layers upon layers as there had been in EHT. Definitely there usually were. There was a lot of brouhaha these days about what some folks called "the deep state." These proponents were sure there was a massive conspiracy—systematic and institutionalized collusion between the political leadership and the captains of industry and finance.

I, for one, couldn't say it was impossible. Quite to the contrary, I had had a glimpse of such arrangements with EHT.

I thought about what I would merely call corruption. It was there. It was here. It probably, in many contexts, abounded everywhere. But it did not occupy my time. It did not get into my head.

Maybe it should have?

I thought of Rodney Mills and his endeavors, along with those of his colleagues, to fight international corruption. I had never seen him again nor had I made any efforts to contact him (maybe I should have, maybe I knew things I didn't know I knew). Nonetheless, every so often I did think back to our exchanges—his vehemence regarding "bad actors and bad acts on a very big scale." I thought that he could likely, if ever allowed to speak in candor, tell tales of the deep state—or whatever hush-hush structures might exist at any point in time—there were undoubtedly lots of nasty things out there—everywhere.

People like Rodney carried a heavy burden. People like Rodney knew more than most of us. They knew so much but could say so little. They were like the Agyō and the Ungyō, the guards of the Japanese Buddhist temples. They tried to ensure supplicants had sites of peace in spite of concealed violence and unseen manipulation.

Still, the shrouded guardians aside, my lifetime experiences had definitely shown the impact of hidden hands that all too frequently pulled strings in very unequitable, often illegal, ways. I saw these covert powers as inherent yet opaque forces that touched nearly all we did—certainly including our current efforts to combat poverty.

I wished we interacted more with those in the know like Rodney—those who could put the inconceivable happenings in the shadows in proper perspective. But this was definitely not to be. The shadows protected their own.

Still, I had enough to do to just deal with what was there on the surface without digging deeper to find more headaches and frustrations. Time was too short, my clock was running, and I wanted—I needed—to get a lot done. The Square Deal Project was proving to be on track—to be a pathway to my hopes and expectations. I needed to be on board to see others savor the fruits of our efforts—to savor these bittersweet fruits myself.

When I reached my own first anniversary of living on Burning Tree Drive, in the height of the run up to the 2018 midterm elections, in addition to the intense political fervor, I had a more private but no less intense matter—one I would most happily have never known.

This was certainly a burning brush if not a burning tree.

One interpretation of Moses' encounter with the burning bush on Mount Horeb was that God, as represented by the fire, was promising to be a part of the people, as represented by the bush, without totally consuming them. In other words, I guess, you could be a faithful follower of God without having God eat up your life. It made sense—at least to me.

This seemed to apply to a lot of the religious (Christian and others equally) people I knew. They sought spiritual assurances—faith—but also desired to lead their own lives. Religious zealots, of all colors and stripes, of course existed—they truly were individuals who were spiritually, emotionally, and socially consumed by the flames of their version of their religious beliefs. They ultimately were burnt to ashes—sadly, all too often taking others with them in the pyre they ignited.

Bringing all this heady discussion to a more personal level, down the street from me there was a Sudanese family. I didn't know them well, but (exceptionally) I occasionally chatted with them when walking with Tally. I had the most contact with the father, Alhaji Omar—the other family members more reserved and probably more hesitant to befriend outsiders due to far too many bad experiences given the level of Islamophobia in many segments of our society.

Alhaji was a UK-trained doctor—a radiologist. He worked at the Tyson Corner Medical Center, on the other side of the Leesburg Turnpike from our neighborhood. He and I would have short, but stimulating, discussions about Africa and African problems.

August twenty-first was l'Aïd-el-Kébir, the Muslim Feast of the Sacrifice that follows Ramadan. Alhaji and his family had gone to mosque at the McLean Islamic Center about two miles from their home. His son, Sadan (meaning happiness) was with a group of pre-teenage boys outside the Center when a sixty-three-year-old car salesman from Fredericksburg got out of his late-model pickup, shouldered his AR-15, yelled, "Here's sacrifice for you!" He killed Sadan and seven other boys before tearing away in his vehicle. He was killed by police at a roadblock on the I-95 bridge over the Occoquan River.

The bush (or the tree) had burned to ash.

I visited the mourning family.

There were no words.

When I was leaving, true to custom, Alhaji accompanied me to the threshold. After thanking me for coming, through red and swollen eyes, he stared at me, and asked, "Are the barbarous acts and slaughter of Darfur any different than those of McLean?"

We both knew the answer.

As things unfolded, apparently the killer of Sadan and the other boys was a fundamentalist Christian who claimed to be heeding the call of his god and his leaders to attack the "Islamist mob"—in particular, kill the young men before they could procreate. It was a terrible, but horrifically, growing story—a story of hate.

And, it only added to the tales of death from Virginia and the country at large. At the time of Sadan's death, Richmond had reported thirty-five homicides for the year (and, it was noted, this was a decline over recent years).

In spite of the sobriquet of "shithole countries" so brutally applied by the same leaders that seemed to have influenced Sadan's killer, it was becoming very clear that, in many cases, these very underdeveloped places were far safer, far more humane, than this land whose icons, at calmer times, proclaimed proudly, "give me your tired, your poor, your huddled masses yearning to breathe free" (remembering, as I often tried to do, the poem on the Statue of Liberty, *The New Colossus*, penned so beautifully by Emma Lazarus in 1883 with hopes and visions that were seemingly challenged today).

Possibly, just possibly, shitholes appeared in places one would never have suspected.

References to shitholes, of course, made me go back in my mind to the wonderful times I had had in all the (shithole) places I had been fortunate enough to work or visit. I, in my view, benefitting far more from the generosity of those with whom I connected than they professedly had gained from my presence. These thoughts, knit with concerns about Sadan's death, the apparent fading of the dream of *The New Colossus*, and our reportedly "great" new world, recalled the fact that nearly all of us were immigrants.

This xenophobia, blatantly obvious to all, but painfully so to a cultural anthropologist, seemed so out of place in a country of foreigners. Foreigners, from all points of the compass, who had done their best to eradicate the indigenous peoples they were replacing. Foreigners who, in turn, had frequently suffered to gain a foothold in their new world.

My mother's family (unaccustomed visions of my childhood in Middle America appearing from I didn't know where) had come to this country from Poland at the beginning of World War I. For generations, her family had lived in Kalisz. Then, in August 1914, the Germans razed the town, killing or driving away 60,000 of the 65,000 residents. Mother's newly arrived American forebearers, among the vanquished, felt lucky to be alive. They felt blessed to have made it to these shores.

My father's family had landed far earlier. His progenitors had come in 1780, according to family rumor, fleeing the household of the Earl of Harrington where the couple had scrubbed flagstones and swabbed-out stables. These same rumors hint that these good folks may have fled across the Atlantic with a few pieces of the good Earl's silver. No one was sure.

In any event, thieves, refugees, or lowly serfs, they were my roots and they were a goulash befitting a country of aliens.

This brought a flashback of Kouroussa, where Joel and I used to take some of our irregular jaunts. We would go to a rather clandestine bar (what the Ghanaians would have called a spot—Guineans probably had a similar epithet, I just never knew it or have forgotten it, along with a myriad of other tidbits) referred to by locals as Chez Elise—alcohol not a readily accessible commodity in many quarters due to the dominance of the Muslim culture. On Saturday evenings, Chez Elise offered what was billed as a special soup. It was, in fact, the floor sweepings of the abattoir. It was a spicy broth in which floated all variety of cow parts—eyes, testicles, ears, noses—you name it, it was there. A bit difficult to get used to, but once you did, it was tasty.

This was the way I, anthropologically-speaking, saw our country. We were a special motley soup—sometimes a bit difficult to get used to. Yet, because it was special, because it was multiform, it was stronger, and it was bolder. If we lost our specialness, we would lose so much.

Like the oft-spoken warning given in Nigeria, we needed to take time. Things, all too easily, fall apart.

Everything was, or so I felt, fragile. Everything was, or so it seemed, intertwined. Hate, ignorance, intolerance, anxiety—all fueled by people whose lives repeatedly failed to meet their own expectations (real or imagined). This was certainly multidimensional. Nonetheless, as with most human endeavors, money was a key element. Our developed, our high-tech, our twenty-first-century lifestyles were expensive. In the majority of cases, it was hard to get by.

Those getting by may not have been poor. But definitely most weren't wealthy—not even close. And, a lot were still poor—even if working poor.

Poverty remained a core piece of the puzzle—the puzzle, if not countered, leading to expanding pictures of intolerance and injustice.

Our work remained important.

Doable solutions remained to be seen—felt by some to be an illusion.

The faint of heart succumbed to fears that the status quo was too intrenched—its roots too deep.

Others remained committed to (if not totally confident of) positive change.

Those peering through rose-colored lenses maintained, "We're almost there!"

The realists cautioned, "A step at a time."

Still, regardless of our individual frames of mind, we carried on.

We carried on.

And, it was not a monotonous drudgery like dragging barges down the Erie Canal.

It was intellectually and professionally stimulating.

It was socially dynamic.

It was a good place to be.

One night, lounging at home with Tally—sipping a big glass of Châteauneuf-du-Pape—listening to my favorite Nigerian musician, Fela Kuti (yes, streaming through my smart phone via my in-house Wi-Fi and not on a six-inch cassette player like I had had decades ago in Fomi—albeit the music was nearly the same)—I realized how lucky I was—how lucky I had been. It was just possible (and, I would not dare go into any probabilities) that I would ultimately be able to make a difference.

It seemed to have been worth the wait.

But I have to candidly admit, I'm still not totally sure what "it" is or was. I suppose it was my life. It was, I guess, my life on the balance of time. It was adding up the pluses and the minuses. It was testing where I felt contented—where I felt vindicated. It was, ultimately, accepting that the view from above was still cloudy—very cloudy most days—but recognizing that I was where I felt I understood at least some of what was beneath the clouds.

Maybe it was just getting old.

❖❖❖

As if to underscore the rapid passing of time, José gave me a present—a celebration of our years of friendship. Knowing of my long history with Albert Schweitzer, she gave me a copy of his 1922 book, *On the Edge of the Primeval Forest & More from the Primeval Forest.*

I was most grateful, not only for José's thoughtfulness, but also for having a chance to read the words of the man who had so captivated my mother—the man I had found "interesting," yet worthy of only a fifth-grade report. Reading about Africa nearly a century earlier, reading about those early days in Lambaréné—it fascinated me. It made me wonder, would I have been able to survive then and there.

I knew vaguely, since my ears did prick-up at the mention of Schweitzer's name, that the Nobel winner had been criticized when viewed through a lens of modern social and cultural sensitivities. I had heard he had been called paternalistic, colonialistic, and even racist by some (afflictions not uncommonly attached to the periods of European domination). Still, my mother's clipping hidden somewhere in their now tattered manila envelope seemed to outweigh any serious censure. Therefore, as I read, I learned. I dared not judge hundred-year-old values, but through my eyes, Africa had seemed very different than it had apparently appeared to Dr. Schweitzer those decades ago. Possibly due to my anthropological background, I was particularly taken by (I won't say shocked) some of his passages in Chapter VII, entitled *Social Problems in the Forest.* A few excerpts really stood out to me:

> The negro is a child, and with children nothing can be done without the use of authority. We must, therefore, so arrange the circumstances of daily life that my natural authority can find expression. With regard to the negroes, then, I have coined the formula: "I am your brother, it is true, but your elder brother."
>
> When, before coming to Africa, I heard missionaries and traders say again and again that one must be very careful out here to maintain this authoritative position of the white man, it seemed to me to be a hard and unnatural position to take up, as it does to every one in Europe who reads or hears the same. Now I have come to see that the deepest sympathy and kindness can be combined with this insistence on certain external forms, and indeed are only possible by means of them.

The man of peace had obviously had different views of those with whom he shared his life. While these may well have been in line with contemporary thought, they definitely were contrary to my perceptions of current reasoning. Maybe, in some ways his critics were right. Nonetheless, we are all vulnerable to finding ourselves under others' microscopes—especially when we are dead and gone and not able to defend ourselves.

What's more, as I had all too often witnessed in the years long after the good doctor's passing, he had had no monopoly on what might be considered by some as narrowmindedness or intolerance. Patronizing and bigoted views were shared by far too many in all corners of present-day society. In so many ways, and in spite of so much effort, up to today, much of mankind remained, at the very least, ill at ease with those seen as different or vulnerable—considering these less-desirables as coming from shitholes or being otherwise unworthy.

I guess some things never change.

Nevertheless, with regard to the honorable Dr. Albert Schweitzer, I tried to remember the wider personal philosophy of his later years targeting a "reverence for life" (tenants with which I generally agreed). I tried to minimize my analyses of his perhaps questionable—I would say, based on my own experiences, not seldom wrong—assessments of his African congregation, patients, and neighbors. I tried to concentrate on how life was lived those years ago. In so doing, I was able to really marvel at how different life was today (yet, in some ways, still similar).

And, as always, life went on.

The mid-terms came and went. However, they went very slowly as there were numerous recounts—numerous protestations (from all sides). In the end, there had been at least a modest redistribution of power that hopefully would affect positively accountability, transparency, and good governance.

We had a cool, but erratic, fall, followed by a wet and snowy early winter. There was snow on the ground when, on December nineteenth, I went to José's for a pre-Christmas bash. She had invited a hodgepodge of friends and colleagues, serving a multicultural meal including kimchi, Murgh Kari (Indian chicken curry), jollof rice, avocado and quinoa salad, and Thai spring rolls—all accompanied by Tej—Ethiopian mead (I have no idea where José found this delicious and potent honey wine, but I welcomed its addition to the menu).

Always ready to volunteer, I did more than my part in helping finish the stores of Tej. By the time I left, about eleven o'clock, I was more than a little tipsy—I was three sheets to the wind.

Possibly because of my somewhat loose inebriated state, when I hit the ice patch on the sidewalk in front of José's, I kind of kicked in the air, pirouetted, and fell in a heap like a rag doll. In my mind, all was OK—simply a slip. I'd get up and get home.

Unfortunately, this was not to be the case.

I had slammed down hard on my left hip. It had shattered like a porcelain bowl. Apparently, as I was to learn later, my struggle with *Naegleria* had weakened my joints and bones—kind of like osteoporosis. While certainly affected by age, my own condition was considerably worsened because of my history with my satanic protozoan.

I couldn't get up.

I was in mind-boggling pain that sent lightning bolts across my eyes.

José called an ambulance.

I was carried to Inova Fair Oaks Hospital in Fairfax.

Here began my second journey into the clouds of medicine and health.

As I had just turned sixty-five, I could only think, "At least I've Medicare!"

I had complex fractures that required over two weeks of hospitalization—amassing bills that could easily bankrupt someone without some sort of assistance.

I had constant and acute pain. I was prescribed opioids. I entered nether worlds where I floated above calm pink seas, seduced by soft breezes, caressed by soothing arias.

I left the hospital in a wheelchair and with a bottle of painkillers.

Once again, José had made the arrangements and I went by ambulance (this time, no flashing lights nor siren) to Saint Helena Convalescent Center to be looked over by another saint and looked after by another flock of do-gooders who truly had little skill at doing good.

What's more, they seemed uncertain when something was done, let alone have any inkling of when it might have been done well. And, they couldn't even concentrate long enough, always playing with their phones or other gadgets, to be able to tell you what they thought they'd done or tried to do.

Many who shared the ministrations of these proclaimed caregivers with me said, "It's just the new generation."

I said, "To hell with it all." Then I'd catch myself and say, "This too will pass."

I just had to be patient.

I just had to wait.

I still hated to wait.

Post Script

Humanitarianism consists in never sacrificing a human being to a purpose.

—ALBERT SCHWEITZER

AFTER FOUR MONTHS OF healing, on April 19th, 2019, Good Friday, Paula Patterson was picked up at the Saint Helena[1] Convalescent Center in Annandale, Virginia, by her good friend José Collins—Paula's dog Tally was waiting in the car.

Paula walked with a cane.

It was raining.

She walked very carefully, so as not to fall.

She didn't want to slip before she got to where she was going.

---

1. Saint Helena is the patron saint of new discoveries.

www.ingramcontent.com/pod-product-compliance
Lightning Source LLC
Chambersburg PA
CBHW061502030726
47503CB00005B/1778